BLOODWORK

Stories by Samuel E. Cole

Joe —

Thanks for coming to the
book launch. Love seeing you —
let's hang more often —
your pal,

Samuel E. Cole

ISBN-13: 978-0-9988476-1-0
ISBN-10: 0998847615

for more books, visit Pski's Porch:
www.pskisporch.com

Printed in U.S.A

For My Mother, Vaida Faye

Contents

The Cognomen Affair

Janet loved Harvey more than she loved herself. She'd always been an ancillary character. Someone else's support system. Calm softness to Harvey's chaotic vibrations. During their honeymoon, she was glad he bought a crimson-colored sweatshirt from the Harvard University bookstore. The cashier gave him forty-percent off the original price, given his baritone radio voice, which reminded her of her father who made her very, very happy.

"I'll take good care of it," Janet said.

"Don't ever wear it," Harvey snapped. "It's mine."

Janet washed it with Tide and dried it with Bounce. It faded: crimson to crayon red to weathered brick to fading flame to cinnamon toast crunch to a sad sort of pink that makes pink look sort of sad. Similar to Janet's parents and siblings, time moved faster than she could keep up. Had anyone taken a second to ask if she took enjoyment in reflection, she'd have said yes. For some reason, looking back brought her closer to the future. Harvey talked a lot on the radio about the good ole days. But never at home. Perhaps he considered their life bad: bad ole days. Early on, especially during dinner, she asked if he was happy. He never answered, squinting at her as if she'd asked him to pass the potato salad, the one item that wasn't on the table.

During the crayon red years, they bought an A-frame stucco house with a crimson-colored mailbox. Harvey wore the sweatshirt to Sipp's Country Club, Golf USA, sporting events, and to Doctor Hoeffel's office, places where opinions mattered. To wear Harvard was to have attended Harvard. Which was a lie. But Harvey was a showman. And Janet accepted his ostentatiousness.

"Never knew you were a Crimson man," Doctor Hoeffel said, pointing to an x-ray scan of Harvey's persistent laryngitis. "Figured you were more of an Institute of Technology or Emerson guy."

Harvey shrugged. His response in lieu of telling the truth.

"You must be an early eighties grad?"

He shrugged. Janet sighed. He hadn't attend college. But he was still the main reason she got up in the morning. Was she the main reason he got up in the morning? Did he love her as much as he loved the sweatshirt? Someday, she thought, he'll tell me.

During the weathered brick years, they moved across town and into a two-story home with a fireplace. Harvey, much like the washing machine, spun fast and frequent, wearing thin everything and everyone. Janet, in between washes, smiled, happy the childhood dream of having a two-story home with a fireplace had come true. "Call me Harv," Harvey said during dinner. "Harvey sounds like a dad's name." Which he was becoming. Like or not.

"But I love the name Harvey."

"Well, I hate it."

Harv was an absent father. Which might have bothered another woman. But not Janet. She knew who they were. And weren't.

Their children, Haley and Harv Jr., despised hearing Harv talk about the sweatshirt and loathed watching Janet wash and dry it. They often stayed overnight with friends, coming home only to gather coins, clothes, and comestibles. Harv extended in North America his radio show from 5am to 8am in 239 cities to 5am to 9am in 281 cities, while Janet learned how to cook Salt-Crusted Fish and Macarons. Harv smoked Cuban cigars that stunk up the house and yellowed his teeth, while Janet sat in the kitchen and shuffled through photographs, relieved to have taken so many pictures of the kids when they were little.

During the fading flame years, Janet talked Harv into buying Kenmore laundry appliances. She giggled like a little girl cutting the red ribbons. Haley missed another Christmas, skiing in Colorado with Connor Barwin from Missoula, MT. Harv Jr. also missed Christmas, but at least he phoned on Janet's birthday in March. Harv's laryngitis, and frantic-grumpiness, forced him to take early retirement. Even during the summer, he napped in the sweatshirt: a woolly cat in front of the fireplace. His mother, Delores, two months before she died of lung cancer, flew in from

Plano, Texas for Thanksgiving. She told Harv to please not wear the sweatshirt at the table. He disobeyed, and then wore it to her funeral, burial, and reception.

During the cinnamon toast crunch years, Harv played computer games all day. And night. Janet and Haley picked out Vera Wang plates, champagne flutes, and the perfect first-dance song for Haley and Landon Prescott's wedding in October: *Fools In Love*. Harv Jr. joined the Peace Corps and went to Rawanda where he couldn't be bothered with American nonsense like weddings, champagne flutes, and tuxedos. Harv agreed, walking Haley down the aisle in the sweatshirt. Haley begged him not to wear it. But he wore it. She cried for a few a days, but eventually got over it.

During the sad sort of pink years, Harv wore the sweatshirt twenty-four seven. His forgetfulness worsened, as did Janet's quietness, leaving them both with even less to say and share. Haley became pregnant and miscarried, while Harv Jr. doled out HIV medication in Liberia. Haley got pregnant again and gave birth to a baby boy named Stanford Graham Prescott, while Harv Jr. backpacked the Orient with some Korean fellow named Leo Choi. Stanford spent many weekends at Janet and Harv's house. "Gramp's sweatshirt is super vintage," he said with every visit. "I hope he gives it to me when he's finished with it." Haley and Landon got divorced in January, the same month Harv. Jr. married Spencer Holmes, a democratic political strategist from Des Moines, Iowa. Janet and Harv Sr. weren't invited to the wedding. Which didn't bother Harv. Sr., who disliked Spencer, because Spencer bragged about attending Yale and called Harvard an overrated institution for lazy louts. Even still, Harv Jr. (and Spencer) phoned Janet every Tuesday evening at 7pm to say hi. Haley, after an elopement to Jamaica with James Baldwin, a co-worker, phoned Janet every Tuesday evening at 7: 10pm to say hi. Every time Janet finished talking to the children, she pressed the phone against Harv's ears and lips and asked him to say hi. He never did. Not even a groan.

"We should go back to Harvard," she said at bedtime. "Tour it again and get you a new sweatshirt."

"This one's perfect."

"But a new one would smell so fresh and look so good."

"You can't replace a classic."

"I'm not asking you to replace it."

"Than what are you asking for?"

"For you, Harvey. I'm asking for you."

He shrugged, removed the sweatshirt, and closed his eyes.

Harvey James Stout Sr. was buried in a black suit. Two days later, Janet gave the sweatshirt to Stanford who carefully tore it into tessellate parts and sewed a quilt in honor of his mother's death to breast cancer and Uncle Harv's death to pancreatic cancer.

Janet and Stanford lived for many years, reflecting on each one as it passed. Stanford grew tall and kind, falling asleep at the wheel one night after work, a professor of Comparative Theology at Harvard, dying from a traumatic brain injury in the hospital with Janet by his side. Janet died on Christmas Eve. Finally surrounded by everyone she loved.

It's Worth Exploring

It was the first openly gay restaurant in downtown Minneapolis, aptly named GAY RESTAURANT, located across the street from the two largest gay bars in Minnesota. The Chinese have theirs. Mexicans. Italians. Germans. Polish. Vietnamese. Jews. Ethiopians. Even one Senor Frog. It was time to reach out and feed the fabulous-foodie-fags and their tag-a-long-hags. The neon sign outside over the front door proudly blinked: *straights welcome*. It was that kind of atmosphere.

The grand opening coincided with the annual PRIDE festival in Loring Park; well within walking distance. The Minneapolis Star and Tribune wrote, "In name alone, it's lecherously cliché, but the food is delightful and the serving staff, named after gay icons, is a hoot and a half."

We served fun appetizers: twinkie fries, husky bear claws, hot-top monster dogs, bottomless boneless wings, and the colossal onion-laser-peel served atop an oversized Botox coupon from Laser Peels, Inc.—buy one pint get the second pint half-off. Lunch and dinner entrees included The Out & Proud (served on pumpernickel bread, because sourdough sounded too homophobic); The I'm-Here-Queer-So-Delicious-Reuben; The Finger-Snapping-Salmon; The Cher-Broiled Chicken Linguini; The RuPaul Bunyan Brisket; The Elton Smelting John; and The Right-to-Wed Waldorf Astoria salad. Leather-chested bartenders shook or stirred drinks: The Pink Triangle-tini; The Same-Sex on the Beach; Cocks between the Sheets; The Quadruple Screaming Orgasm; The Cosmo Climax; and The Woo Woo Waterloo. Fantastic stuff. Uproarious. Catchy.

Our first TV commercial, produced by an openly gay film student at the University of Minnesota, was robustly colorific: Leave nobody out. Bring everyone in. Flirt a little. And be sure to laugh. The eight-foot talking rainbow was the perfect spokesperson.

The back of the menu offered a smorgasbord of informational

tidbits: where to get tested, open and affirming churches, the brief history of Stonewall (and affirmative action). Calling all demographics. Uber-inclusivity. Totally bi-partisan. Friday night comics. Tuesday afternoon balloonists. Thursday evening karaoke. All day Sunday open-mic poetry slams.

But the gay community took insult, rebuking both the food names and the open-door policy. One gay-rights activist wrote in a gay-rights blog, "I refuse to patronize an establishment that, through mocking parody, solicits profit from downgraded sexual orientations."

A representative from OutFront Midwest Diners Club told three different news anchors, on three different networks, "This restaurant typifies the shallow greed of clueless individuals who seek to further exploit the already exploited." The Minnesota HRC Chairman expressed to the food critic at Mindfulness Magazine, "Serving moderately flashy food on the broken backs of the LGBTQI community, GAY RESTAURANT shines as a flaming beckon of what to never do, say, be, or eat."

And then they wonder why no one takes us seriously.

The Governor's Table

It was a magnificent table. Which is why I hated it, and chose to make it suffer.

My father built it from a large maple tree that his father-in-law, my grandpa, the scariest man I've ever encountered, dropped off in the backyard during the night. Much like my mother, my grandpa came and went as he pleased.

My father sliced with speed and fury the scary looking branches with a scary sounding chainsaw: safety goggles magnifying the size of his eyes, hairy arms covered in wood shavings, customary red and orange plaid shirt and coveralls, and brown-scuffed boots. Working-class distillation.

"Everything has a purpose," he said, dragging the branches through thick snow to the woodshop's front door. "Even skinny things."

But he couldn't lift the log. "Goddamn it." His neck and forehead veins bulged. I'd never before heard him cuss. Perhaps my mother's assessment of him was true. Perhaps he was weak, profane, and filthy. Perhaps he couldn't move anything of importance, regardless how hard he tried. Perhaps he was in permanent trouble.

Two days later, two bigger, stronger men came to the house and tossed like a plastic toy the log into the back of a big, yellow pickup truck. My father referenced having a bad back and some messed up knees, but I knew he was lying. He'd have told me, as I was his sounding board and he was my learning curve. We jumped into our blue pickup truck and followed the yellow pickup truck to a sawmill where two bigger, stronger men lifted and stuffed the log into a gigantic, gray machine that gurgled and steamed and coughed and moaned until eight flat boards popped out in a cloud of haze. Then the men loaded the boards into a commercial dryer and pushed a big, green ON button. It was the greatest movie ever made.

"Three days should dry 'em out," the biggest man said, lifting me until he and I were face to face. "As for this one." He smiled, exposing chipped yellow and brown teeth. "He looks pretty dry already." His breath reeked of sour cream potato chips and cherry soda pop. "You don't say much do you?"

I didn't say a word. Neither than nor during the drive home, wondering if being dry was the same thing as being weak, profane, and filthy. As often as my mother compared me to my father, I couldn't shake the notion of inseparability, nor the familial DNA careening through my (and his) limbs and brain.

Over the next three days my father and I stirred inside the small woodshop which sat in its saggy metal skin forty small hops behind the house. I played tag with a stuffed rabbit, Woody Woodshop, a birthday gift from my mother, while my father worked on projects already in progress: a birdhouse with a tin roof; a chair that became a step stool when flipped over; a fireplace mantel; a tall curio cabinet with six windowless window slots waiting for windows. My father never asked for my help and I never volunteered a finger, content to watch (or not) from any distance of my choosing.

Two days later, back at the Sawmill, my father slid with his own hands the eight boards into the back of the pickup truck. "I'm not weak," he whispered (over and over) on the drive home. I kept quiet, trying to guess what he was going to build. Something for me? Or better yet, a welcome home gift for mother.

"When you're making a table for someone important," he said, stacking the boards like a pack of gum, "You can't just shove things together and start gluing. You have to do first things first."

First, he ran each board through a metal plainer, twice. Burnt woodchips twirled and swirled the air like confetti on New Year's Eve. So fun, until he swept every last chip into a brown dustpan and tossed it into the woodstove which I'd named, Belly of the Beast, an evil wizard who took great pleasure in luring poor, harmless creatures inside only to eradicate them by fire to ash. "A clean room is a wise house." He looked directly into my eyes. "You got that?" As young as I was, I got it.

The next day, he switched one board with another until a rough tabletop took shape. "I gotta get this one just right," he whispered. "It's gotta be magnificent."

Over the next week, he wielded with agility hand saws, power drills, and various size electric belt sanders. Back then, mechanical noise was the one constant reminder of where, how, and who I was.

"Edge-to-edge you need to use eight clamps to get it good and tight." He sat beside me and watched glue dry. We shared a few slivers from a cube of white cheddar cheese and a warm A&W root beer. Then he stood and sat at a small metal desk beside the woodstove, where he shook woodchips from his hair and shuffled papers.

The next morning, in between sanding and re-sanding, he said, "Always go with the grain so you don't ruin her natural beauty." His hands moved forward and backward in a steady dance of determination. "Smooth as a flower pedal," he whispered. "Soft as silk."

The following afternoon he became entranced by a lathe, creating an edged lattice design that upon completion smelled as scorched as it felt divine. With a fresh, white cloth he applied a thin coat of varnish and then, once again, sat beside me to watch glue dry. This time, we shared a turkey sandwich and a semi-cold Pepsi. "Just two more coats and the business of the legs and then she'll be ready to go on her way."

"On her way," I said, wondering if all wood is female, or is it just female in a male's hands. "To where?" He didn't respond.

The next day, he shaped, glued, clamped, and lathed four 1x4 pieces of wood into four uniform table legs. "Great legs should complement a table. They should never be the focal point. Amateur carpenters worry about the legs and end up losing their mind."

A week later, he stood in the middle of the room and waved a hand over the table like a magician. "Magnificent, yeah?"

I nodded.

"It's crazy what the earth gives up for creation," he said, patting me on the head. "I do hope she's going to a good home." At the desk, he scribbled on a yellow piece of paper: INVOICE. His cursive was as bad as mine. Benjamin Tressell. Raleigh, North Carolina. February 4, 1985.

"Who's Benjamin Tressell?" I had come to believe the table was ours. The small, round table inside the house was old, wobbly, and plastic. Not one uniform chair. Not one ornate design. We needed a new table. We deserved a new table. Mother would love a new table.

"A customer." My father folded the yellow invoice and stuffed it inside a purple folder. "A governor to be exact."

"What's a customer?"

"Someone who pays cash for a job well done."

"What's a governor?"

"An important man who can afford to buy nice things."

"Is Raleigh close to us?"

"No. It's more than a thousand miles away."

"Why can't he get one there?"

My father took Woody Woodshop from my hands and placed the stuffed animal on his right knee. Then he lifted and set me on his left knee. And bounced. "Because I'm the best at what I do and some people in this world are smart enough to understand, and want, that." We sat quiet and stared at the table as the rain came, all of us trembling in our own way.

"Why can't we keep it?" I asked.

"Because that's not who we are."

"Who are we?"

"Some say easy to forget but I say well on our way...up."

Later that night, after my father had fallen asleep on the coach with a toothpick in his mouth, I took Woody to the woodshop to say goodbye to the table. I rubbed the table's intricate designs and caressed the four legs, top to bottom, thinking about my mother's legs and floral dresses and raspy voice and reddish-pink lipstick and cold-fingertip-touch. Perhaps she'd come back (and stick around) if he made for her a magnificent table. "Fuck Benjamin Tressell," I yelled over and over (and over).

I set Woody beside the woodshop door and grabbed from a shelf a piece of 300-grit sandpaper. Rough and raw in my hands, it begged me to be mischievous. I surrendered to the impulse and climbed atop the table and began to sand, turning light and dull with friction the polish and grit of my father's skillful handiwork. "This one's staying put," I said, painfully aware that sanding wasn't enough. I needed to do more. I jumped off the table and tried to push it over, but my puny arms and legs were no match for the table's power. I wasn't meant to move it. I wasn't meant to touch it. I wasn't meant to understand its worth. Or was I?

I held things I had only seen my father hold. Handsaws. Screwdrivers. Hammers. A gallon of varnish. Then I saw it hiding on a bottom shelf behind The Belly of the Beast. A cordless drill. I grabbed its weight and pushed the green ON button. Tiny curlicue wood bits spun off the metal bit. I stood atop the table and drilled holes in the air, testing things, cursing Benjamin Tressell. Then I got busy marking up the table. Forward and backward. My own steady dance of determination. Rebellious exhilaration washed over me. I was possessed. Obsessed. Repressed. And on fire.

After I'd finished leaving my mark, I took to my knees, not to pray for forgiveness but to split with a hammer the drill into three hot, metallic pieces. I jumped down, grabbed Woody, and laid face up on the table. Woody sat on my chest as I sucked my thumb, until my eyes, and mind, went blank.

I awoke the next morning to my father's roar. I tried to squeeze Woody for comfort, but he'd fallen overnight onto the floor.

"What have you done?" My father brought me face to face. His voice, like his grip, grew tighter. "This is how we eat. This is how we survive. This is how we prove." He paused. "Her wrong."

He set me down and snatched the piece of sandpaper and the drill's broken pieces, tossing each into the trashcan. Then he lit a match and a corner page of newspaper, which he threw into The Belly of The Beast. Things quickly began to snap, crackle and pop; the evil wizard blazing with red heat. Then my father snatched Woody from the floor and threw him into the stove, leaving the woodstove door wide open. Watching Woody disintegrated into soot, something inside me shifted, replacing the last traces of naivety with profound, disturbing maturation. "Now we're even," my father yelled. "Now we're the same."

That night, I went to bed hungry, the first of many hungry nights. I didn't scream or cry or apologize. I simply buried my face in a pillowcase and pounded my fists on the mattress. And then I made two vows. One, to never speak to my father, or my mother, again. Which I didn't keep. And two, to never enter the woodshop again. Which I did keep. Losing all interest in my father's world while he lost all interest in mine.

Jonathon's Tunes

The old lady's gasping had been testing the parameters of Ken's patience all afternoon. Her modus operandi, he thought. Every client has one. So why was he letting her bother him? Not his modus operandi. His boss, Lyle, during Ken's latest performance review, said Ken possessed the rare balance of outer confidence and inner control. "Does nothing rattle your chain?" Lyle asked, to which Ken replied, "Not at work." No, Ken didn't mind moving other people's belongings, as long as they stayed out of the way. Unfortunately, many of them stood directly in the way. Like today.

Garth, Ken's assistant of three years, grabbed the opposite side of the grand piano and helped Ken tip it on its side. The beast creaked, hummed, and moaned as the old lady gasped. "That's totally normal," Ken said. "Nothing to worry about." Strings plucked themselves errantly, producing dissonance that matched in intensity the old lady's vocal range.

"Please be careful with it," she said. "It's the second most valuable thing I have."

Ken attached the three legs, positive the first most valuable thing she had was stalking blue-collar day laborers. The old lady's hands and head shook as she placed on the floor in front of the bay window three carpet-protection coasters in which Ken and Garth set the roller-ball toes. Late sixties, Ken guessed her age. Or early seventies. Maybe eighties. Maybe ninety-nine. Regardless, she belonged to his least favorite age group. And for three good reasons. In this line of work, clients with more wrinkles than skin are notoriously bad at giving space, compliments, and tips.

"How many times have you moved a piano?"

"Hundreds of times," Ken said. Which was true. And false. Ken had moved hundreds of pianos. Garth had moved five. "Not one complaint yet." Which was true. So far.

"The last guys I hired were really rough with it." She placed her palms on the window. "Which is the exact opposite of what it needs."

Maybe she suffered from dementia. It happens. Or maybe she was a secret shopper. Lyle talked freely in staff meetings about recruiting random clients from the community to serve as spies who were paid a small fee to report back any, and all, unprofessional behavior. "You ever used our company before?"

"It's almost one-hundred years old." She sat on the windowsill. "My father bought it for my mother for their wedding. They were a marvelous couple. Such love between them. Not one fight in almost seventy years. Not one day spent apart. Not one cruel word said in anger or judgement or misunderstanding."

Ken scanned the living room, much smaller than the Victorian ballroom in which the piano sat earlier in the morning, with a layer of dust on the lid. An easy move. Heavy son-of-a-bitch. Seventeen miles across town. Gated mansion to a run-down rambler. "This a second house or something?" He crawled underneath the piano and attached the rods and pedals. Of all the lessons he'd learned from the moving business, one bubbled at the top: people, when given the chance, love to talk about themselves. Especially rich, white women. In return, all he had to do was fake a smile and offer an occasional "ah" or "gotcha." Similar to his blue work shirt, khaki pants, and steel-toe boots, wearing mandatory pleasantries may get old but they never wear out.

"I'm here for good now." She sighed. "That other house isn't me anymore."

"Well, it is the age of downsizing."

"Privilege ruined us." Her voice cracked and petered out. Like Ken's joints and stamina. Being a mover was hard work. It punished the body. It mocked set hours. It payed for shit. What's a pension plan or a 401K? The oldest mover by ten years, maybe fifteen, his muscles were continually shedding the younger days of youth's potency. How much longer before something gave out, or worse, breaks? There's not a lot of employment options for a guy without a high school diploma.

"Ready to get the lid, Bingo," Garth said. Bingo. Garth's nickname for Ken. How unprofessional.

"Did you call him Bingo?"

Garth chuckled. "It's a funny story, actually."

"Have you guys worked together for a long time?" She sat on the edge of a pinstriped wing back chair beside a round, wooden table. A glass lamp and a gold-edged picture frame brightened the table. Inside the frame was a black and white photograph of a young man. Maybe twenty-one. Handsome enough. Mischievous eyes. Striking lips. Facial softness some men might call gay.

"We're sort of related," Garth said.

"How can you be sort of related?"

"I was married to Bingo's sister for a short time. A very short time, thank you very much."

"Just the lid and a few signatures and we'll be on our way," Ken said.

The old lady pressed the picture frame against her chest and set it in her lap.

"Is that your husband?" Garth asked.

"No." She thumbed the frame. "It's my son, Jonathon."

"Nice looking guy." Garth rubbed his own bald head. "He's lucky to have so much hair. As you can see, me and Ken here ain't so blessed."

"Are either of you boys married now?"

"I'm on a permanent break," Garth said. "Maybe forever."

"What about you?" She looked at Ken. "Are you married?"

Garth snickered, quickly turning it into a cough.

"Nope. Just me, ma'am." Nosey hag. Ken's relationship status, however nonexistent, was none of her, or Garth's, business.

"It's hard to believe those clothes and that beard bat for the other team, isn't it?"

"Other team?" She squinted. "Oh." Her shoulders raised. "Oh." She smiled. "Other team. I get it." She kissed the picture and set it on the table. "You boys want some lemonade?"

"Hell yeah."

"We've got three more jobs," Ken lied, glaring at Garth. "We better not."

"It's freshly squeezed." She disappeared into the kitchen. Humming. "You'll really like it. I promise."

"If she tips us even a dollar, you ain't getting one cent," Ken said half-way to the truck.

"I was just trying to cheer her up."

"You shouldn't ask personal questions. And stop calling me Bingo."

"She seems sad." Garth shrugged. "I don't know. I kinda like her."

Ken liked Garth right away: sprightly voice, right-lip smirk, and lanky demeanor. Not unattractive, but much closer to simplistic-boney than wife-beater muscle. A strut, jam-packed with self-sufficiency. One-hundred percent natural flavors. Kosher. Satisfying. Consumable. Ken hungered for Garth. Not for his body. But for his mind. His capacity for genuineness and openness. No one was too small and no topic was off limits. Ken's sister fell fast for Garth, cannibalizing Garth's heart with the same pace with which she injected heroine into her veins. Ken knew about her struggle but kept it to himself. Another family secret he chose to ignore through omission. At first, Garth asked Ken about a girlfriend, a mistress, a stripper, a prostitute. "Not my thing," Ken said. Garth asked Ken if he wanted to meet a biker babe or two from his motorcycle club. "Not my thing." Garth asked Ken if he someday wanted a wife and kids. "Not my thing." Garth asked Ken if he batted for the other team. "Bingo," Ken said. Garth said Ken didn't look or act gay. "I'd like to keep it that way." Garth said he was cool with gay people and that he didn't see Ken as different or less. "I hope that's true." Neither brought it up again. Until today. In front of a client who gasps, an old lady, a bitty hobgoblin with a hundred year old piano. Creaky mother fucker.

"Think she'll let me use the bathroom?" Garth asked Ken at the truck. "I really gotta go."

"She's a secret shopper. I know it. Let's just finish up and get the hell out of here."

"But I gotta go. Like now."

"We're almost done. Can't you just hold it a little longer?"

Garth jumped in the truck and started the engine. "This shit can't wait." He locked the doors and rolled down the window. "I'm pretty sure that dude in the picture also bats for your team. I say it's the perfect time to go in there and ask her all about him." Garth rolled up the window and sped down the street, leaving a trail of smoke pouring from the noisy muffler.

Ken whispered a few expletives and sat on the curb. Bat for the other team. What a condescending phrase. But truth. Sweat beads slid down his cheeks, back, and crotch. The whistling wind scattered oak leaves and pine needles across the front yard. Cardinals sang and Swallows flew as he plucked and sniffed a dandelion, his mother's favorite, replaying in his head four images from boyhood that clung to him like air: picking summer flowers for his mother; dueling winter shovels beside his sister; moving spring trees with his father; hiding behind the bleachers at every autumn school dance in order to discreetly watch Kevin Kramer, a boy, not a girl, dance with girls, and not boys. Fascinated. Enamored. Turned on. And there was no way for him to wrap his arms around Kevin's waist. Or to stare into Kevin's blue eyes. Or to rest his head against Kevin's chest as they swayed to the music. No clear possibility to escape the clandestine web of being visibly invisible. No chance to show up, show off, show everyone that boys who like boys are no different than boys who like girls. No idea how to connect to his own wiring. No occasion to find self-acceptance and build a life beyond midnight shadow dancing with married men at ill-lit gay bars across the state line and unmarried closet cases in X-rated bookstores in neighboring towns and anonymous horny truckers and travelers stopping in for a quick blow-and-go in rest stop bathroom stalls along the highway. And now it's too late, impossible to achieve freedom from the many years of self-entrapment. So much running. Moving. Hiding. Gasping.

The truck chugged back down the street, Garth bopping in the driver's seat. The brakes screeched as Garth parked and opened the door. "Yo Bingo. McGafferety's happy hour goes until 7pm." He jumped out of the truck. "I say let's go and get good and wrecked."

"Not today." Ken stood.

"Since when do you pass on McGafferty's happy hour?"

"Did my sister ever say anything to you about me?" Ken felt vulnerable and weak, in his mind, a gay man's mind. He unlocked the truck's back door and threw it open. "When you two were still together."

Garth nodded. "All I know dude is if I were gay, you wouldn't be single."

"Gay." Ken said it. Strange rolling off his tongue. Like a foreign language. But the release made him feel a little lighter. And a tad bit stronger. He jumped in the back of the truck and grabbed one side of the lid. Garth jumped in and grabbed the other side. They walked in silence to the house and carefully set the lid atop the piano.

"I used to make lemonade with powder," the old lady said, carrying into the living room a wooden tray with two glasses of lemonade and a small plate of cookies. The lemonade sloshed and the cookies rattled as she set the tray on the coffee table. "But now I only use real lemons." A few cookies fell off the plate. "Only one-hundred percent authentic stuff for me from now on."

Ken wiped with a blue terry cloth wayward fingerprints from the lid, wishing to erase every hint of himself from this odd lady's home.

"Do either of you play piano?"

Garth shook his hands. "Not with these stumps."

"What about you?" She looked at Ken. "Do you play?"

"I know a few chords but I'm no pianist."

"A few chords, huh." She smiled. "Do you boys live in the area?"

"I live in Montgomery and Ken here lives in Auburn."

"Local boys. How nice."

Ken drank fast—thankfully Garth did too—relieved to see that every phone jack in the living and dining room was empty. Maybe she wasn't a secret shopper. Or maybe she was. Whatever. They'd be finished and gone in less than five minutes. Ken noticed two rainbow-colored yard flags leaning against a box in the dining room. He hadn't seen them before. Because they weren't leaning there before. "Clients usually like to try it out before we leave." He set the empty glass on the tray. "Feel free to give it a go."

"I can't." She folded her arms. "It's not mine to play."

"You don't play it." Garth set his empty glass on the tray and grabbed a handful of cookies. "You're breaking my heart." He leaned against the doorway. "Why don't you play it?" His cell phone rang. He paused and looked at the screen. "I gotta take this but it was really nice to meet you, ma'am." He looked at Ken. "See ya at McGafferty's, Bingo."

Ken pulled an invoice from his back pocket. "Looks like she's tipping in all the right places." There was subtly, and then there was Ken's approach.

"Sorry if I bothered you today."

"Just a quick signature and we'll be out of your hair."

"Is your phone number on the invoice?"

"The main office phone numbers on it."

"Do you have a direct number I can call?"

Crazy bitch. "Guess I can give you my cell phone number."

"Wonderful."

Ken jotted the cell phone number on the back of the invoice and handed it to the old lady.

"I'm Delores," she said, setting the invoice on the round, wooden table. She grabbed the picture frame and brought it close to Ken's face. "My Jonathon's like you, too."

"What?" His stomach dropped. Walls started closing in. Fingers. Flags. Piano keys. Garth's big mouth. "The office address is on the invoice." He stepped back, bumping into the piano. "Sorry." He blinked. Trying to focus. Right foot. Left foot. Control. Breathe. He bumped into the piano. Again. "Take care, ma'am."

"Jonathon won't talk to me about it either." She grabbed Ken's hand and set it on the piano. "This is his piano and he hasn't played it in ten years."

Ken pulled his hand away. "If you need a piano tuner, Janice in the office can hook you up." Everything was dizzy. Fuzzy. The opposite of outer confidence and inner control. He bumped into the wall. "Forgive my clumsiness."

"Would you mind it terribly if I gave Jonathon your phone number?"

"What?" He tripped over his own feet and fell to his knees.

"Do you need a cold towel?" She pressed her hands against his forehead, cheek, neck, arms; the same way his mother used to press her hand against his skin whenever he was ill as a boy. "My Jonathon gets really dizzy too, sometimes."

"I'm okay, but thank you." He stood and bumped into the piano. Again. It didn't matter. The job was compromised. He'd been outed by Garth. The old lady was harassing him, soliciting from him things of which she had no right to meddle.

"He needs someone gentle like you." She stood in the doorway. "Someone who pays close attention to detail and follows through."

"I can't help you." Why couldn't he be rude and push her away? Why couldn't he have been born that way? "You've got the wrong guy."

"You're exactly the right kind of guy. I know it."

"I'm not."

"But how do you know? I mean, you haven't even met him."

Ken's shoulder brushed against the old lady's shoulder as he exited the doorway. The wind cooled his neck and the sun warmed his cheeks as he walked to the truck. Which wasn't there. Shit.

Alone, he spun round and around. Goddamn it, Garth. Really.

"See that little red house down there on the left?" she asked, startling him, her boney finger almost touching his nose.

Ken sat on the curb and sighed. Why not. It's all fucked up anyway.

"That's my Jonathon's house." She sat beside him. "He hardly ever comes out anymore and when he does he's always in his pajamas. I watch from the window hoping someone will show up and talk to him and maybe even go inside, but no one ever does." She paused. "I wouldn't even care if it was a guy."

Ken studied the red house. Peeling paint. More weeds in the yard than grass. Every window curtain was closed. A toppled-over bicycle laid in front of a tan-colored garage door.

"It's just a phone number," she said. "A simple idea that may or may not work."

They sat quiet for a very long time.

"Do you know what a secret shopper is?" Ken asked.

She nodded.

"I actually thought you might be one."

"I am one." She smiled. "My ex-husband and your employer Lyle Carlson go way back. I've only met him a few times but when he recognized my name in the appointment book he called to ask if I'd participate." She patted a hand on Ken's leg. "You have nothing to worry about. No one has ever been as tender and gentle."

Ken picked another dandelion, wondering whether Lyle had asked her to spy on him or on Garth. Maybe Garth had outed him to Lyle, too. Maybe recruiting her as a secret shopper was Lyle's reaction? Maybe the discrimination Ken had fought so hard to avoid through concealment was now playing out right in front of his face. The old lady flung a lump of gray hair from one side to the other and wiggled red toenails. Like a nervous girl around a nervous boy.

"He may not even like me. I mean, what if I'm not his type."

"He will like you." She sniffled. "You're soft-spoken and deliberate and I hope I'm not overstepping my bounds but you're quite handsome." She dabbed her cheeks with a sleeve, staring at her son's house. "He's been mishandled so much during his life. I just want him to find someone who doesn't act that way."

They stared at Jonathon's house for a few minutes. Handsome, Ken thought, and gay. Like Jonathon.

"After he told us he was a homosexual, his father and I told him that he wasn't and that he was to never use that word around us, because it was sick." Her voice cracked. "But now that I'm sick, I've come to realize he isn't sick."

"How are you sick?"

"Parkinson's." Her hands shook. "It gets worse every day. I can't drive anymore but at least I'm not in a wheelchair." She turned and looked at her own house. "The only reason I didn't sign the invoice in there is because I didn't want you to see me scribble my name like a kindergartner."

"It's okay."

"It's hard for me to show weakness," she said. "I've always been a pretty stubborn gal."

"I understand weakness and stubbornness."

"I actually used to think gay meant weakness. But I don't anymore. Parkinson's of all things helped me see that. People stare at my twitching. Kids laugh at my tremors. Teenagers snicker whenever I drop something in the store. Men, by not looking at me at all, look at me as if I'm already dead. Illness changed me, and even though I'm not sure gay means strength, I sure as hell know it doesn't mean weak."

"I don't talk to my parents about it either."

"Do you think they'd respond negatively, like I did at first?"

"My mom's pretty disconnected and my dad's not much of an open-thinker."

"How did your friend find out?"

"He pestered it out of me."

"He seems like a sweet fellow."

"He is."

They sat quiet for a short time.

"Can you hold on for another second?" She shuffled to the house. Leaving the front door wide open. Reappearing holding the two rainbow-colored flags. "Would you mind helping me put one in my yard and then go with me to put one in Jonathon's yard? I've wanted to do it for a while but I haven't had the nerve. I only recently found out through the internet that rainbows are your guy's symbol for being out and proud of who you are."

Out and proud, Ken thought, watching the old lady struggle to push the flag in the grass. In the middle of the yard. "I'm neither of those things, ma'am."

"Good thing today's a new day," she said.

"Did you say your name's Delores?"

"Loeffler." She nodded. "Delores Loeffler."

"I'm Ken Talbert." He walked beside her down the street and stepped into the middle of Jonathon's yard. "Put your hands on top of mine and let's do it together," she said. Ken obeyed. "One. Two. Three." Her porcelain skin felt smooth and cold against his hot, callous palms. The flag began to flutter. She stepped back and smiled. "Perfect. Right?"

"I hope it works out."

"It has to. He has to come and play his piano again. I have to see his fingers and kiss his neck and tell him I love him." They stood quiet for a short time. "I have another idea, if you're up for it." She smiled. "Would you ever want to come visit me again?"

Hell no. "I'm pretty busy, but yeah, maybe that's something I could do."

"I'm not even sure how I'm gonna get your phone number to Jonathon, but in case he does call, his full name's Jonathon Phillip Loeffler, okay."

"Jonathon Phillip Loeffler," Ken said. "Got it."

"Do you think he'll connect the two flags and understand what it means?"

"I hope so."

"No matter how many people say you and Jonathon are less, I don't believe it anymore."

"Thanks for the lemonade and for letting me help with the flags."

"Come visit whenever you want and bring your friend, too." She laughed. "Okay, Bingo."

Ken laughed, turned around, and walked and walked (and walked). Four miles. To McGafferty's. Past McGafferty's. Three miles. Past his sister's apartment complex. Two miles. Past the Love-Tenders adult bookstore, Hickman Park's public restroom, and Albert Saxon's house, the town's closeted gay mayor who Ken regularly fucked on weekends. One mile. Past his parent's house. Past the junior high school. Stopping in front of his own little red house. Without a flag. Or a piano. Or a Jonathon. For now.

Which Face Today?

Another ad campaign. A basic job. Seven or eight hours. Hundred bucks an hour. Come sober and showered. No makeup or hair products. Subtle piercings and tattoos are fine. Snacks and water provided. Don't be late.

The studio set consists of a green screen, a child's writing desk, a thumb tack, and a pair of sharp tongs. Tools I've seen before and understand the purpose of their fashion.

"This campaign isn't about comfort," the photographer tells me and six other men as different as six men can be except for our naturally thick hair and facial boyishness. It's apparent that I'm the tall, skinny choice. Number 1 according to the headshot storyboard.

The make-up dude, practicing what he preaches, says, "Smear a bunch of black eyeliner underneath both eyes and tousle your hair like a wind storm meets Abercrombie."

"Number one." A voice calls from above. I sit on the writing desk. Tight, white boxers ride up my ass.

"Now cry." The photographer drops to his knees. "But don't ugly up your face."

"Like tears-tears?"

"Last time I checked, this wasn't an acting class." He lies on the ground and switches camera lenses. "I need real tears from a place of real pain. Do you have that in you or not? If not, use the tools to make some."

"I don't need tools." If fifty-odd theater gigs have taught me anything, it's how to cry (and laugh) on cue, the surest and fastest way to get a call back stapled to a paycheck. More, I have the images of my mother's swollen face and my father's beer bottle hands to get the waterworks started.

"Excellent. I can see real pain in your eyes."

The camera flashes pop like strobe lights at a dance club.

"Now put your fingers over your face like a spider and let the tears and mascara bleed together."

I push my fingers into my face, weeping the brokenness spanning my own history.

"Genius. Whatever you're thinking about, don't stop."

The other men come in and whisper among themselves. Nobody likes to be outdone. Upstaged. Praised. Over-modeled.

"God, you're so fresh and exciting right now." The photographer clicks. A step stool appears at his feet. "I'm gonna shoot down on you but don't look up. Stay focused on whatever it is you're feeling. It's totally brill."

Two days later, walking home from another casting—everyone's got something to sell—I see my face plastered on the side of a city bus, underneath the words, *don't-let-your-sad-old-car-ruin-your-life*. Fingers spread apart. Black mascara running down my cheeks. Real pain oozing from my eyes. Had I not just been smiling for Crest, I might have sat on the bench at the bus stop and wept.

The Weebies

Walker Weebie understood setbacks, both in theory and in practicality. The upcoming weekend had the potential for setbacks, although he couldn't imagine any worse-case scenario than being sunburn, tired, stinky and wet. He brought the cell phone back to his ear and listened to his older sister, Janelle, beg him to join her and her family (J.R., Jeremy and Janessa) along with Walker and Janelle's older brother Ronnie, and Ronnie's family (Rhonda, Rylan and Ricki) at Huntington State Park for a three-day Fourth of July weekend celebration.

"Celebration? Okay. If you say so," Walker said.

"In case you forgot where it is," she said. "It's off Highway 91 by that big-ass rock that looks like a dildo."

"What can I bring?"

"Just bring your sleeping shit and some water stuff and we got the rest covered."

"It'll be nice to see you." He paused before saying, "And Ronnie too."

"Come around three, okay?"

"Three it is." He hung up the phone, comforted by the excitement in Janelle's voice. It had been six years since their last visit. He scanned the home office, admiring the textured walls and complimentary furniture, everything designed with a sense of purpose and order. Unlike Huntington State Park, a three-mile trek from his boyhood home—if a poorly constructed trailer house can even be called a home—where he played hide and seek with squirrels, floated the river on twisted branches, and climbed trees in which he often slept overnight, preferring oak roughness to the squeaky full-size metal-framed bed he was made to share with Ronnie. Ronnie? What a rotten name. And boy.

Nestled in bed against his wife, Laura, Walker dreamed overnight of frightening things he ignored in daylight. He awakened at 6:30 am and slipped out of bed, adoring for a few minutes Laura's sfumato face, tan-brown hair, and High Renaissance body of which Da Vinci's paintbrush would find greed and creed in painting. He showered and dressed in blue jeans and a favorite Handsome-Dan Yale t-shirt. Back in the office, he thumbed through a stack of cover letters and resumes from unemployed teachers looking for work—there were always so many. At 8:30 am, he went to the garage and carefully packed camping gear into the Porsche Cheyanne, last year's Christmas gift from Laura—Doctor Laura Livingston from the New Hampshire Livingston's—and stared for a long time out the den's bay window at the row of pine trees in the backyard, wondering if forgiveness, like forgetfulness, is something only people who don't need, find.

"Just remember who you are and who they are not," Laura said, blowing kisses as he backed from the garage. Such a lucky man. Blessed even. Flourishing. Way ahead of most. A-OK.

10:45am

Driving past ever-expanding tree groves confined to sparser and sparser small towns, he rubbed a thumb over the pink post-it note Laura had stuck to the dashboard—"Install GPS and don't get lost." So funny. So thoughtful. So sexy. But he didn't need GPS. He liked finding his own way. She knew this. There were no secrets between them. Well, almost none. His cell-phone rang. DAD appeared on the screen. The hands-free Bluetooth took over. "Hey dad."

"Laura says you're going camping with them." He coughed. "Tell me it isn't true."

Damn it, Walker thought. She promised not to tell him. "Did Laura call you or did you call her?"

"She said she's not crazy about you going there."

"I haven't seen them since mom's death."

"They're still the same." He coughed (and coughed). "You could have at least taken Laura along."

"The hospital needed her," he lied. She could have come if she'd wanted too. Walker exited Highway 91 and turned into an Exxon station. His hands quivered against the steering wheel. "But I do appreciate the concern."

"I'm sorry I failed you when you were little."

"You didn't fail me."

"You're too forgiving, Walker."

"Have you tried the Nicorette lozenges I sent? You do like spearmint, right?" Walker wanted an answer, and he wanted it to be yes. One present-day yes to counterbalance so many long-ago nos.

"They're bad eggs, son. They don't see things like you and Laura do. Please turn around."

Walker first saw Laura in the Yale University library, sitting in a cubicle studying the twenty muscles in the foot. He was finishing a research paper about Commerce and Ethics and The Role of Big Government in the American Public School System when a lavender scent, his mother's scent, caught and held his attention. The small part of his heart that still belonged to his mother sought out the scent, and led him to Laura. Standing behind her, he closed his eyes and bathed in his mother's memory. A fingertip tapped his shoulder. It was Laura.

"Are you okay?" she asked.

He hadn't realized he'd been crying. "You and my mother wear the same perfume."

Laura winked, and whispered, "I'm heading to the snack shop for some fries. You wanna tag along?"

In the time it took them to walk from the library to the snack shop, Walker knew he wanted to keep walking. With her. Forever. Fast friends. Boyfriend and girlfriend. Yale's cutest couple 1997. Walker enjoyed learning about Laura's childhood: book-reading mornings, pink bicycle afternoons, and firefly nights in the backyard beside an in-ground swimming pool with underwater neon lights. Walker spoke more coolly of childhood, careful neither to overshare the impoverishment nor understate the squalidness of his parents, Bob and Jeanine, and his two step-siblings, Janelle and Ronnie, who did whatever they wanted, however they wanted, whenever they damn well pleased.

Walker focused instead on what he called "The Illumination Outcome," a concept grounded in the notion that although family dysfunction is a combination of genetic factors and environmental conditions, the dysfunction can be overcome through determination and hard work. Whereas Janelle and Ronnie were only half-blooded Weebie, he was full-blooded. Whereas Janelle and Ronnie quit school at the age of fifteen, he excelled at line leadership duties, Charles Dickens, the FOIL algebra system, public speaking, senior-class salutatorian, and tuition-free academic scholarships to Ohio State, Yale, and Cornell. His dissertation regarding Twenty Key Disadvantages of Children Reared in Cyclical Systemic Poverty in Small Town Rural America earned him both a second doctorate and The Fannie and John Hertz Foundation Prize for outstanding achievement in thought leadership writing. No other Weebie had made it past the ninth grade.

"Promise me you'll keep your phone handy, okay, son?"

"You do like spearmint, right dad?"

"I wish you'd go back to Laura."

"Janelle's gonna be there so it'll be fine."

"That girl's worse than Ronnie is."

"I gotta go, dad. Goodbye."

"Did you forget what he did to you?"

"I gotta go, dad. I'll call you later." Of course he hadn't forgotten. Or forgiven. Another reason he had to go. Time to right the wrong. Time to repair what still hurt. Time for everyone to grow up and move on and, goddamn it, love.

1:51pm

Walker laughed out loud at the sight of the dildo—more like an erect piece of limestone jutting from a slate of sandstone—but the comparison, however rudimentary, was satisfactory. Odd that he'd never noticed it, he thought as he turned onto a narrow dirt road and followed two deeply imbedded tire tracks through monster trees, meddlesome critters, and a collection of human beings embellished in all manner of swim trunks, fair food, and perspiration. Campsite 27 slowly came into focus, every bit as provincial and vulgar as The Valley View Trailer Court where Janelle and Ronnie still chose to reside three manufactured doors apart. He parked in the only available spot, in between a dull-red Pontiac Grand Prix—the side mirrors were attached by duct tape—and a dilapidated black station wagon—with no back seat or radio. He saw Janelle, on her knees, rummaging through a blue suitcase. She wore a sheer, cream-colored nightgown. A red-tipped cigarette hung from the left corner of her mouth. Barefoot and 4'10 at her peak, she epitomized dense relegation. Dark varicose veins amplified her swollen legs, arms, and neck. So little. So sad. Fifteen or twenty feet may have stood between them, but the distance seemed like a million miles. Walker often questioned the privilege he'd come to find with Laura, unsure if it was on loan from someone else's life: someone who'd lost their way; someone who was making a comeback; someone who was going to sneak up behind him when he wasn't aware and snatch it away. For keeps.

He tossed the cell phone, wallet, a second wristwatch, and all of his dad's and Laura's apprehension into the center console, ready to forge ahead and secure some kind of familial alliance. If it was possible. And if it wasn't possible, then he was finished. For good. All or nothing this time. No more floundering in the middle ground for the middle ground. He opened the car door and ground a new pair of Timberland work boots into the rutty soil. The wind stirred mercurial aromas: ragweed, pine, smoke, and liquor. He had to catch his breath. Twice.

"I wondered if you'd really show," Janelle yelled, jogging toward him.

"Just point me to the outhouse and we can mark this weekend as officially started."

She wrapped her arms around his waist, reeking of a successful tobacco industry. "I always forget how gorgeous you are until

I see you again."

"I see you're still keeping our mother's fashion statement alive." He stayed with her hug for six seconds: five seemed dismissive: seven seemed heavy-handed.

"It's outdoor camping, Walker." She released her grip. "It's not a fashion show."

He wished he'd have said something complimentary. Laura, albeit insincere, would have complimented Janelle's cerulean-blue eyes and the blonde and black highlights in her hair travelling to and from any number of greasy split-end destinations. Laura was the better word-savvy-savant. At their wedding reception, before the final tango, she'd lifted a champagne flute in front of the beautifully dressed crowd, and said, "To a man who overcame an unlucky childhood with a slick-oil brain, lifetime eyes, and a cute little ass that gets the privilege of cuddling up to mine for the rest of his. Now I ask you, is he not the luckiest man alive?" Everyone cheered, except for the Weebies, whose invitations were misplaced and never mailed, an accident Laura promised to make right—ASAP. Which she still hadn't done. Failing to fulfill a vow made during a most sacred time in married life, at the beginning, when spoken words become the traction hope utilizes to cultivate more.

"How's Laura doing?" Janelle asked, standing beside Walker in front of the outhouse. "When am I ever gonna meet her? I mean, sometimes I wonder if she's even real."

"Hospitals and sick people don't get holidays off."

"Get your ass outta there." Janelle pounded the outhouse door. "Walk's here and he needs to shit."

"No, I don't." Had he said this to her? "Did I say 'shit'?" He'd forgotten she called him Walk.

"You totally did. Like a second ago. Don't you remember?"

He didn't remember. Nor did he remember walking to the outhouse. And he didn't have to take a shit. "You do know who's inside there, right?"

"He's been in there like for an hour." She stroked an invisible cock. "We all know what you're doing in there, you horndog weirdo."

"Fucking leave me alone," a male voice yelled back. "Goddamn stalker."

"If you're anything like your father you should have been done like fifty-five minutes ago."

Walker laughed. He couldn't help it. "All I have to do is pee." He surveyed the campsite, looking for the nicest, cleanest spot to set up camp. "So, where is everyone?"

"Swimming or fighting probably. I'm just glad for a little peace and quiet. Don't jinx it."

He decided to pitch camp on a patch of dusty-dirt to the right of a large purple tent. "Is that your tent?"

"Nah. It's Ronnie's." She looked over her shoulder. "That mess over there is us."

Pitched directly across from Ronnie's tent, similar in distance to and from the fire pit, Janelle and J.R.'s dark-beige tent sat off-kilter and unsteady. A commanding breeze could end it all. Sweatshirts, bras, CD cases, beach towels, and flip-flops encircled the tent like a moat. So very, very Weebie.

"How's Ronnie been acting?"

"Ronnie's Ronnie. How else would he be acting?" The specificity of her words and the composure in her voice made it clear that over the years, years Walker had been away and years she'd been close by, she'd come to understand, tolerate, and accept Ronnie's ways and means. Perhaps she even liked him. Perhaps she even loved him, too.

"Did I really say 'shit'?" Expletives were forbidden at school; frowned upon by church friends; super tacky according to Laura.

"It's just the word 'shit,' Walk. I mean, everybody says it and does it. It's even allowed on TV these days."

"Is it?"

"Don't tell me you don't have cable."

"We don't actually watch much television."

"Must be nice to live the dream instead of having to watch everyone else live it."

He wished he'd have hugged her without restriction. Why couldn't he do that?

"You do remember how to piss behind a tree, I hope." She pointed to an oak tree leaning sideways across the gravel road, its branches stretching skyward as if pleading with heaven to uproot it and take it away.

"Truthfully, it's been a while."

"It'll all come back to you soon enough. You ain't that far gone."

3:09pm

After Walker peed on the zigzagging roots of an oak tree, he setup camp beside Ronnie's tent, which was furnished with all sorts of expensive- looking camping gear. Walker couldn't help but wonder how much of it had been stolen. Ronnie was a notorious shoplifter in youth. He'd been caught stealing outdoor camping gear from Walmart, Gander Mountain, Cabela's, and Sears more than a dozen times. Felonies. Without a record. Thanks to their mother's speedy fake-tear involvement.

Walker pumped air into the mattress, made the bed, and refolded the clothes in the suitcase. He shook out the welcome mat Laura had rolled up and tucked into the backseat, saying, "Try to at least keep some of their Weebiness out of our tent." How disparaging and mean-spirited. He rolled up the mat and stuffed it inside the rusty brown trashcan sulking beside the outhouse.

"Just my tent this time. Sorry love."

"Looking pretty homey there, Walk," Janelle yelled from inside a square, white canopy—the makeshift mess hall—encumbered with metal tables, antiquated cooking contraptions, and various-sized cardboard boxes Walker hoped held more food than alcohol. "I knew you still had a little Weebie left in ya." Sweat beads pockmarked her face as she washed and rinsed white tube socks and long underwear in a five gallon bucket. She had always exceled at manual labor. Growing up, she washed and dried the clothes, nuked meals, vacuumed carpets, cleaned toilets, straightened rooms, beat rugs, made beds, and sewed bedroom window drapes from random pieces of clothing. Not their mother, but Janelle, shorter than every Weebie by a good seven inches. How could his dad say she was worse than Ronnie?

A swarm of yellow jackets from a hive high in the oak tree swooped down and encircled Walker's tent. Like a warning call, letting him know something bad, something far worse than a swarm of yellow jackets was on its way.

"Nothing can be worse than right here," he whispered, wishing he hadn't spoken, bothered by the ears of this place, by the secrets the air knew about him, by the stench of familiarity that loomed like murky, achy nightmares. Yellow jackets are chasers, his ninth-grade science teacher had told the class. And their movements are fairly subtle, so be mindful, because you never know what they're up too.

"So the townie came after all," Ronnie said, walking his belly fat and crooked teeth toward Walker, his soggy family following behind: Rhonda, a chalk-stick wife; Rylan, a runt of a pre-teenager; and Ricki, a twig-twirling toddler doing a decent job of impersonating a snake. Rhonda's long, blue t-shirt was impregnated with empty pop cans and plastic water bottles. "For the less fortunate kids at the boys' school," she said, without being asked. "Not every kid has it as good as ours." Scorch-red hair emphasized her emaciated leather-tan face and ragamuffin body. Ouch, is all Walker could think.

Walker gave them all a quick smile. He considered giving a hug or offering a hand shake. But he didn't. With so little to consider standing before him, it was easy to stand there and consider very little. And more, they were sopping wet. He said the only thing he could think of. "Seems like you guys got everything under control."

"We know how to do some shit, too." Ronnie unzipped the tent

35

and pushed the boys and Rhonda inside. He turned around and pointed to Walker's Porsche. "Those your wheels?"

"A Christmas gift from Laura."

"Some people, man." He disappeared into the tent, his plump shadow zipping the zipper in one quick blow. Not even a simple hello.

4:29pm

"Screw the pooch, he is alive," J.R., Janelle's husband said, standing between Jeremy, dressed in head-to-toe black, including a Fedora, and Janessa, dressed in a neck-to-knee leopard t-shirt and dark purple Croc's. "Didn't figure I'd ever see you around these parts again." J.R. grabbed a Miller Lite from a red cooler, one of eight red coolers strategically placed around campsite 27: Weebie territory—intruders beware. Walked nodded at Jeremy and Janessa, who nodded back and walked away, whistling in different directions.

"Can I interest you in a cold one?" J.R. asked.

"Nah. I'm okay."

"It's hard to do this sober."

Walker smiled, surprised by J.R.'s lucid deduction. Neither a complete idiot nor the worst drunk in the bunch, J.R. did fall well within the range. "Maybe later." Walker lied. He knew firsthand the ill-effects of alcohol's dangerous misapplications: how it had anesthetized his mother's common sense and manipulated his father's best intentions and deteriorated Janelle and Ronnie's bodies and minds, inside and out. If there was any chance of reconnecting with these people, country folk with hard faces and sad eyes, the task necessitated sobriety. At all times. He had to find out if the weekend held within its actions anything beyond cessation proving to extinction the true meaning of split apart?

4:51pm

Friday evening drifted along smoothly. Everyone except for Walker adding little substance to a chinwag discussion about pop-culture comparisons: Adidas versus Nike, Lebron versus

Curry, Vikings versus Bears, WalMart versus Target, Idiot Trump versus Crooked Hillary, Menthol versus Pectin. The logs inside the fire pit crepitated and spit up like a little baby, adding hedonistic flavor to the moon's gleaming sheen. J.R. and Ronnie drank as many Miller Lite as Janelle and Rhonda smoked Marlboros. The teens made s'mores and paid close attention to their IPhones and ear-buds while Ricki turned a fascination with twigs into a triangle that no one noticed until Ronnie kicked it over and Ricki started to cry.

"Fucking bully." Janelle slapped Ronnie's bare shoulder. "He's like five. I mean, Jesus Ronnie, leave him alone."

"Kids gotta get his head outta the dirt sometime. It ain't right."

Rhonda grabbed for Ricki but Janelle was quicker, bouncing Ricki on her knee until he surrendered to spasmodic spurts of laughter. "Don't fuss little guy. One day you'll be tough enough to kick his ass for all of us."

Ronnie flexed and kissed both biceps. "Ain't nobody here got what it takes to bring me down." He looked at Walker. "But I invite anyone who'd like to give it a try."

Walker stood and pulled from his back pocket nine computer-printed copies of 20 Fun Things to Do While Camping, happy and surprised when no one scoffed, declined, boycotted, stood in defiance, or left in a huff. Even Ricki begged for a copy.

"I thought we could go around one at a time and read each number aloud and then decide which, if any, are doable over the weekend. I can start, if that's okay."

"Tell Early Bar-o-key ghost stories." Janessa said, skipping numbers one through five. "What's Bar-o-key mean?

"It's pronounced baroque. It relates to a style of European architecture, music, and art from the 17th and 18th centuries."

"How retarded."

"Janessa Renee." Janelle released Ricki back to the ground. "Can you not be a snot for one minute?"

"Check ya'll bitches later." Janessa threw her copy into the fire.

"Have fun talking about retarded music no one's ever even heard of."

"Sit your ass down you little brat," Janelle said.

"I'm so not hearing you right now, mom."

"Fine, leave then, but that Spencer's gift card is mine."

"If you can find it, you can have it." Janessa slowly faded into a sheet of mist hanging ominously low and thick at the entrance of the woods.

"Total mind of her own," Janelle said, then yelled, "Don't you go too far in there, missy. I mean it. I'm so not playing with you anymore."

"Fuck off."

"Fuck you, too, then."

"Should someone go after her?" Walker asked. "It's easy to get lost in there, especially in the dark."

"Does she look like she's afraid of the dark to you?" Janelle said.

Walker stared at the mist. She didn't seem afraid of the dark. None of them did.

"Use words that begin with a vowel and make up silly songs about nature," Rylan read sluggishly, skipping numbers six through seventeen. "Lame." He gave his copy to Rhonda and pushed white ear-buds into his ears. "Now this is a song."

"Number 18." Janelle brought the paper to her nose. "Play hide-and-seek using neon glow sticks, solar-powered night wands, or battery-operated flashlights." She giggled. "What are solar-powered night wands? I mean, seriously, Walk, where did you get this list?"

"From camping dot com." He looked up. "Is this not what people do outdoors anymore?"

"We never did these kinds of things."

"Yes we did." He remembered telling hundreds of ghost stories at Huntington State Park. Had he only told them to himself?

"No Weebie but you would wanna make up songs using vowels," she said. "I always did think you came from another family."

She rattled the paper. "Now I have proof."

"Number 20," Ronnie said before Walker could argue the point. Ronnie brought an imaginary pair of spectacles to the tip of his nose and cleared his throat. "Bring extra cash for Sunday brunch in case of inn-clee-mint rain, wind, or cold weather." His tore the paper in half. "I knew you were outta touch dude but come on, seriously, Sunday Brunch?"

"This list is so you, Walk." Janelle laughed. "I'm so dying right now."

"No real camper does shit like this." Ronnie stood and grabbed the papers from everyone's hands, including Walker's. Then he dropped them one by one into the fire, fell back into his chair, and chugged the rest of the beer. "Some people ain't got a goddamn clue about nothing."

10:07pm

"You know who'd think the list was a real hoot," Janelle said, winking at Walker. "Mom."

"To mom." Ronnie lifted a seventh beer in the air. "She married a son-of-a-bitch and died too young but she was still the prettiest lady I ever did know."

"To mom." Walker grabbed a beer for the red cooler. The bottle felt cold and unfamiliar in his hand. He put it back.

"You think she really is resting in peace?" Janelle clicked her beer bottle against Ronnie's.

"Rest well, Leona Charlotte Weebie." Walker said.

"Here here." Ronnie threw another empty bottle in the fire.

"To mom," they said, each bowing their head. First Janelle, then Ronnie, then Walker. Things always ending with Walker.

10:14pm

"Night everyone." Walker stood. "Thanks for a great evening."

"Laura make you go to bed this early at home?" Ronnie asked. "Pretty short leash she's got you on there, don't ya think?"

"I wish we told ghost stories and sang silly songs," Rhonda said, her voice trailing off by the time Walker arrived at his tent.

Inside, he zipped the zipper and remaining fully clothed, including his boots, laying face up on the clean sheets and fleece blanket. "Night love." He blew Laura a kiss but quickly grabbed it and held it inside a tight fist. "You know what? Not tonight, love. Not tonight."

11:16pm

Listening to the brazen, monotonous, hum-drum sound of Weebies being Weebies, Walker released his fist and gradually, then all at once, fell asleep.

11:58pm

Saturday morning sunlight pierced through Walker's mesh-net roof, warming awake first his face and neck and then the rest of his body. A plume of campfire smog hovered above the campsite, coloring everything gray. He sat up and scratched himself like the indigenous grizzly bear he had dreamed of fighting and conquering overnight. His stomach growled. He was hungry. Hungry as a grizzly bear. Well not quite. But close.

7:56am

The other Weebie's stood around the picnic table yawning, picking pajama fabric from their asses.

"Could easily top ninety-five degrees," J.R. said. "Sure your city-slicker skin can handle that much wear and tear?"

"Three bottles of sunblock ought to do it, yeah."

"Maybe if you swallow it or snort it."

"Breakfast duty time," Janelle said, dispersing the group to prearranged tasks without assigning one to Walker. "What can I do?" he asked. Nobody answered. Ronnie opened the lid to the grill and emptied a bag of charcoal. Janessa cracked a dozen eggs into a bowl of pancake mix which she whisked into a gooey lather. Rhonda bragged about her mom's homemade maple syrup and organic strawberries. With metal tongs, Janelle poked strips of bacon, ham, and sausage that sizzled in a frying pan. Rylan separated black plastic forks from white plastic spoons. Ricki picked at his own toenails. Jeremy tossed white paper plates into the air,

40

finger shooting—pew! pew!—each one as it fell like a snowflake to the ground.

"You know how to work a grill?" Ronnie asked Walker. "Or is the rough and tough smoke too much for ya?"

"Walker's helping me," Janelle said, handing Walker the tongs. "Nobody cares about your stupid grill stuff anyway."

"Shrimp."

"Gimp."

"Tong slut."

"Porn freak."

Walker flipped the meat, thankful for its compliant nature.

After breakfast, energy and noise levels increased until pajamas disappeared into tents only to emerge moments later as colorful bathing suits, beach towels, inner tubes, and a dozen or so long, conical swim noodles. Walker hadn't moved, staring at the sticky plates, toppled over cups, and broken plastic forks strewn across the table—a bunch of leftovers nobody else wanted.

9:22am

"Look what I found in the trash," Rhonda said, holding the welcome mat like a banner. "I can't believe someone would throw this away. It's like brand new."

"Stop looking for shit in the trash." Ronnie grabbed the mat and glared at Walker. "You know anything about this?"

Walker nodded.

"Give it back." Rhonda grabbed for it but Ronnie was too quick. "It'd look nice in front of the tent and keep us from dragging so much dirt inside."

"I better not see you touching this fucking thing again." Ronnie made a fist.

"But it's brand new. It's like perfect."

"I said no, bitch."

"But it's so nice."

Ronnie's fist retreated backward, and like a slingshot, thrust forward and landed on Rhonda's right cheek. "I said no, cunt!"

"Fucking bully." Janelle stood between Rhonda and Ronnie. She snatched the mat from Ronnie's hands. "I mean, Jesus, Ronnie, it's a goddamn mat. Let her have it if she wants it."

"Oh, I'll let her have it."

"All I was saying is that it looked brand new," Rhonda cried.

"If it ain't sports, beer, or strip clubs, men can't see shit." Janelle stuck the mat underneath her arm and walked Rhonda to the purple tent. "I don't mean you, Walk." Janelle yelled. "I know you see things exactly as they are."

9:59am

Floating the rivers lukewarm current, heat pouring down summer's sunny endorsement, Walker and Janelle lollygagged twenty feet or so behind the others who littered the river with expletives, off-key country music songs, and the hand-crushing sound of mutilated beer and pop cans. A few cans bounced against Janelle's inner tube and against Walker's chest before drifting to the community of refuse lining the river bank. Walker drudged barefoot along the sandy river bottom, holding like an umbrella over his head one of Janelle's blow-up lounge chairs. In the rush to get to the river, he'd forgotten to put on aqua socks, apply sun block, or grab the brimmed, collapsible wicker hat. Jagged rocks and other indecipherable sharp objects stabbed at his feet and toes.

"How much farther to the end?" he asked Janelle, spinning ass-deep in an inner tube.

"You used to love the water."

"Did I?"

"You loved it even more than me or Ronnie did. Do you remember nothing about growing up here?"

A beer can bounced against his chest. "So much for Rhonda collecting cans for the boys' school."

"That crazy crackpot prolly don't even know the name of the school."

"Like a few loose screws or she needs better medication?"

"Like cuckoo clock nuts. I mean, she still calls Janessa, Vanessa."

"No, she doesn't."

"Have you not been listening to her?"

He hadn't been listening to her. Nor to anyone. Not really.

"She's like super bi-polar. I thought you being married to a doctor and all would know that."

"Has she been diagnosed?"

"Haven't you been watching her?"

He hadn't been watching her. Should he have been? Maybe she was bi-polar. Maybe Ronnie was bi-polar—that'd explain a few things. Maybe Janelle and J.R were also bi-polar. And all the children. And his dad. And mom. Maybe the whole bunch suffered with mental illness. Laura regularly postulated the theory of Weebie abnormality, linking it to heredities, hyperbole, and hysteria.

"I can't believe how big your kids have become." Walker said. "Jeremy's practically a giant."

"He knows he's fat, Walk." She stopped spinning. "We all know we're fat."

"That's not what I meant."

"We can't afford fancy gyms and personal trainers like some people."

"I don't have a personal trainer."

"Whatever."

"You still work at the plant store?"

"I haven't worked there for three years."

"Is J.R.'s still working at the salt plant?"

"Jeremy don't bring any of his homework home."

"You still playing video games on the Wii?"

"That dumb school put him in summer classes but they ain't helping him a bit."

Walker didn't want to bring out Principle Weebie. Not here. Not now. "Most schools do offer tutoring programs." Weakling.

"Isn't that what those classes are for?"

"A lot of tutors make house calls."

"I don't want some rich, nosey-ass teacher judging our house."

Rich teachers? Walker wanted to laugh. But he didn't. "Just throwing out some options."

"None of the chairs around the kitchen table match and we still don't have a couch. Have you forgotten what our house looks like?"

He hadn't forgotten, staying overnight at Janelle's request the evening of their mother's funeral, made to use the convenience store toilet across the street, as hers was wrapped with blue tarp. The shower head trickled egg-smelling water. The tuna casserole had a long, black hair in it. The fork tines were bent. The one lamp in the living room was broken. And Janessa's white sheets and pillowcase were stained with longitudinal brown lines and latitudinal red streaks. Lucky for Walker, Laura had enough foresight to tuck a set of 800-thread count sheets with two matching pillowcases into the bottom of the suitcase. As he changed the sheets, he vowed to never visit again. A vow he'd kept. A vow he planned on keeping.

"Did you know he was doing so poorly in school?" he asked.

"They sent this weird test home for me and J.R. to fill out." She slapped the water. "Some dumb hundred and fifty questions that don't have anything to do with math or science that's for sure."

Likely an IEP behavioral assessment. "Are the questions multiple-choice?"

"Circle S if he sometimes answers the phone correctly. O if he often hates doing chores. A if he complains about headaches. He's never had a headache in his life. I mean, he has trouble reading. He don't have headaches. It's like they want me to say he's retarded or something. But he's not. He's just unmotivated, and isn't it the school's job to keep him motivated and stuff? I mean, does your school send tests like that home?"

"We administer similar tests."

"Well, what are they for?"

"It's a standardized assessment tool designed to help parents measure and record for school staff their child's behavioral and developmental state of mind."

"Standardized what?"

Dumb it down, Walker. "They want to see him through your eyes."

"One of the questions is does he sleep with his parents. I mean, Jesus, Walk, we're not lunatics."

Walked laughed, instantaneously regretting it.

"Don't laugh at me, Walk."

"Sleeping with parents suggests the same room, not the act of sexual intercourse."

"But it says word for word does he sleep with his parents."

Walker set the blow-up chair on the water. He jumped aboard, paddled to Janelle, and grabbed the inner-tube. "A child Jeremy's age sleeping in his parent's bedroom is considered abnormal behavior."

"He's had his own room since he was a baby."

"Then tell them that."

"But the test only has letters to circle."

"You're allowed to add supplementary comments, questions, and concerns." God, he sounded like a principal.

"What would I write?"

"That he's had his own room since he was baby."

"J.R. told me to bring the test, but I didn't because I didn't want you to think we were all stupid."

"I don't think you're stupid."

"Why don't that school just call me on the phone and ask me if he gets happy or sad or angry really quickly."

"You can phone them, too, ya know."

"Yeah, and say what? I don't know any big-ass fucking words."

"I'm happy to go over the test with you on the phone, if that'd help."

"You ever heard of the Tard-Yard?"

"The what?"

"The Tard-Yard. Some place at school where apparently all the retards hang out." She fell off the side of the inner-tube only to pop her head through the center hole and set her chin and arms on the rubbery shell. "I guess that's the group where Jeremy belongs."

"I've honestly never heard that term."

"It's kinda hard to make him do something I can't even do."

"I can try to talk to him about school if you'd like."

"But you have to be secretive about it. Can you even be secretive?"

Walker made an X over his chest. He could be very secretive. She had no idea.

"Part of me's glad you're not a secretive type of person but the other part of me wishes you'd stop being such a pussy and just enjoy the river for what it is. You know as well as I do how fast the summer comes and goes around here."

"Enjoy the river. Got it." He smiled. She was right. Summer did fly by fast, opposite in every way from the ever-winding river.

Going on and on and on.

1:41pm

Back at the campsite, thanks to The Huntington State Park Volunteer Transportation Patrol, Walker sat lazily on a fold-up lawn chair near the fire pit and listened to loon's call out in melodic timbres, a sound only mother nature could create and the Weebie's could disregard. Laura would insist he change out of his wet clothes and help clean up. But why bother. Sand in his eyes and ass seemed apropos. Even the wildest flowers here refused to blossom. The toughest grass failed to grow. Only yellow jackets flourished here, swooping and buzzing around his face.

Janelle tossed a bag of Doritos and peanut M&M's on the picnic table. "Eat up bitches." Rhonda and Ronnie went inside the purple tent and zipped it up. Rylan emptied the bag of Doritos on the table and turned the bag into a flying carpet ride. Janessa plopped on the ground and braided her own hair. Jeremy disappeared into the outhouse. Again. Rylan shoved earbuds in his ears and laid face up on the dirt outside the fire pit while J.R. mumbled to himself about who'd done what already and who better man-up and help him with dinner. Walker's name didn't come up, making it easier for him to close his eyes, wrap like a turban a beach towel around his face, and cover his ears with his hands.

2:14pm

"Sup," Jeremy said, tapping Walker's shoulder. "You ain't much into camping, huh?"

"What?" Walker sat up. "What time is it?"

"It's like four."

"Is it really?"

"You ever been camping before?"

"Quite a lot actually. I know it's hard to believe, but I guess I've come to enjoy nature more from the perspective of an indoor window or from a sofa in a four-season porch."

"Mom told me to wake you up and say hey."

"Hey."

"Said you weren't having much fun and that I should talk to ya."

Walker smiled. "Go on. I'm listening." He did want to know more about the Tard-Yard—what an ugly word. And image. Kids cordoned by labels. Students at his school did not use this term. Jeremy sat quiet, staring at his own hands.

"Why so much black?" Walker asked.

"Why not?"

"Touché." Walker stood and made his way to the outhouse: a guy can only put off the call of nature for so long.

5:13pm

For dinner, Walker gobbled up Frito's, baked beans, hot dogs, white buns, and four Little Debbie Nutty Bars, proof that sugar makes everything better. Only twenty-two hours to go. Piece of cake. God, for a moist, gluten-free piece of cake. He walked to his car, mainly to check for cell phone messages—perhaps a sweet one (or two) from Laura—but also to relax in the comfort of an ergonomic seat with some fast-blast air conditioning. He stopped at the driver's side door and sighed. A deep scratch was embedded from the door handle to the gas tank cover. He felt queasy. Upon closer examination, the scratch ended in a W. "Perfect."

"That's what happens when you have the nicest car here," Janelle said, tickling Walker's ribs. "I mean, get a rental car next time."

"Why is this place always so difficult?" He retraced the scratch—definitely a W.

"You can't do anything about it now so why waste time fretting about it."

"Who would do such a thing?"

"I wouldn't put it past that sneaky little brat Rylan," she whispered. "God, I hate that kid."

Retracing the scratch a third time, Walker couldn't recall seeing Rylan do anything sneaky. And he didn't consider Rylan a brat. No. That title belonged to Janessa. Walker sighed and turned to Janelle. "I'm not sure if you know this or even care, but dad's health is pretty bad. He's coughing a lot and I don't think he's taking his medication. I ought to check to see if he's called and left a message."

"Bet you didn't know it was him who bought me my first pack of cigarettes."

"No, he didn't. Why would you say that?"

"Ask Ronnie if you don't believe me. Who do you think got him started?"

Unfortunately, it made perfect Weebie sense. "So what if he did?" Walker sat on the ground, in the dirt. Janelle sat across. Like kids. Like friends. Like dirty Weebie's with nothing better to do than be dirty in the dirt.

"His only condition for buying me smokes was that I had to smoke outside because he didn't want any smoke around you." She shook her head. "Didn't care if it was around us, mind you."

"I tell him to call you, to check in, to be involved in some way as a grandpa. I do."

"I'm over it, Walk. He's never liked me or Ronnie. I know that."

"But he's still your dad."

"He's not my dad."

"I don't understand why we can't all get along."

"If you and Laura got married today, would you invite us to the wedding?"

"I put your names on the invitation list."

"Was dad at the wedding?'

"No."

"Did Laura not want us there?"

How to answer. What to say. What not to say. Always tiptoeing between fact and fiction. So many juxtapositions. So many spools of Weebie thread tightening and unravelling. "She grew up very different from us. I don't think she's been camping a day in her life."

"What have you told her about us?"

Train wreck. Insufficiency. Embarrassment. "She's an only child who comes from old money so it's difficult for her to see anything, or anyone, beyond the eyes of privilege."

"Is she a snob?"

"Growing up, she never once heard her parents fight. Can you believe that?"

"I want to ask you a question, Walk, but I need you to promise that you won't get mad, okay?"

"Okay."

"Did Ronnie hurt you when you were little?"

Walker sat quiet. What to admit? What to omit? "Hurt's an ambiguous term."

"What's am-big-u-ous mean?"

"Open to more than one interpretation."

"Oh." Janelle shrugged. "Well, there was this one afternoon when mom and Ronnie and I were smoking inside the house and dad came in with an almost empty bottle of whiskey and he looked pretty jacked up and he came at Ronnie calling him a rapist and said Ronnie was gonna burn in hell for what he'd done. I'd never seen so much hate in someone's eyes and I knew one-hundred percent that whatever Ronnie had done dad wanted to kill him for doing it, but then mom stood up and got between them and told dad if he mentioned it to anyone, she'd blame him and just like that dad shut up and left the house."

"He used the word rapist?"

"A couple weeks later, Mom was really jacked up on Long Island Ice Teas and we were sitting on the couch watching TV and she started yelling your and Ronnie's names into her hands, like her tongue was stuck on replay. She kept calling you a liar and saying Ronnie was a good boy and then she slumped over on the couch and started snoring and I figured it was just drunk talking but then the next morning when I asked her about it she told me if I ever brought it up again she'd make me go back to school and take away my cigarettes and since I wasn't gonna have any of that I just stayed the fuck quiet and smoked outside behind the house. Do you know what she was talking about?"

Walker nodded, sifting sand through his fingers. Janelle sighed, picking grime from her fingernails.

"Did he hurt you?"

"Did he hurt you?" Walker replied.

Janelle stood and pressed her hands against the nightgown. "Do you think it's tacky that I wear these?"

Super tacky. "It's your thing, so no, not really."

"I feel comfortable in it, ya know? Like it's a kind of super hero cape. Like I've got a little bit of Wonder Woman in me too, and even though I don't have a hot body or nice hair or some invisible plane to fly off in, I've still got something to offer. Like maybe someday someone's gonna get hurt and my nightgown is gonna keep them from bleeding to death or warm them up if they're cold. I so much want Jeremy and Janessa to see themselves as

Wonder Woman and Superman but I know they don't and I know they wish for cool cars and lots of money and I feel like that's my fault they don't have those things because me and J.R. aren't smart enough to find a way to get them those things even though we both want to. Do you think I'm weird for thinking that way?"

"Not at all."

"Really?"

"Really."

They sat quiet for a short time.

"Did Ronnie hurt you?" She lit a cigarette and offered it to Walker. "You can tell me."

Walker took the cigarette from Janelle's lips and brought it to his own. "How do I even fucking do this?"

"Just put it in your mouth, suck in, hold the smoke in for a second or two, and blow it out." She laughed. "It's not that hard."

"I'm glad my first cigarette makes you so happy."

"I've never heard you swear before and seeing you hold a cigarette is kinda funny. I guess perfect Walker Weebie isn't so perfect after all."

"I've never claimed perfection."

"Then take a drag, Marlboro man."

"Is there a wrong way to do this?"

"Not unless you plan on eating it."

Warm smoke filled Walker's mouth while the smell of burning ash soured his acidic stomach. How could anyone enjoy this? He coughed. Like dad. Tiny puffs of white-gray smoke escaped his mouth. He took another drag, blew it out, and handed the cigarette to Janelle. "This is definitely a sensation."

"That's the worst drag I've ever seen anyone take in my whole life."

"So there is a wrong way to do it." He coughed. And coughed. Waving a hand over his face.

"If you do it like that there is." She brought the cigarette to her lips. Sucked in. Held the smoke for a second or two. Blew it out.

Perfection. Skill. Wonder Woman. Of sorts. "Does Laura know you swear?" Janelle poked a finger into his bellybutton.

"Fuck no."

"Does she swear?"

"Only on the Bible and on elitist feminists."

They laughed and laughed (and laughed).

"Do you have any idea the pressure I feel whenever you're around?" Janelle asked. "I mean, before you came here, I sat all the kids down and told them what swear words were okay to say and which ones weren't okay and to not be mean to each other around you and don't tell dirty jokes or say sexual things because I didn't want you to feel uncomfortable." She laughed. "I'd never do that for anyone but you."

Walker followed with a finger a line of ants marching forward, each one carrying its own weight, each one united in purpose and cause, each one caring for the other. "If I can get dad and Laura to agree to come here for Christmas, would be open to that?"

"Does Laura think she's better than you because you're a Weebie?"

Walker rubbed a growing beard and looked directly into Janelle's eyes, frightened by the dark-gray bags sagging underneath, and by the hardline wrinkles spreading across her forehead, cheeks, and chin. He wanted to tell the truth. About something. Once. Maybe once was enough. Weebie to Weebie. As it should be. But he hesitated, uncertain if Janelle was the right first person to tell. Did she possess enough intellectual acumen to comprehend both Laura's Weebie prejudices and also the truth about Ronnie's abusive, devilish cruelness? "Let's talk more tonight." He stood. "Maybe after everyone's gone to bed."

Janelle stood and wiggled out of the nightgown, placing it across Walker's shoulders. "Let it help you, Walk. Let it heal whatever's hurting ya, okay?"

"I think I'm gonna pack up and go home."

"Nothing bad's gonna happen here, especially now that you

have the cape."

He wrapped the nightgown around his waist and pulled Janelle into a hug. Ten seconds. The longest hug he'd ever given her. "Thanks, sis."

"We're family, Walk, and that's what family does. Now let's go to the lake and wash up, you stinky man. And don't you dare forget to talk to me later about the mom and Ronnie thing, okay?"

"Talk later. Got it." He knotted the nightgown. Staring at his sister, standing in a tan bra and panties, rolls of fat plopping out from every nook and cranny, he'd never liked, nor loved, her more. "You are a wonder woman. Now get."

"You really don't think it's tacky?"

"Not anymore."

"Yayzers." She clapped, jogging to the tent.

Back at the picnic table, Walker stood behind Rylan, who was playing Solitaire. A half-empty bottle of Jameson whiskey sat well within reach. The campsite was eerily free of every other Weebie. Quietness pervaded the area, quietness Walker hoped might last for the rest of the trip. Janelle reappeared seconds later wearing a light-blue nightgown and lime-green flip flops. "You guys coming to the river to wash up?" She waved a small, mesh bag of mini-toiletries in front of her face. "I'll share."

"I think I'm gonna hang back here for a while." Walker sat on the nightgown, across from Rylan.

"Suit yourself, Walk. Oh, and I am sorry about your car."

He looked at Rylan. Was this little runt capable of keying a car? "You into cars?"

"No." Rylan scowled.

"Got ya last." Ronnie said, sneaking up behind Janelle, behind all of them, knocking the toiletry bag from her hands. Got ya last: a silly game Ronnie and Janelle played as children; a game they apparently still played as adults. If Laura had come, she'd tell Walker to get up and help Janelle pick up the toiletries, be a kind, helpful brother and decent human being. Which he was. And so much more. He wasn't the snob. He wasn't the liar. He wasn't the elitist feminist. He grabbed the Jameson whiskey bottle by the neck and brought the opening to his lips, tilting his head back to allow the warm liquid to fill his mouth, throat, and stomach. Numb it all, mother fucker. Do your worst. Or best. I double-dog dare you.

Ronnie's large hand came fast and hard at Rylan's head, smacking the back of it, messing up Rylan's swooped-to-the-right hairstyle that Walker believed was a bit feminine for a boy who already looked more feminine than most boys. "Keep your ass on this bench, talking to your mother like that." Ronnie smacked Rylan's head again. "Yeah, she told me what you said. I hear you've moved even an inch from this table, you ain't gonna be able to sit for a week. You hear me, you fucking little smart-aleck?"

7:07pm

"You know how to play Rummy?" Walker asked Rylan. Another drink.

"Rummy's lame."

"It's a game of skill and strategy."

"I said it's lame, dude." Rylan played another game of Solitaire while Walker set the bottle on the ground and placed his hands, palms up, on the edge of the table, a compliant position he often used at school whenever he conferred with a child who had recently been hurt by a peer, a teacher, a sibling, or a parent. It happened a lot more frequently than people realized.

"We haven't talked much, you and me. How about we remedy that over a game or two of." Walker paused, "if not Rummy, what about Kings in the Corner?"

"That's lamer than Rummy."

"Then let's play Rummy."

"You play with ten or thirteen cards?"

"Ten." Walker had never played with thirteen. Was that even allowed? Another drink.

Game after game, Walker lost and Rylan won, happy to play the victor's role: fist bumping the air, his own knuckles, and the

54

top of the picnic table. "You suck at this, dude."

"Any fun plans for the rest of the summer?"

"I'm gonna see Kid Rock at the fair next month."

"Is he a rapper?" Another drink.

"Rock and roll, dude. Rap's lame."

"Noted. So what grade are you going into next year?"

"Fuck school."

"That's one way to approach it."

"Math and science are lame but geography's okay when it's on Russia."

"A man of the world, are we?" Another drink. "I like adventuresome people."

Rylan won. Again. "You tired of losing, dude?" He yawned and outstretched his arms. "I can't wait to leave this lame town and go to Russia and never come back."

"Why Russia?"

"I'm gonna be a spy for the KGB."

"Why not spy for the American CIA or FBI?"

"American spies are lame."

"How many American spies do you know?"

"I own like seventy-five spy movies."

"Who are you gonna spy on in Russia?"

"Bad people who deserve to be caught."

"Caught for doing what?" Another drink.

"Criminal shit, what else?"

"Like stealing stuff or murdering people or…"

"First," Rylan interrupted. "I'm gonna machete every man who beats on ladies and kids and dogs and then I'm gonna hijack some money from some big banks and buy a big house with a big swimming pool and find some hot chicks who wanna get naked and party hard inside of it."

"You ever heard of Russian Nesting Dolls?"

"Dolls." Tiny wrinkles spread across his forehead. "Like dolls for girls."

"They're not Barbie dolls."

"Dolls are dolls, dude."

"A lot of men own them."

"Who. Men like you?"

"Yeah, like me. Like your dad. J.R. All types of guys."

"I said dolls are lame."

"You say 'lame' a lot. Why is everything lame?"

"Lame. Lame. Lame." He crossed his arms. "Lame."

"I don't think KGB spies say the word 'lame.'"

"They would if what they were looking at was."

"Nice rejoinder, but I still don't think they'd say it." Another drink.

"Whatever, dude." He looked toward the river, at the tents, at the fire pit, at Walker. "So what word would they use then?"

"Lame suggests an appetite for apathy."

Rylan shrugged.

"Do you know what apathy means?" There was a short silence. "It's the condition of indifference, a lack of interest or concern. You don't seem indifferent to me."

"I don't care how anybody sees me."

"Wanting to save women, children, and dogs from abuse is far from lame. It's actually quite noble. As for hijacking money from a bank, that's a bit more lame than noble but it's not entirely lame if the end result produces a few hot, noble chicks who want to party hard inside a big swimming pool. You feeling me, dude?"

Rylan giggled. "You're weird."

"Maybe I am, but I still think hot, noble chicks are better than hot, lame chicks. Do you agree or disagree?"

"As long as the chicks are hot I'll agree with you on anything."

"Smoking hot, my man." Walker set the bottle on the table and squeezed the air around his chest. "Jugs the size of fully-fwilled, I mean, filled water balloons."

Rylan's posture, and eyes, softened. "So what's so great about these Russian dolls?"

"To the naked eye, it appears to be one doll. But it's a deception." Walker sliced a finger across his chest. "The first doll can be opened, thus revealing a well-kept secret."

"Can you open it with a knife?"

"Do you have a knife?" Another drink.

"What kind of secret's inside?"

"Do you have a knife, Rylan?"

"I ain't got shit, dude. Either tell me the secret or I'm leaving."

"You're dad's not gonna like that very much." Walker looked toward the river, as the tents, at the fire pit, at Rylan. "Does he hit you a lot?"

"Mom gets most of his shit."

"Does he hit Ricki?"

"I don't want to talk it about it, dude." A mixture of acceptance, permanency, and disgust underpinned his voice. "Adults are so fucking lucky. You get to go and do wherever the fuck you want and nobody can tell you what you can and can't do."

The campsite started spinning: horizontally, vertically, sideways, tumbleways. Walker couldn't blink it away. The action, like excessive drinking, was pointless. He stared at the tip of Rylan's nose, trying to find measure and balance, flinching when Rylan's nose turned into a fist that came fast and hard at Walker's nose.

"You okay, dude?"

Walker slapped his own cheeks. "The secret of the dolls is that there are several smaller dolls hidden inside the biggest doll."

"Do these dolls talk if you squeeze them?"

"But people never want to look inside things."

"Are they all pink and shit?"

"People forget the bigger dill is supposed to protect the smaller ones."

"I hate purple. Are any of them purple?"

"Bigger is supposed to watch over smaller."

"They better not be any rainbow colored ones."

"Bigger is supposed to be a guardian." Another drink. "A

watchman. A superhero."

"Do you have any of these dolls?" Rylan touched Walker's arm.

"What?"

"I said do you have any of those dolls."

"Sorry, kid. Go on. I'm listening." Walker went to take another drink but found the bottle empty, drained, finished. He tossed it on the ground and unleashed from his chest a loud burp. Laura would be mortified. He did it again. Louder.

"Gross, dude."

Walker's face and chest felt hot and wet. "Sorry, dude."

"You ever been to Russia?"

"Twice actually." Another burp. Louder. Riper. Pungent. Uncouth. Hilarious.

"You ever see any KGB's?" Rylan's eyes widened, his voice trilling with excitement.

Walker closed his eyes. Darkness eviscerates spinning, right? Not today. He blinked and blinked. He cracked his neck and knuckles. He took in a deep breath and exhaled. "I didn't see any KGB's but I wasn't exactly looking for any either." Blatant drunkenness. In front of a child. How stereotypically Weebie.

"Were the dolls expensive?"

"A thousand rubles or so."

"What's a ruple?"

"Ruble, with a B. It's Russian money."

"Is a thousand rubles a lot?"

"Not really. You should go online and check it out." His stomach churned. And gurgled. And his heart hurt. So much.

"We don't have a computer."

"Your school has to have one."

"I'm not allowed in the computer lab anymore."

"Maybe you could use one of your friend's computers?" Trees started coming at him. Squirrels. Red coolers. Moats. Snakes. Yellow jackets. The scratch in the car. The W. Who did it? Someone had to do it. Someone had to know. Someone had to pay.

"I ain't looking up dolls on my friend's computers. You want me to get beaten up even more than I already do?"

"I got beat up when I was a kid, too." Walker bent over and freed from his mouth dinner, dessert, and every bit of the Jameson Whiskey. Pale greens, dull yellows, and bright reds pooled and mixed on the ground. "I'm not an experienced drinker like your dad and J.R." He unwrapped the nightgown from his waist and wiped his mouth, flicking remnant vomit from his forearm. Rylan didn't move. Or say gross. Or mock him. Or scowl. "I'm not normally like this, Rylan. You wouldn't even recognize me if you saw me at home."

"My dad says you think your shit smells better than ours. Is that true?"

"Does he do more than just hit you, Rylan?"

"He says you're lame, that you ain't a real man."

"Men come in all shapes and sizes."

"He says your spine curves like a woman's."

"Does he now?" Walker set his hands, palms up, on the table. Balance was returning. As were the five senses. Four. No five. Three. No five. Breathe. Exhale. "I could easily prove the theory of ancestral spines."

"Ancestor what?"

"Let's say my spine does curve like a woman's. If it does, there is a high probability that so does your dad's. Why is that, you might ask? Because we share similar DNA. Some of it exact. How do you think he'd respond to such an analysis?"

"Why does he hate you so much?"

"Does he use the word 'hate'?"

"He's been saying it for like two weeks."

"You being a good KGB spy and all, why don't you tell me why he hates me so much?"

"I think it's cuz your teeth are white and cuz you drive a car without duct tape."

"Have you been hanging around my car?"

"No, but it's all he talks about in the tent like every goddamn second."

"What's he been saying?"

"None of its very nice."

"I can handle it. You can tell me."

Rylan shook his head. "It's too mean, dude."

"I promise to not take offense."

"Mom tells him to stop saying mean stuff about you, but he listens to her about as much as he listens to me and Ricki."

"Does he hit your mom a lot?"

"Yeah. Sometimes."

"Does he hit Ricki?"

"Why does he call your car the faggot-finder?"

Walker laughed. "Faggot, like homosexual?"

"Mom says you're not one but dad says you are one and I don't really care either way, but are you?"

"No, I'm not. Are you?"

"Fuck no. Faggots are gross."

"How are they gross?"

"Because they do to a dude do what they could do to a woman. Which makes no sense."

"You sound pretty homophobic and misogynistic. Is that how you want to sound?"

"He also says he has proof that you've done butt stuff in the past." Rylan wrinkled his face. "Have you?"

Walker paused. Yes. He had done butt stuff in the past. Not by choice. But by Ronnie's cruel hands. And force. And tools. And twisted brain. "Your dad hurt me a lot when I was your age."

"Like how?"

"I guess you could call it butt stuff."

"My dad wouldn't do that. No way."

"Just because you don't want to believe it doesn't make it less true."

"That's fucked up, dude."

"It is, isn't it?"

Rylan and Walker sat quiet for a very long time.

"Has he ever done anything besides hit you, Rylan?"

"Fuck no."

"You promise?"

Rylan nodded. "I think the real reason he hates you so much is because he wishes he was you and the only reason he calls you shit is because he feels so much like shit himself."

"I think you're gonna make a terrific spy."

"Sup losers," Janessa said. Walker and Rylan jumped a little off their seats. She pulled a piece of beef jerky from the front pocket of her jean shorts, ripped it open with her teeth, and spit the wrapper onto the ground. "It smells like a fucking outhouse over here." She sniffed, staring at the pile of vomit on the ground. "Ew. Is that what I think it is?"

"Go away." Rylan shot her the middle finger. "Fat moose."

"Fuck you, short round." She grabbed the nightgown from Walkers hands. "What are you doing with my mom's nightgown?"

"She gave it to me."

"Why would she give you her nightgown?"

Back at home, at school, inside beautiful, sturdy stucco walls, Walker handled every situation with decorum, culture, and diplomacy. But out here, removed from scholastic rules, daily protocol, Laura, and basic human kindness, he was just another silly Weebie reliving the cycle of a poor, unfortunate past.

"Two props on my stage." Janessa said. "Players getting played."

"Yeah, well you're fat and ugly." Rylan yelled.

"And you're a fucking dwarf."

"Do you know how to play Rummy?" Walker spoke without meaning to.

"Does it look like I'm talking to you, you fucking dorkwad?" She stuck her hand in front of Walker's face. "You ain't nothing but a hoity-toity know-it-all with a nice car."

"You been hanging around my car?"

"Fuck your car. Mom's the one who can't stop talking about the fucking thing."

"You're too retarded to play Rummy anyway," Rylan said.

"Sissy."

"Rhino."

"Midget."

"Elephant."

"Anal wart."

"Seriously, you guys, enough."

"Stay out of it, douchebag."

"Do not talk to me like that."

"Fuck you."

"Leave him alone, Janessa."

"I ain't moving one inch, tiny Tim." She chomped louder, swinging the nightgown like a lasso. "But go ahead and try to move me and find out how good I am with this here whip that I'll use to tie you up and ram my fist up your ass."

Ram my fist up your ass.

Walked exploded.

"Why don't you fuck off, you fat fucking cow? Nobody here likes you or wants you around, because you're nothing but a snotty, conniving lard-ass little snot-nose who has a disgusting body and an even uglier attitude." The words flew out of Walker's mouth so fast, so easily, so coherently, he didn't have time to grab each one back, though he desperately wanted to. Verbal slushiness from a sunburn, tired, stinky, wet man who had stooped to the lowest form of cruelness by way of bruising a child's fragile self-esteem. How unbelievable. How Weebie-wrong.

"Fuck you, you stupid jerk." She ran toward the river. Crying. Loudly.

Walker and Rylan sat quiet for a short time. Walker removed sand particles from his hair while Rylan shuffled cards and stared at the river.

The swarm of yellow jackets swooped down, this time stinging

Walker's neck, back, and legs. One flew up his nose, but he didn't move, swat, blow, shoo, or cuss them away. Rylan waved a hand over Walker's face. "Dude, doesn't that hurt?" He squeezed Walker's arm. "You need to get outta here before anyone comes back."

"I wish things were different for you, Rylan." The yellow jackets retreated to the hive, leaving Walker swollen, red, and sorrowful. "I wish things were different for all of us."

"My mom has a bee-stingy-healer-thingy in the tent if you want me to get it."

"Nah. I'm okay."

"Don't the stings hurt?"

"You'd think they would, but they don't."

"She deserved everything you said about her."

"No one deserves being called names."

"But she started it."

"I'm sorry your dad hurts you."

"You rotten no-good mother fucker!" Ronnie yelled, running toward Walker and Rylan. Rylan ducked underneath the picnic table while Walker sat still. Ronnie grabbed a handful of Walker's hair and pulled him to the ground, smooshing his nose into the pile of vomit. "Piece of shit." He punched Walker's spine. "How dare you bully little girls around?" A left jab to the ribs. A right hook to the jaw. "Faggot."

Ronnie beat a path of tight fists across Walker's back. Walker's body, but not his mind, grew numb. As if he was looking through a View Master camera, Walker saw frame-by-frame color images of Ronnie's fist thrust into his rectum. Hammers. Cucumber. Screwdrivers. Pliers. Corncobs. Pushed with such force and frequency, Walker began to accept the routine as inescapable. If Walker ran, Ronnie caught him. If he hid, Ronnie tracked him down. If he groaned, Ronnie stuffed underwear in his mouth. If he cried, Ronnie laughed. If he refused to sleep in the same bed, Ronnie made him sleep naked beneath the bed. It went on until the pain became intolerable, forcing Walker to vomit the truth to his mother who slapped his cheek and called him a liar, even as blood dripped from his rectum in the bathtub.

After his mother, Ronnie, and Janelle left the house, and after he plugged his rectum with toilet paper, he went to the garage where he found his dad building a birdfeeder. He showed his dad the blood and the toilet paper, groaned as his dad carried him to the car and sped to the clinic where a tall nurse squeezed ointment onto a cotton ball and rubbed circles around his wounds before a fat male doctor gave him four stitches and chatted with his dad about weather patterns and the civil war in Russia.

"Clumsy kids these days," his father said, after the doctor asked what happened, inquiring neither about the reason for the wound nor the result of the blood. Which worried Walker. If nobody talked about it, it might continue. It couldn't continue. It had to stop. Ronnie had to be confronted, punished, and made to make restitution. Promise to never do it again. And if he didn't keep the promise, he had to be purged. From the trailer. Forever. Sent away. Far, far away. To the invisible places bad people on TV shows and the movies are sent to never return.

Back home from the clinic, Walker laid in front of his dad on the couch and watched TV until 10:36pm, the exact time his mother's noisy car engine pulled into the driveway and sputtered out. His dad stood and paced the living room floor, pounding his fists into his own palms. His mom threw open the door and went to the kitchen, to the sink, where she stood and lit a cigarette. Walker had never seen her smoke. Nor had he ever seen his father punch his mother in the back. Nor had he heard them scream a litany of expletives, for an hour—arguing, punching, stumbling around Walker as if he wasn't even there.

At 11:58 pm, hoarse and exhausted, they called a truce, a cease fire, a period of utter silence in which his mom smoked at the kitchen sink while his dad rested on his knees on the kitchen floor. It was the first time Walker understood the meaning of Weebie brokenness: some people don't possess the necessary insight to overcome the ruination of their own past in order to change the outcome of their own future. At 12:37 am, his mother yelled, "If you even think of involving the police, I'll blame you so fast and then whose gonna watch over your precious fucking Walker Weebie." She slammed the front door and drove away, staying away for two weeks and two days. Taking Ronnie. Leaving Janelle. And Walker. And his dad's tears.

"You ain't any better than us." Ronnie turned Walker's body face up. "You were a sissy back then just like you are now." He punched Walker's face. Walker faded in and out of consciousness. He could feel muscles tear. Veins pop. Bones snap. His left eye swelled shut. Just as it had been in boyhood, fighting back wasn't in his genes. Then he heard other Weebie voices: Rhonda call out to God; Janessa laugh; J.R. yell, "Fight back, Walker. Show that mother fucker what you're made of!"

Walker took a first swing. Air. Another swing. Wood. Another swing. Flesh. Another swing. Bone. He prayed it was Ronnie's. He stood, staggering to find balance, boxing the air. Another swing. Chest. Another swing. Neck. Ronnie's fatness fell to the ground. Blood dripped from both their noses. The small part of Walker's right eye that could still decipher shapes enjoyed seeing surprise, anger, and disbelief on Ronnie's face.

"You go Walker! Show that mother fucker who's who!"

"You can do it, Walker." Rhonda yelled. "Keep fighting back."

"Use this." Rylan put a thin, warm metal object in Walker's right hand: the knife. Walker took a swipe. Air. Another swipe. More air. Another swipe. Flesh. The blade hooked bone and scratched a long line across solid yet pliable skin. "This is for fucking with my car," Walker yelled, stopping at the spot he hoped was Ronnie's heart, force-feeding the blade, his own heart beating wildly in his feet. Then he let go of the knife and collapsed. Ronnie kicked at the dirt and cursed the world to hell. Neither could stand on their own. "I never touched your fucking car."

Walker laid still. Who else could have done it? The yellow jackets swarmed the area, this time focusing their time and talent on Ronnie.

"You need to get here quick," Janelle yelled into Walker's cell phone.

It looked like his cell phone. Were those his keys in her other hand? Was that his wallet, and wristwatch, and small square plastic container with a yellow lid in which Laura had filled with fresh fruit, telling him, "If things go sour, be sure to eat sweet." Was that his collapsible brimmed wicker hat sitting atop Janelle's head? No. It couldn't be. He wasn't seeing things clearly. How could he, given the circumstance?

"Both my brothers are seriously fucked up," she yelled. "Like seriously fucked." She wiggled out of the light-blue nightgown and laid it across Ronnie's body. Then she stepped back and grinned. At Walker. Snatching from Janessa's hand the nightgown she'd given him—a superhero cape meant to heal his wounds.

"Dad," he whispered.

"Laura," he cried.

Mom.

Nothing but a bunch of Weebies standing around yawning, picking fabric from their asses.

Preacher Victoria

As a small girl, Victoria practically lived in the tree house, higher than the roof of the real house, playing church service with her six favorite dolls. She healed the sick; fed the hungry; clothed the naked; forgave sins; served communion; taught the choir how to sing. Everything she did was a great big success. Whatever she touched turned out better than alright, but glory be to God on high.

"You shall call me Preacher Victoria." She demanded, pointing to each doll as if to say, don't call me anything else for this is who I am, and nothing else.

But sometimes—stupid weekends—she had to climb down the ladder and eat turkey and green peas with her turkey-and-green-peas-obsessed parents, leaving the spiritually nurtured dolls in the ever-watchful eye of the Lord.

"Someone is always watching," she told the dolls. "Don't try anything funny."

"Have you practiced your ballet?" her mother asked, removing some of the green peas from her plate. "You'll never be any good at it if you don't try."

So she tried, but she wasn't any good at ballet, soccer, hula dancing, chess, synchronized swimming, horseback riding, knitting, or even reading books about wild horses knitting ballet shoes for swimmers in the winter ballet.

"You must never give up," she told the dolls during a lengthy afternoon sermon titled, *Let's Keep Going*. "You must stay the course. You must fight the good fight." But the dolls seemed unimpressed with her homily, each one falling over in laughter, determined to do things their own way. Soon they became sick, hungry, frail, and unforgiving. They refused to take communion. They didn't move their lips once during choir rehearsal.

Sometimes she snuck in food at night, not turkey or green peas, but stolen milk duds, whoppers, and dill pickle potato chips by Frito-Lay. "Eat up, ladies. You mustn't lose your strength."

But the dolls were losing strength. Little by little, things like eyesight, hairlines, and cheekbones were growing so thin, so fast, none of them had enough strength to eat milk duds, their favorite snack of all.

"These dolls look disgusting," her mother said, scooping them up and stuffing them into a black trash bag, walking around the tree house, and the girl, pointing out everything that must go. Which was everything. "Honestly, this is no place for a lady."

The next day, watching from the bedroom window her father remove the tree house piece by piece, she decided to stop talking altogether, figuring she had nothing important left to say. To anyone. Ever.

Years later, during an evening jog, she heard a little girl's voice preaching salvation high in a tree house. Running in place, she smiled whenever the girl yelled Amen and wept when the girl climbed down the ladder and ran toward her mother who was waiting with open arms, as if to welcome her home from a long, perilous journey.

Syntax

As a boy, I listened carefully to my parents, who talked openly in the kitchen about everything. I was rarely the topic of conversation: a face seated at the table; a vexation with a big appetite; a house pet who wore my father's ski-slope nose and my mother's bottom-heavy ass; a squeaky fulcrum on which their tiny world swung. And missed. Sometimes they laughed. Oftentimes they stared at each other menacingly, as if to erase the other altogether.

When I turned ten, I sat atop the kitchen table to practice spelling words. My parents didn't yell me off the table or point me upstairs. Indistinctness: a word I could spell, define, and draw upon. With refrain.

One night, creating a top 10 favorite vocabulary list of 1991, I overheard my mother ask my father, "I wonder if rain ever wishes to be something other than wetness."

1. WETNESS

"God, you're dumb," he said, leaning against the baker's rack. "Rain becomes snow if the temperature gets low enough."

2. TEMPERATURE

"How cold does it have to get before that happens?"

"It depends on the amount of humidity in the air and the rate at which precipitation falls. Do you know nothing besides broccoli and chicken?"

"Don't be mean to me."

3. PRECIPITATION

"Speaking of rain." His voice turned cavernous. "I'm feeling a downpour coming on myself."

4. DOWNPOUR

"Henry." My mother snapped, stirring with a spatula broccoli and chicken. "Don't be a pervert."

5. PERVERT

"Said the biggest dick tease in high school." He laughed.

"Miriam Bensworth was the biggest dick tease." My mother

turned around and threw a dishtowel at his crotch. "I was the biggest seduction."

He threw back the dishtowel which landed on my mother's face before it fell into her hands. "Miriam Bensworth was a dick thesaurus who knew all the freakiest words to explain everything I needed," he said.

6. FREAKIEST

"Miriam Bensworth was a classless slut."

"No." My father shook his head. "She was simply unwilling to change her character."

"It's time we both got over her."

"Still threatened, I see."

"A rose isn't threatened by a skunk cabbage."

"You, a rose." He stepped forward and wrapped his fingers around my mother's waist. "No, I don't think so." He squeezed her neck. "But you and your ways won out."

7. ROSE

"You can be so vile sometimes."

"Say it." He squeezed. My mother stood quiet, her cheeks turning red. Water poured from the faucet as he slapped her ass. Again and again. He buried his lips in her cleavage. She shrieked. Her boobs jiggled like Jello. "I said say it."

8. CLEAVAGE

"You said last time was the last time."

"I lied. Now say it."

She stared at the floor, and whispered, "Whore."

"Now come upstairs so I can show you what a real rainstorm looks like."

9. WHORE

My mother turned off the stove and covered the pan with a dinner plate while my father's face took on the wild lust my sexual adulthood would become. Embedded. Combative. Disturbed. So very.

10. UNWELL

Re-Release

George carefully set his wife June's favorite cup and saucer on the nightstand. He didn't want to wake her. He dipped the Chamomile teabag a half-dozen times, watching honey swirl and blend at the bottom. Little curlicue wisps of steam rose and disappeared into the air. Afternoon sunlight trickled in through small slits in the wooden blinds, warming the already warm room. June rarely slept during the night anymore, wanting instead to talk all night, and often all day. It didn't matter that George slept less than June, and never in the same bed. He was alert, still cognizant enough to know that the more he struggled to be quiet the more he trembled out loud.

Thick pieces of June's brown wig rested unevenly across her forehead, cheeks, and neck. Her face wore the vacant expression of thin skin and amorphous coloring, augmented by well-travelled wrinkles that had been painted on by life's toothpick. Her eyelids flickered and her chapped lips sputtered. Her tarnished hands, interlocked across her belly, rose and fell with every snort-in and hiss-out. Age had found them. It said it would. A promise offered. A promise kept. George placed no blame on age honoring its word, although he did take issue with its decision to steal many of June's memories before she had a chance to remember the final ones. Similar to the ache in his elbows and knees, aging was a real pain in the ass.

Rummaging the nightstand for lip balm, he inadvertently awakened June.

"Have I been out long?" She sat up, checking an imaginary wristwatch. "Have I missed the show?"

"Had I known you'd fallen asleep, I'd have stayed away longer." He offered the cup.

"Who are you? Why are you standing over me?"

"It's Chamomile, my love."

"I prefer earl gray. I can't smell chamomile."

"Drink as much as you want but be careful, it's still a little hot."
He kissed her cheek.

"Oh, hello George." She took the cup and brought it to her lips.
Drops of water spotted the duvet cover. "When did you get here?"
She sipped. And sipped. "Mmmmm."

"I live here, sweets. We're married."

"We are." She sipped. "Is it winter outside?"

"No, it's the middle of June, June."

"Did you know the last movie I filmed was in Alaska during the
winter?" she asked. "The wardrobe department was completely
ill-prepared for all that snow and all that cold. They had to go out
and buy me a brand new blue parka and white fluffy earmuffs."

George helped June set the cup in the saucer on the nightstand.
"Were you some sort of actress?"

"I was part of the union. A real bona fide player."

"Are you hungry?"

"Did I ever tell you who won the best actress Oscar race in
1968?" She struggled to push her hair back; such sorrowfully
shaky, crooked hands.

"You haven't," he lied, sitting in the recliner by the large bay
window which overlooked the empty backyard pool with a broken diving board. "But I do hope you'll tell me all about it."

"1968 was the year Katherine Hepburn and Barbara Streisand
tied for Oscar gold."

"Wow." He grabbed The Complete Unofficial History of The
Academy Awards Book from the wooden table beside the recliner. The book fell open to 1968. "Did they tie for Lion in Winter
and Funny Girl?" He knew they did.

"Have I told you this before?"

"Perhaps, but at our age who can remember?"

"Well, I sure remember." She scoffed. "Ingrid Bergman stood
on stage and announced it to the world. I could see on her face
that she was completely stunned."

"Do you remember who won best actor that year?"

"Peter O'Toole should have won but it went to Cliff Robertson for Charly. What a shame." She sighed. "And Jack Albertson won best supporting actor and Ruth Gordon won best supporting actress."

George flipped a few pages ahead. "What do remember about 1984?"

"Let me see. Amadeus won best picture and best director, and, oh, yeah, that man with the terrible skin won best actor, something like Abraham Morey or Murphy or..."

"Is it Murray?"

"Yes. F. Murray Abraham. Rather unknown actor up until that role. Very nice man but not attractive. Really bad teeth, too."

"What else do you remember?"

"Sally Fields won best actress and." She paused, closing her eyes.

"You okay?" George asked. "Sweets?"

Outside, the irrigation system turned on. Overhead, a jet plane roared. Inside the room, a bulb in the ceiling fan light burned out, making George and June a little darker.

"I think I'm gonna rest," June said. "I feel like I should sleep."

"Rest well, my dear." He ear-tagged the book to 1989. "We can talk more about movies or anything else you want tomorrow, okay?"

"My favorite year was 1941," she whispered. "Such a marvelous time for us."

He reopened the book, but quickly closed it. "June." He stood. "June, what day is it today? What are our daughter's names? Where do we currently live?"

"I was happy to give it all up for you and the girls," she whispered. "I never felt an ounce of regret, not once. So many people tried talking me into leaving you, but I knew you and the girls were my greatest role and my biggest achievement."

"June, is that you?"

"You were better than any Academy Award."

"June, what year is it?"

"But I'm tired now."

"What day is today?"

"You, Susie, Leslie. You are my rolling credits."

"Please June, tell me it's you." He kissed her cheek.

"Have I been out long?" She sat up, checking an imaginary wristwatch. "Have I missed the show?"

The Good Life

His eating habits annoy me. The constant humming. The way he child-holds a fork—stop stabbing everything. The way he separates side dishes from the main entrée. God forbid a pumpkin seed touch poached salmon. He talks with a full mouth. Slurps Merlot as if he's drinking Coke. Refuses to use a napkin. Drums forks on the tabletop. And beneath the table his hairy, bare feet tickle mine like crazy.

Ten years together, we've broken lots of bread. Spilled lots of beer. Spread tons of sweet potato hummus on Pits chips. Grinded sea salt. Cracked pepper. Licked sour cream from each other's lips. We've fattened up quite nicely, not that either of us we're ever skinny. Our natures aren't inclined to eat a healthy diet or walk for sport. Thinness means self-controlling larger portions. Less is bad, especially conversations. God, can we talk and eat. So fluid. So engaging. No awkward silences when we're chowing down. Deep ideas. Strong points of view. Compassion. Understanding. Questions questioned and answers answered. The entire world's cured of every ailment during dessert. We hate hateful ideologies and love loving philosophies. Think about us like this: ¼ cup of olive oil, ½ cup of fresh basil leaves, 4 ripe tomatoes, 8 ounces grated mozzarella cheese, a few chopped Kalamata olives, two baguettes, and some roasted turkey. Sounds delicious, right?

Last week, during dining at Sensario's—the buffalo blue cheese pizza is to die for, btw—he said my sleeping habits annoy him. The constant snoring. The way I hog the sheets—stop pulling everything. The way I snot-rocket a stuffy nose. God forbid I throw a Kleenex's in the trashcan. I talk with a full mouth. Gurgle Pinot Noir like Listerine. Sing show tunes off-key. Drum fingernails on the tabletop. And beneath the table my dry, bare feet tickle his like crazy.

Ten years together, we've washed lots of dishes. Folded lots of sheets. Fluffed lots of pillows. Played lots of games. Watched hours of The Food Network. Argued until we cried. Cried until we had make-up sex. Had make-up sex until we became two fat, sweaty old bodies in need of a cold shower, roomier pajamas, and a box of dark chocolate with fresh strawberries, our favorite after make-up sex treat. We've slept quite nicely, not that either of us we're ever insomniacs. Our natures aren't inclined to agitate overnight. Sleeping sound means self-nurturing satisfying dreams. Less is bad, especially slumber. God, can we sleep and eat. So fluid. So engaging. No awkward silences when we're chowing down. Deep ideas. Strong points of view. Compassion. Understanding. Questions questioned and answers answered. The entire world's cured of every ailment by dessert. Sounds like contentment, right?

I wish this were true. I wish we were friends. I wish we had deep conversations and ate chocolate with strawberries after having make-up sex. I wish we slept in the same bed. Or in the same bedroom. But we don't. And we haven't for years.

Instead.

We repress.

We deny.

We implode.

Great Lengths

He had known her for only a moment, a quick breath in his thirty-nine years, a shiny copper penny tossed into his teenage wishing well—the only one really—that over time became buried beneath a troubled life and defective heart that more than one doctor said had very little thump left in it. But they had connected. They had talked in the school cafeteria. They had walked through Barnes and Noble at The Resington Mall. They had drove to the beach one Saturday afternoon in July in her mauve colored Pontiac Grand Am and had eaten cheeseburgers, onion rings, and chicken nuggets in the Burger King parking lot beside the abandoned Montgomery Ward's. Memories so vivid there was no dream to dream. He had loved her. And she had loved him.

Google, Yahoo, and Ask.com couldn't find her. MySpace came up empty. Twitter was really difficult to muddle through and Classmates.com was even muddier. There were never any pictures, just random states with ages and outrageous fees for criminal background checks.

"Try Facebook already," one of his support group friends said. "If she's out there, Facebook will lead you to her."

He set up a quick profile, added a blurry photo from his phone, typed AMY JOHNSON—each letter a promise of hope.

Hundreds of Amy Johnson's appeared. None with red hair. None with skin the color of summer butter. None with a smile so contagious it became an antidote for sadness. He tried Amie. Ammy. Ame. Johnsen. Jonson. Johnston. He didn't know her middle name. He typed Lynn. Anne. Lisa. Louise. Names he thought paired well with Amy. Nothing. No one came close.

"Stalk other people's pages," another support group friend said. "That's what I do when I'm looking for the past."

He had only attended Stone Mill Academy for two months, not nearly long enough to remember anything substantive like last names, except for Amy Johnson. He vaguely recalled one

Kim Bushay, but like Amy, Kim was nowhere in the land of walls, photos, or flashing subscription enticements. Bushaey, Bushaye rhymes with fung shway. He was really losing steam.

April. May. June. July. Nothing but a chest cough and weakened muscle mass.

August 17. Kim Busfray. Friend Request.

Busfray. Ah. He clicked confirm and sent a private message.

Kim! Thanks for friending me. Hope all is well. How r u? I was just thinking about u and Stone Mill Academy the other day. Off chance, do u have any idea what ever happened to Amy Johnson (I think its Johnson. Is it?) U 2 always cracked me up. Let me know what's going on. I'm glad we're friends. Seth.

September. October. November. Nothing but bloody diarrhea and cracking skin.

December 8. No Kim Busfray. Unfriended. WTF?

The shiny copper penny began to spread toxins into his heart. What had he done, or said, to make her unfriend him? There was no good reason. No way of finding out. No capacity in which to respond with anger, sadness, or blame. Cut off like a lung. Paralyzed by the swift click of a mouse. There was cruel, and then there was Kim Busfray.

"Maybe it's time to let her go," an inebriated support group friend said at the annual New Year's Eve party. "It's obviously not meant to be."

"It's only been eight months. There's still time."

"What you need is a good case of reality," the friend said, sipping cheap white wine from a box at the bar. "Reality's what's we all need, friend, cuz that's where we're all headed anyway."

"Reality Schmalady. She goes way beyond that."

January. February. March. Nothing but bedridden in ICU and a hideous pair of grandpa-white orthopedic shoes.

April 26. Kim Busfray. Friend request.

Kim! Hey. Glad 2 hear from u again. U haven't posted in 5 months. Is everything okay? Ur pal. Seth

May. June.

July 4. No Kim Busfray. Unfriended. Again.

"That's it!"

"You must really be bonkers for this Amy chic," a new support group friend said, pulling up to the curb at the airport. "How much did the ticket cost?"

"What's Citibank gonna do, bring me back from the dead and make me pay for it?"

"She must be something special."

"Cereal's special. She's lobster bisque. No. Filet Mignon."

"When's the last time you ate steak?" The new friend asked.

"It's been awhile."

"Sure you can do this by yourself?"

"I'm not sure of anything save Amy Johnson."

Off the plane, already exhausted, he phoned Uber. The driver dropped him off at Amy's old house. He rang the doorbell three times, knocked on the front door, and peeked inside the side windows. Nothing. Then he slid open the sliding glass backdoor and walked straight through the kitchen, the hallway, up seventeen stairs, one by one, resting (he had to) every few seconds. He pushed open the wooden bedroom door—tap tap tap—bouncing against the rubber-capped door stop. Empty. Even the drapes were gone. Quiet. Like sorrow in a child's tear.

He sat on the carpet and banged his head against the yellow wall, light-blue when they were friends. Dust floated the air while rays of sunlight poured in through the window, adding spotlight to four small round divots where a dresser once sat, though not anymore, but why and where and when and how. The ceiling seemed lower. The closet doors smaller. The baseboards were way too thick. No sign of Amy Johnson remained, not even one tini-tiny drop of Electric Youth by Debbie Gibson, her (and his) favorite. He stood and stared out the window. Nose touching the warm glass, fingers tapping the wall, his thoughts descended to the blues of loss. In the closet, back pressed against the wall, he watched the light bulb flicker on and off until everything, eventually, went dark.

By Robert McClintock 2017

Dressed in matching white linen shirts, khaki shorts, and open-toed sandals, Harold and Hannah strolled from their car to Square Pines Park, the epicenter of summer community activity in the idyllic town of Alexandria, Minnesota. Hannah enjoyed craft fairs while Harold enjoyed the many food vendors peddling their greasy wears at the very end. So did Hannah—a fact she kept to herself. But he knew. So very well.

"Slow down." Hannah blocked his belly-bump with her cane. "You know I like to stop and see people's work." She sighed. "Why do I always have to remind you?"

She was right—she did always have to remind him—not that she needed any reminding. "I wish you wouldn't block me like that," he said.

"I'm not blocking you. I'm simply directing us."

Hundreds of white tents, lining both sides of Knife River, were filled with artisans selling pottery bowls, decorative silverware, hand-blown glass vases, chunky wool-knit scarves, and other artsy-fartsy whatnot. Hannah pulled Harold into the first tent. Colorful metal flowers attached to thin metal poles were lined like soldiers in the grass. "Oh, honey, look at this," she said, thumbing a large tulip. "Wouldn't this look great in the rock garden?"

"Get it if you want it."

"Hmm," she said, her typical 'no-thanks' reply, spending money only on items 75-percent off the original price and then only if she had an additional 20-percent off coupon. When they were young and planning to wed, Harold valued Hannah's thriftiness—quite dissimilar from the other women he'd dated. During their wedding ceremony at Square Pines Park, huddled inside the smallest shelter with a green-shingle roof and eight picnic tables, Hannah had held a wild flower bouquet, wore a gently-used veil, and served the twenty-three guests fudge brownies on paper plates and Peach Sangria in Styrofoam cups. Frugality at its finest.

A budding savings account was the best wedding gift they could give each other. After Holly, their only child was born, who clung to Hannah the way a runny nose clings to sinus allergies—one simply cannot live without the other—Harold and Hannah were still able to save more money than they spent. Before he retired on June 12, 2014, working for twenty-seven years at Ridgewater College as a professor of economics, Harold brought home a modest yet comfortable salary of 75K per year. Hannah, who chose not to work, didn't have to work. He'd been a wonderful provider for his family, not that he needed any reminding. A fact he kept to himself. But Hannah knew. So very well.

"Oh, honey look at this," she said, thumbing a twenty by fourty pottery bowl.

"Get it if you want it."

"Hmm."

"Oh, honey look at this," she said, thumbing a lace tablecloth.

"Get it if you want it."

"Hmm."

"Oh, honey look at this," she said, thumbing a 20x40 photograph of a lighthouse bound to a copper-colored frame. "Well, aren't you gonna tell me to get it?"

"Hmm." Harold slid rimless bifocals to the end of his nose. He stepped closer to the photograph, scanning the obvious panoramic intention and architectural interest captured by the photographer, Robert McClintock. Harold outlined with an index finger the dark-blue sky and inhaled the sea-salt danger crashing into a stone-edge cliff. "I'm gonna stay here for a while."

"It's a stupid lighthouse." She yanked the back of his shirt collar. "What's there to see?"

"I wish you wouldn't yank me like that."

From her fanny pack, she brought out a yellow coupon. "Pronto pups are buy one get one free between two and four." Irritation amplified her voice. "I know that's the only reason you come."

Harold glanced at his wristwatch, a black Timex, a Christmas gift from Holly in 2004. "It's not even one-thirty. All I want is a minute or two."

"These craft people are built to talk you into buying stuff you don't need."

"I'm simply observing." He blew on the lighthouse door. "You can leave or stay but I'm not moving."

"I guess I can go look at those silly, overpriced Adirondack chairs."

"Get it if you want it."

"Don't be coy, Harold. It doesn't suit you." She huffed and walked away.

Harold didn't care if people thought he was making out with an old lighthouse. He was, in fact, infatuated.

"Took that one with a Canon D-20," a low voice whispered from behind. "They even let me go down by the rocks to take it, and there isn't a bit of Photoshop on it either. That's the way God intended the day to look."

"Is it the Split Rock lighthouse?"

"Indeed it is."

"Never been."

"How much you've missed."

"You must be Robert McClintock."

"Thousand words or not, some pictures exist beyond language."

"How much you asking?"

Robert pointed to a clearly visible sign taped to the bottom of the photograph: *$350.00. No refunds. Checks accepted with proper ID. Preference to cash.*

"Any without a frame?"

"Sorry. Archival integrity still matters to me."

Harold turned and searched the grounds for Hannah, who was nowhere close to the Adirondack chairs. Nor was she among the small crowd circled around a group of ponytail pan flute players playing pan flutes. "Hold onto it for me, okay. I will be back."

"It's the last one, just so you know."

Harold found Hannah seven tents down on the left, haggling with a young Native American woman who was selling colorful yarn, three for five dollars. "Five for five and we have a deal," Hannah said.

Harold pulled a five dollar bill from his wallet and set it on the card table. "We'll take three and be on our way."

Hannah grabbed the five dollar bill and scoffed. "Mind your own business."

"I want you to come back and look at that lighthouse. I think it needs a new home and I think it outta be ours."

"We have tons of nicer pictures already." She exited the tent, without any yarn.

"None of a lighthouse." Harold offered his right hand. "And I need the checkbook."

"Absolutely not." Hannah squeezed the fanny pack, walking in the opposite direction of the lighthouse. Harold walked directly toward the lighthouse. Hannah sighed, turned around, and stood defiant. Harold kept walking. "I'm not following you," she yelled. Harold sighed, turned around, and stood defiant. "Get over here. Now."

"We don't need a lighthouse."

"Please." Harold turned around and stared at the lighthouse, a sly smirk upturning his lips.

"Glad to see you came back," Robert said. "Had a guy earlier willing to pay cash for it, but I told him it already belonged to its rightful owner."

"Rightful owner?" Hannah said, standing beside Harold. "I can't leave you alone for five minutes."

"I wish you wouldn't mock me like that." He glared at the fanny pack. "Give it."

Hannah, as if slicing from her gut a most prized possession, unzipped the fanny pack and brought out the checkbook and blue pen. "A preschooler could take a better picture."

"Now turn around."

"For what?"

"I need a rigid surface to write on."

"Not on me you don't."

"Ninety degrees please." Similar to the merry-go-round on which Harold pushed Holly on in childhood, Hannah creaked and groaned as she turned. Harold's smirk expanded into an outright smile, happy to remind the muscles in Hannah's body that he still had a say in things, too.

"Get it if you want it," she whispered. "Never again."

Robert carefully wrapped the photograph in cellophane and slid it into a large, blue bag. "Hope you enjoy it and thanks again."

Hannah snatched the checkbook and tossed the yellow coupon on the ground. "I'm leaving in ten minutes so if you're not at the car by then you can find another way home." Quite nimbly—cane-free—she power-walked toward the parking lot.

Harold, however, wandered with ease, strolling in and out of tents, carrying the photograph above his head, at each side, and then finally in front of his chest.

"Someone's having a good day," a middle-aged woman walking a puppy said.

"What do you mean?" He set the photograph on his toes.

"You seem happy is all." She picked up the puppy and tickled its head. "Like Mister Hurricane here."

"His name's Mister Hurricane?"

"Oh, he's got a wild side. Don't let his calm facade fool you."

"I suppose we do call things exactly as we see them, don't we?"

"It's very American." She laughed. "Very Midwestern."

Harold scratched Mister Hurricane's head. "I'd have named him little-bit or tiny-tim or something diminutive because of his size but you're a lot more than that, aren't you, Mister Hurricane?"

The puppy growled, showing teeth.

"See what I mean." She stroked the puppy's head, bringing calm to its quivering lips. "So what's in the blue bag?"

"I guess you could call it my wild side."

"Now I have to know what it is." She laughed.

"It's a photograph of the Split Rock Lighthouse."

"A lighthouse is your wild side?"

"Don't let the calm façade fool you."

"Ah." She set the puppy on the ground. "Maybe we aren't what we seem, after all"

Harold jogged to the car, smiling and laughing. Is this what happiness feels like? Damn it, it had been a long time.

***

Slouched in the driver's seat, Hannah gripped the steering wheel as if to never let go. The air conditioner teased her fine, vanilla-colored hair. Her skin, once tightened effervescence, had attenuated into the look of a crusty, flaking bread roll. The trunk lid popped open. Harold laid the photograph face up and took a deep breath as he slid into the passenger seat. "Thanks for waiting."

"You had forty-one seconds left."

"Would you have actually left me behind?"

"Don't blame me if we run over a pothole and that stupid thing shatters into a million pieces."

"I need to make a quick stop on the way home."

"For what?"

"An accessory or two for the accomplice."

"Who was that lady back there with the dog?" She readjusted the rearview mirror.

"Just some woman who asked about the lighthouse."

"Why were you touching her dog? You hate dogs."

"I don't hate dogs."

"Then why did you never let Holly have one?"

"Because I knew she'd tire of it in a week and ignore it forever."

"You never gave her the chance to prove you wrong."

"I told myself, if she ever asked three times in a row, I'd get her one. But she never did, so I never did."

"Children shouldn't have to ask three times for anything. Once is more than enough."

"I want to drive home," he said. "You ever done a Chinese fire drill?"

"What's gotten into you today?" Hannah huffed, opened the door, and limped around the front of the car while Harold skipped—sorta—behind. He repositioned his seat, his mirrors, his wheels, his turn signal, his speed, driving faster than usual, taking a different (and more scenic) route home. Hannah occasionally mumbled, "waste," "simply observing," and "three-hundred and fifty dollars," which Harold ignored, preoccupied with where to hang the lighthouse. He pulled into Ace Hardware, put the car in park, and left the engine running. "In and out," he said, offering the palm of his hand. "Now you can give it to me nice and easy or I can go in there and dig it out myself. That's one choice you do get to make."

"What are you gonna buy?" She stared out the passenger window, squeezing the fanny pack.

He touched her arm, relieved when she didn't pull away. "Not once have I ever told you what you could or couldn't buy. All I'm asking is for the same courtesy."

"Courtesy." She tossed the checkbook onto the dashboard. "I think our definition of that word is quite dissimilar."

"Be back before you can count to three hundred and fifty."

After eight minutes and nineteen seconds, Harold emerged from the store carrying two gallons of paint, two paint rollers, two paint trays, and two wooden paint stirrers. He set the items on the back seat and tossed the receipt on the dashboard. Hannah didn't look at it. Or touch it. Or grab it when it slid off the dashboard and fell into her lap. Instead, she blew at it until it fell onto the floor mat. Harold turned on the radio and hummed a pop song he didn't know. "Can't wait to get home and get things started."

"Rightful owner," she whispered. "What a clever, clever man."

***

At home, Harold assisted Hannah up the twenty steps to their bedroom, her favorite late-afternoon spot to take a nap and do crossword puzzles. He could feel in her tight grip and body odor a substantial tantrum brewing. Maybe a storm. He offered a kiss, which she refused, covering her lips with both hands. "I do not kiss irrationality."

Harold undressed, including his underwear, placing each article of clothing atop the bed—pushing boundaries— as nakedness, like sexual intercourse, was something that happened only underneath the quilt after the lights were turned off. Another one of Hannah's rules.

"Harold James Krippayne," she snapped. "No, no, no. This will not do."

"If you don't like what you see, then don't look." He grabbed from the bottom dresser drawer blue jeans and a sleeveless white t-shirt—he couldn't believe they still fit—clothes he hadn't worn since he'd painted Holly's room three months before she was born: twenty-eight years ago next month.

"You look ridiculous."

"Should I close the door or leave it open so you can slam it after I leave?"

"Whatever you're planning on doing, you better not be making a mess."

"I will be making a mess and I can assure you that I will be cleaning it up." He shut the door, opened it, and shut it again.

"You look ridiculous."

As if walking a plank, he made his way down the hallway to Holly's room, a place he hadn't visited in years, mostly because he hadn't been welcome inside for years, but also because he hadn't wanted to go inside for years. But he knew it was time. To walk. And jump in. And change. Things. Today.

***

Teetering between flabbergast, vertigo, and anger, Harold stood shaking his head at the swollen hoard suffocating Holly's room. He could barely see the dark purple wainscoting or the cream-colored carpet beyond the stacks of totes brimming with quilting materials, romance novels, naked dolls without eyes, turtleneck sweaters, khakis (some with original tags), scrapbooking albums, and lidless shoeboxes overflowing with 4x6 and 5x7 pictures of Holly and Hannah making funny faces (often painted) in funny costumes (often matching) at funny places (the Red River Zoo, Zanzabar Water Park, Easter Egg Baskets, Shrine Circus, DMV, Dog Shows, Horse Shows, Bicycling, Beach, Softball, Church Choir, New Kids on The Block Concert, Tiffany Concert, Prom 1990). He sat on the edge of the mattress and shuffled through the pictures. He was in none of the pictures, nor had he taken them. So who had? He'd have gladly gone to a water park or a horse show and wore a funny costume with a painted face. If only he'd been invited. To participate.

Armfuls at a time, he removed the contents of Holly's room to the garage, leaving for tomorrow the full-size mattress and six, large wall posters of Jodie Foster—whoever she is—a woman with a strong jawline whose face had been framed and outlined with red-marker hearts. Sweat beads dropped from his chin as he crawled beneath the bed and pulled out a sewing machine, decompressed silk flowers, stuffed animals, and two additional lidless shoeboxes filled with more pictures of Holly and Hannah. But not of him.

"What are you doing under there?" Hannah asked.

He hadn't heard her enter the room. "Spring cleaning." He popped out his head. "Looks good, huh?"

"This room belongs to Holly and me."

"It's wrong to treat a room like this." He stood.

"I'm glad you have sense enough to leave her Jodie Foster posters alone."

"Did Holly draw those hearts around her face?"

"She's a movie star, Harold. That's what kids do to movie stars they love."

Harold shrugged. "But she's a girl movie star. You don't find that a little strange?"

"What's strange is your intrusion into this room."

"Everything's in the garage for you and Holly to go though." He paused, debating whether or not to laugh. He didn't. "At your leisure."

Hannah groaned and sat on the edge of the bed. The mattress springs squeaked from the supplementary weight. "Does this have something to do with that stupid photograph?" Her eyes and lips tightened. "Where is that silly thing anyway?"

"I want to hang it on the best wall with the best light." Harold scanned the room. "Or do I? I mean, it's already a lighthouse so I guess it doesn't need any more light. But still, I want it to feel at home and well taken care of."

"This room has never looked more un-at-home-like."

"This room has never looked better."

"Why would you want to remove my and Holly's memories from the house?"

"I'm not removing you. I'm simply liberating the carpet and setting free the air vents."

"She's gonna be really hurt the next time she visits."

"When's the last time she visited?"

"We talk on the phone every week."

He picked one of the lidless shoeboxes and sat beside Hannah. "Why am I in none of the pictures?"

"They were of me and Holly. They weren't about you."

"Did you omit me on purpose?"

"You can't omit something that wasn't available."

"Who took them?"

She stood. The mattress springs exhaled. "Do not remove the Jodie Foster posters. I'll deal with it by myself. Like I always have."

"I was too available."

"Are you taking out the mattress?"

"Probably tomorrow."

"Believe or not, that's one decision I'm okay with."

"What about Holly are you're not telling me?"

"I can tell you this. She never once put a heart around your face."

***

For the rest of the day, while Hannah kept to the master bedroom, and while Harold painted the walls light brown and the wainscoting dark brown, he thought a lot about Holly—who she is, isn't, was, and wasn't. Families grow apart and separate. Children move out, on, and up. Holly was no exception. Evolution evolves. He knew this. A triangle can never know the fluidity of a circle. Nor should it. It goes against its nature. But a lighthouse knows fluidity, even with its edges and sharp points. It knows how to keep things safe and on course, even during times of storm and drought. Everyone knows this. Hannah and Holly knew this, too. So very well.

***

"You need anything before I turn off the lights and crawl into bed?" Harold asked Hannah, as he towelled off after a shower. His skin smelled of lilacs and daisies, similar to the ones blooming around the lighthouse. "I used some of your body wash tonight. Hope that's okay."

"Taking over everything." She fluffed a pillow. "Just hurry up."

"The bedroom's pretty much finished." He checked his teeth in the small oval mirror and pulled out a few gray hairs poking from his nose and ears. "A little touch up paint and then removing the bed and that'll be that."

"It's more of a bathroom print if you ask me."

Harold laughed. They both knew the photograph was far too large to occupy any one of the three bathrooms. He kept on laughing, because he realized, at that very moment, that laughter amplifies quietness, something Hannah had misinterpreted over the years as agreement. No more holding his tongue, following along, and being omitted from the picture. He'd never considered Hannah capable of meanness, but perhaps she was mean, perhaps she'd always been mean, perhaps she was always going to be mean. He disrobed and laid naked atop the quilt.

"Put some clothes on and get under the covers already."

"Do I ever occur to you?" he asked.

"I've washed your underwear for thirty years, Harold. Of course you occur to me."

"I don't think you and Holly have ever really seen me."

"Oh, I see you, and I can tell you right now you are quite unappealing."

Harold stood and walked out of the bedroom only to return a few minutes later holding the photograph. He took to his knees on Hannah's side of the bed. "What do you see when you look at this?"

"Insistent vulgarity."

"Goddamn it, Hannah. I'm being serious. Tell me what you see."

Her eyes widened. "Swearing now, too?" She sat and pressed her back against the headboard. "What's gotten into you tonight?"

He set his chin on the top part of the frame. "Tell me what you see." He spoke soft. Soft is always better than hard. Right?

"Since when did you become so self-centered?" she asked.

"Can't you see how it sits there all alone?"

"That's what a lighthouse does, Harold."

"How close it lingers to the edge." He thumbed the peak of the biggest wave. "The right storm or the wrong ship could take it down so easily. It's a lot more vulnerable than people realize."

"A lighthouse knows the risks and rewards involved in its job."

"There's no reward in being taken for granted."

"I knew this thing was gonna be a problem. I saw it in your eyes when you were looking at it."

"You did. What did you see?" He sat on the edge of the bed, turning the photograph so both of their reflections were staring back. "Please tell me."

"It's the same look you used to give me whenever I asked you to watch Holly by yourself."

"What kind of look was it?"

"I don't know, Harold. It was you." She pointed at his reflection. "The silver-haired, once frugal man, who should be wearing his reading glasses so he doesn't strain his eyes."

"No, I mean how did I specifically look?"

"You only have one look."

Harold tapped his forehead against the glass. "I'm sorry, old friend. I am trying."

"I'm tired, Harold. I want to go to sleep."

Harold stood and walked to his side of the bed, leaning the photograph against the wall. He sighed and once again laid naked atop the quilt. "Just once I wish you could see the bigger picture."

"You've never been a bigger picture, Harold. And neither have I. That's not who we are."

"I hope you'll come see the bedroom tomorrow once I've hung up the picture."

They laid quiet for a very long time.

"Dim," she whispered, turning off the bedside lamp. "That was your look."

Harold turned onto his side and stared at the lighthouse. "I don't want to go with you anymore to Square Pines Park."

"That makes two of us."

"Why did Holly draw hearts all over that movie star's face?"

"Go to sleep, Harold."

"What are you not telling me?"

"Everything, Harold. Now stop talking and leave me alone."

"I'm not dim," he whispered to the photograph and slowly fell asleep. Overnight, he dreamed a rolling wave was plowing toward the lighthouse, carrying with it a large ship spinning like a merry-go-round. Hannah and Holly were there, too, blocking the spotlight with their bodies, until darkness fell, and every scrap, lie, exclusion, and picture toppled into the sea.

Potion Number Us

Scott pushes open the Venetian-style front doors with the kind of exuberance normally meant for Vegas honeymooners or surprise birthday parties, neither true nor upcoming. He throws his jacket on the floor and leans against the kitchen doorway, trying to imagine life without Donna, his wife. He sighs and thinks about the word loneliness.

Donna, sitting on a leather stool at the center island, slips a blue pen up her sleeve and a white piece of paper into the middle of a Bible, neither original nor unfamiliar. Trying to imagine life without Scott, her husband, she sighs and thinks about the word companionship.

Wanitta and James, Scott and Donna's children, run up the staircase and talk over one another about who loves the movie best. Both wants the other to shut up. No you. No you. No you.

Scott and Donna, unaware that the other is thinking about the word goodbye, give each other a quick smile. Not too big. Not too small. But just right. So unlike the wrong they've become.

"If we could concoct a potion to help us fall in love again, what would it include?" Scott asks, standing behind his chair at the head of the kitchen table. He points to Donna's chair, directly across.

"Let me smell your breath," she says, unmoved.

He continues to point. "I'm not drunk talking. I'm being serious. What would you put in it?"

"Potions are for children's books and chick-lit movies."

He swirls his hands over a deep-blue, art deco glass bowl sitting like hardened brine in the center of the table. A wedding gift he gave her twenty-three years ago come November. "Tonight they belong here, to us, to 1936 Donegal Drive."

"Which is it, then?" She smirks. "Crack or Smack?"

"Don't belittle me. Not tonight."

Donna thinks about the word belittle. Scott thinks about the word crack.

"Seriously, what would you put in it?"

"I sure don't want cancer again."

"This isn't a cure for disease." Scott thinks about the word Sarcoma.

"So you do prefer me dead." Donna think about the word remission.

"Not exactly. Now focus."

"You know I detest playing games."

"Think of it as a riddle, then."

"I hate riddles even more."

"You said I lacked spontaneity. Well, here it is."

"I said that like twenty years ago."

"Better late than never, right?"

"More like once upon a time."

Scott opens the sliding glass door and steps onto the deck. Inhaling the backyard scents of elm trees coated with snowfall, he thinks about the word scream. Donna opens the refrigerator and pulls out a short plate of eggplant tartines. Chomping an icy tune, she thinks about the word exasperation.

"You're letting all the cold in. Close the door."

"Only if you agree to make the potion."

"Leave it open then." She stands. "It's your heating bill to worry about now."

"Why can't you just play along?"

"Fine." She sits in her chair. "Play."

"I want specific items." He closes the door and sits. "Good times in the past that'll help brew better times in the future." He flicks ten fingers into the bowl. "You start."

Silence fills the kitchen, interrupted only when the furnace kicks on. Scott stares at the bowl and thinks about the word shallow. Donna sets the Bible on her lap and thinks about the word forgiveness.

"I guess I'd throw in those first few Valentine's Day cards," she says. "If I'd have kept them."

"Poof." He flicks ten fingers over the bowl. "What else?"

"I think we can both agree we love the sesame chicken at PF Chang's."

"Poof."

"Definitely a Dirty Martini from Georgette's."

"I like those, too." He smiles. "Food and drink always brings people together, right?"

Donna thinks about the word together. "Tell me what you and the children talked about at the movies."

Scott thinks about the word children. "You're not supposed to talk at the movies."

"What movie did you see?"

"It really got me thinking, that's for sure. When the kids at Hogwarts have a problem, they simply concoct a potion to change the outcome."

"What grade is Wanitta going into next year?"

"Seventh. No, eighth."

"She's gonna be a freshman, Scott. How do you not know that?"

"Fine. You win and I lose."

"What's James' favorite movie?"

"Harry Potter."

"How can you be so clueless? What the name of his karate buddy's who's over here almost every weekend?"

"You know I'm terrible with names."

"You don't know it, do you?"

Scott and Donna sit quiet, each thinking about the word clueless.

"Maybe you can put in a dash of leniency?" he asks.

"I've put in way too much of that already."

"So, are you saying you don't have any more to give, or that you don't want to give any more?"

"I'm saying that I lost it all after the first affair."

Scott thinks about the word Meridith. "She was more toxin

than potion."

Donna thinks about the word Meridith. "She was more tramp than anything."

"I probably shouldn't have done that."

"Then why did you do it again? And again?"

"I never set out to do it either time."

"She scoffs. "How many times were there? Really?"

Scott thinks about the word aging. "I should have complimented you more."

Donna thinks about the word appearance. "Neither of us will ever be twenty-five again."

"Those women made me feel even less relevant," he says. "Less young."

"They did the same thing to me."

Their eyes meet, and an unexpected pulling and tightening of strings between husband and wife erupts. They quickly look away. Donna thinks about the word relevant. Scott thinks about the word Sharla.

"Did you love either of them?"

"Nothing lasts forever."

"I get that know."

"Me too." Scott thinks about the word vulnerability. "There's lots of things I wish I could go back and redo."

Donna thinks about the word redo. "Did you ever bring them to the house?"

Scott brings the bowl to his chest and thinks about the word house. "Did I ever tell you my father was homeless for a spell in his early twenties?"

Donna stares at the bowl and thinks about the word twenties. "Did I ever tell you my father cheated on my mother with a girl who was half her age?" She sighs. "What is it about a girl at nineteen men can't refuse?"

Scott offers his hand. Donna shakes her head. Scott withdraws. Donna brings the Bible to the tabletop.

He pushes the bowl to the center of the table and thinks about the word religion. "Since when did you become religious?"

She thinks about the word religious. "Having a creed is a good thing, Scott. You outta try it."

"I'd put in our wedding vows," he says, flicking ten fingers over the bowl. "Speaking of creed."

"You can't put in what you failed to keep."

Scott stands and runs up the staircase. Running back down, he carries two black pens and two blank sheets of paper. "Let's write new vows," he says. "Ones we promise to keep this time."

"What have you done with my husband?"

"So you're still Mrs. Marsden, Mrs. Marsden?" He flicks ten fingers, ten times, into the bowl.

"Someone call 911." She looks around the kitchen. "Anyone. Hello. Are you seeing this?"

"Poof. Poof. Poof."

"Forget it, call a straight-jacket instead."

They laugh and laugh (and laugh), their voices resonating as one.

Donna thinks about the word resonate. "Were their only two?"

Scott thinks about the word Mandy. "Yes."

"Promise?"

Scott stands, opens the refrigerator, and finishes the chicken salad congealing in a Tupperware container. He tosses the container and metal fork into the stainless steel sink and thinks about the word clash. Donna pulls from her Bible the white piece of paper and removes from her sleeve the blue ink pen and thinks about the word consequences. Scott opens and closes random kitchen drawers, pulling from the scrap drawer a red ink pen which he sets atop the Bible.

"You want blood, fine." He offers both wrists. "Slash away."

"I'm finished cutting you, and me, down."

Scott sighs, sits in his chair, and runs a finger over a long groove in the table. Donna sighs and does the same thing. Their fingers meet, touching for the first time in over a year. They pull away and retreat into the boundaries time has drawn between them. In the beginning, they wanted so much to be what the other needed. And wanted. Underestimating the power of dissatisfaction, acrimony, and secrecy. Each wonders, if their marriage does come to an end, and likely it will, who will the children blame and who will the children claim?

"I'm gonna write new vows." Scott scribbles across the page the way a doctor fills out a prescription pad. Donna turns over the white piece of paper. Scott leans forward and sniffs. Donna shoos him away.

"I've already written my new vows," she says.

He uncaps the red pen and writes on the palm of his hand. "Done." He makes a fist. "You start."

Donna thinks about the word start. "I could have handled one affair, but not two, Scott. If that's really how many there were."

Scott thinks about the word Heather. "Think whatever you want, but I know the truth."

"Did you ever really love me?"

"If you don't think I did, you don't know me at all."

Donna slides the white piece of paper into Scott's chest. "Here's the ingredients in my potion."

Half the cash in the money market account.
The Lake House, pontoon, and ski boat.
Full custody.
Monthly alimony of $8,000, plus $1,500 per child per month.
The Lexus coupe and Mercedes.
The Waterford China.
Sole proprietorship of the children's college fund.
The divorce papers: signed, sealed, and delivered.

After a few minutes, Scott stands, loosening the fist.

"What did you write on your hand?" Donna asks.

"Disclosure."

"Disclosure of what?"

He takes to his knees, lays his hand on the table and gradually, thumb to pinkie finger, opens his fist: *There were five. Now you know.*

State Lines

Then he died, Azim, Fatima's favorite co-worker and fag: sad, witty, lean, and closeted as he was. She loved him, the way he listened with open-minded ears (and eyes), the way he haphazardly stocked shelves as if sundries infuriated him, the way he swooped his wild hair to the left and wore more eyeliner than she did. A few years ago, they fancied opening a Burka shop. He could sew and she could sell. Combine talents to make a mark and follow the trail of profit. Silly now, now that they knew marks leave scars and profits stretch only far enough to break. Not so different from Iran after all. Still trapped by their shades of color. And thick, giveaway accents.

Fatima didn't ask Azim where he was going for a drive after work. He was always driving off, rarely telling her (or anyone) where he was going. His car was a mess. He couldn't go far. Oftentimes they met up and took the bus, chatting in Persian, laughing whenever native business suits and bag-lady Q-tips moved one (or two) seats over while rolling their eyes. Being ostracized hurt Fatima more than it hurt Azim. Which is why after three dates she married Alan P. Chambers, a colossal-muscle dentist, who promised to help her fit in to society and look after Azim. "Azim needs me," she told Alan. "I'm all he has."

Azim, quite out of character, told Fatima something top-secret. "I've been seeing someone. He's like so OMG hot. Bulges for days. I'm jizzing so hard. So fast. It's like, damn."

He's become so American, she thought. So sensational. So dramatic. So queer. Maybe someone will kill him.

That night, as she laid on the foam mattress with sateen sheets beside Alan, Alan whispered, "You're pretty quiet tonight. No update about Azim?" Alan's comment surprised Fatima. He'd never before mentioned Azim first. Or ever, now that she thought about it.

"Do you like Azim?" she asked.

"He has good teeth, but he's needy and." He paused, squeezing her hand. "Below us."

"I guess he met someone. Maybe that'll lift him up."

Alan sat up. "Who did he meet?"

Fatima shrugged. "Whoever he is, Azim's in love."

There's a type of dying no one sees, Azim had thought for years, especially after he started having sex with Alan, his خروس قشاع گرزب—*huge cock lover*—who had turned the grimace in his heart into a smile on his lips. Alan liked Azim's smile, said he had good teeth, said he had *good everything,* during a teeth cleaning. "Let's keep that between us," Alan had said. Azim agreed, understanding both the reason why and the logic behind it: some people have to keep secret what they can't divulge.

It took two months for Fatima to let Azim's death settle like aches and pains into her bones. Some things in life can't be raised. Her first feeling was one of relief, that a fight with Azim about fate (or the lack thereof) had been avoided; that there was no family to mourn his passing; that Alan had agreed to pay for the funeral and a burial plot. Her second, and altogether persistent feeling, was one of culpability. She should have asked for a name, demand to know where Azim was going, phone him to make sure he got home safe. Their friendship, like her marriage to Alan, was one-sided. She took whatever he gave—which happens to those who grow up with nothing. Azim, if he were still alive, would agree with this sentiment.

"This'll take the edge off," Alan said, handing Fatima two light blue pills. "Take two at bedtime. Three if things get really bad. But be careful. Xanax is an addictive drug."

Three months earlier, Azim had driven his fist against a stop sign and sunk to both knees in exhaustion. "Alan," he'd yelled at a forest of trees where they routinely had sex, trying to free himself from Alan's smile. And hands. And forest scent. And terms. Unsuccessful. Doing nothing but losing his voice while simultaneously diluting his friendship with Fatima, Alan's wife. Stupid wife.

How could she not see? Or know. Or care enough to ask.

"Night husband," Fatima yawned, enjoying the drug-induced collapse of unwanted emotions. "Can we skip sex tonight?" she asked Alan. Sex. So American. So sensational. So dramatic. So queer, she thought. Maybe someone will kill him, too.

"You're thinking about Azim, aren't you?" Alan asked. "See how he always interferes."

"Hottie bulge wants to meet up at some new spot tonight," Azim had told Fatima two months ago. "And in a pickup, too." Azim paused, squeezing her hand. "I know it's cruel to not tell you his name, but trust me, one day you'll find out."

Sitting in the pickup truck, staring at the forest of trees, Azim had told Alan that Fatima had a right to know about their affair, their love. Alan pushed with one hand Azim's head down onto the dirty floor of the old pickup truck and kept the other hand on Azim's legs. Azim inhaled the musk of cigarette soot smoldering in the dashboard ashtray. "I can't let you tell her," Alan had said. "She needs me. I'm all she has."

For many months, Fatima had chosen to believe Alan (and Azim) didn't smoke cigarettes, blaming strangers with bad habits for the lingering scent of smoke on their clothes. A dentist, of all people, wouldn't participate in such a stinky exercise, and Azim, sweet Azim, said he hated the smell of smoke. She'd never brought it up. Until now. "How long have you smoked?" she asked Alan, snuggling her head into the pillow. "I think Azim smoked, too. I never asked him, but I knew he did."

Alan scoffed, pretending to be shocked. "Why don't you trust me as I trust you?"

"Why don't you love me as I love you?" Azim had asked Alan in the pickup truck, Azim's nose melding into the car mat, his hands trying to slap loose the open air, until he could no longer slap. Or trust. Or hear. "I don't love you, Azim." Or breathe.

The events, cloudy to some, clear to others, temporarily dissipated overnight. The next morning, sober and undressed, Fatima wasn't sure if what had happened was accurate. Or equivocal. Or hers. Or Azim's. Or Alan P. Chambers.

Fifteen

Desire stirs in him like medicine, moving everything he knows, and some things he doesn't, closer to the outdoors. Awareness tempts him to go farther. Mind games are abuzz. He's alert & acute & auspicious. Adolescence grows both above and below the waist.

In his bedroom, free of nighttime noise, he plays with roles, fantasies, and costumes. Emotional acts of mental passion released by physical goo into a thin black towel.

Daylight is getting stronger, calling out like a song. Boundaries feel more like boundless possibilities. There's a flux in the force. Premonitions of promise. Inclinations to do something wild.

Monday arrives and he counts forty-three steps to the mailbox. Tuesday comes and he does it in a bathrobe and sandals. Wednesday is too thick with summer wind. Thursday uproars like a corporate-espionage-movie-marathon playing in the den. Friday rain and Saturday gloom keep him in the kitchen, helping mom and gramp-gramps cut pasta strips for lasagna. Sunday—God needs veneration—is rife with slamming doors and mom's hurry-up gesticulations and dad's anger with gas prices and who has any energy to do anything but keep quiet and follow the routine until Monday reappears and reopens its doors for business. Model Monday—saturated with surprise. Ah!

Sunday night arrives, and he plans what to wear—what not to wear—how to dance the dance he wants to dance without ever being taught the dance. He puts on a record and disrobes, slapping junk against curly tufts of brown pubic hair. He dedicates the dance, reflected in a rectangular mirror, to all men, like him, who need and love to dance. In his dreams, a band of tall, rain-soaked walking sticks stand upright in crisp, white navy uniforms.

Monday smells triumphant. The mailbox lid sits closed. The red flag points upward like a fire alarm. Dance, he says. Dance out the screen door and all the way to the street. Come on. Don't be ᴏɴ. Dance. You have to.

Five cars drive by the house in less than one minute. Two black SUV's and three brown moving vans. 11:26. 11:38. 11:53. 11:59. Down to whitey-tighties. He flings open the screen door. Leaps into the grisly wind. Birds sound happy. Sun beams bright. He stands beside the mailbox like a package waiting for collection. An advertisement—buyer must have strong hands: must possess car: must love to dance. Three cars honk. A bicycler scowls. A mini-van put on its brakes and squeals to a stop, slowly drives backward, forward, backward, forward. "Can I help you?" the driver asks, sending the boy into a fit of fully-expanded ambition. Bouncing into the middle of the yard. Waving. Go. Go. Go. Not the right dance eyes. Not the right nose.

A bright red Ford pick-up truck stops and rolls down the window. The man winks and leans his head sideways. "Hey buddy. Watcha up too?"

The boy smiles. The dance—more hip-hop than jazz—has begun. Inside the truck, the boy bounces on the black leather seat and waves goodbye to the house and mailbox and boring week-days he will never forget. Or miss. The man puts a hand on the boy's leg, sending pleasure-shivers to places the boy can't reach in the shower.

"You're quite the cutie." He moves the hand upward. "I don't usually drive this route home but I'm glad I did today. Why don't you take off those underwear and let me see what's happening underneath."

The boy smiles and obeys. Then he frowns. For a moment. He knows there will never be another first dance. No brighter sun. No happier birds. No way to leap out and start over.

Is there?

No, there isn't.

Not when you need to dance. Like this.

Do You Know What I Mean?

She found his serious tone awful and awkward. Not like him at all. Sitting across from him on the bed, she tried looking through him, as if to see farther into the future, trying to decipher whether she needed to get around him, under him, or over him.

"Have you told anyone else about Yowl's Reef?" he asked, biting his fingernails.

"I told the officer I was at the mall with my mom the whole day."

"I didn't want to do it, you know."

"Don't tell me anymore." She covered her ears with her hands. "What if the officer asks me about it again?"

"Those dudes dared me to do it and I didn't have time to think about the end result."

"Stop talking."

"Nothing bad happened, though."

"Really." She twirled her bangs. "They're a pretty weird bunch. I don't know why you hang out with them."

"But they're really funny sometimes."

She held his hand while he scanned the bedroom, his eyes landing on the wooden armoire standing tall in the corner of the room. "What's inside that thing?"

"Junk mostly. Oh, and a broken TV."

"Why don't you get it fixed?"

"It's just a dumb old TV. Mom said I can get a new one when we have more money."

"Maybe I could fix it."

"It's not worth it." She scooted closer. "So tell me, now that it's over, was it worth it?"

"I thought you didn't want to hear any more about it."

"Just tell me if it was worth it."

"I can tell you it was as fantastical as it was dreadful."

"I'm glad I wasn't there."

"You should be. You wouldn't have enjoyed it."

"How was it fantastical?"

"You'd have been super freaked out."

"I don't freak out that easily."

"Boo."

She jumped.

"See."

"That's not fair. I wasn't prepared."

"Neither was I. I mean, not for the feelings part afterward."

"Feelings part?" She held his other hand.

"You know, feelings, like regret and shame and confusion."

She shrugged. "Does that mean you're sorry for what you did?"

"Not exactly." He squeezed her hands. "But kinda."

"Did they give you money to do it?"

"I did feel shame, though, but not for very long."

"Do you feel shame right now?"

"Not really."

"Then what do you feel?"

"Mostly like I need to take a break from getting in trouble with them." He stood, jumped out the window, and crawled to the edge of the roof.

"I'm glad you're okay," she said from the window. "Now come back in. Please."

"You wanna know what I really felt, I mean more than anything else?"

"Be careful or you're gonna fall."

He pretended to lose his grip. She reached for him. He steadied himself. She grunted. "You're so bad."

"That's how I felt." He leaped from the roof and landed flat-footed on the grass. "Asta La Pasta, Quora."

"Come back tomorrow." She watched his shadow move like nighttime mist down the street. A burglar who had yet to be caught. A schemer who had stolen her heart. In the beginning, she'd given the pieces of her heart so freely, believing her pieces could help his pieces tick clockwise. Once again. That's what he said he wanted. With her. For a long, long time. Finally, after she was unable to see his shadow, she laid down, whispered goodnight, and programming another night and day: moon and sun: her and him.

Elder Mistrust

Hey there, gramps. My English professor mentioned you in class today is what I think I hear my granddaughter say over the cellular telephone tucked between my right shoulder and ever-softening jaw line. At my age, and in my condition, talking on the phone while simultaneously decapitating green sprigs from the tops of ripe strawberries requires the cunning mélange of centrifuge eyes and ambidextrous wrists, which, much like my hearing, worked a lot better in my mid-seventies. But I always take her call, even when I'm fruitlessly wielding a sharp, pointed instrument with my one good hand.

I figured she'd mention you at some point is what I think I hear her say as I mumble a reply, my only option anymore, as my communication system is eternally distorted by buzzing, clanging, and a continual popping sensation in both eardrums. God, I miss hearing the credulous lilt in her voice, like a Mariposa Lily emerging from desert sand. More, the television volume in the living room is turned up to one-hundred percent because I refuse to wear hearing aids and because I am interested in the subject matter. If some half-wit in Estes Park, Colorado, wants to give me a power chair for free (in most cases) heaven forbid I stand in Medicare's way. I'm incurable, not naïve. I outta jot down the one-eight-hundred number except that I can never find a writing utensil. JoAnn, my daughter, hides them. A tactic meant to induce exercise. JoAnn's always had an affinity for playing hide-and-seek with my things. I'm not bitter, nor do I blame her for being obsessive-compulsive. We're very much alike—two bottomless wishing wells devoid of a sturdy bucket or a tight rope.

My professor said you were really dense in your day is what I think I hear her say when I notice a new stack of bills sitting on the center island. JoAnn bought me from the dollar store a spongy-tip water-dotter so as to make it easier for me to seal my bills, walk them to the mailbox, and raise the red flag. Doctor Pleshanko's lab reports have confirmed a compromised circulatory system. JoAnn has threatened to stick me in the malodourous nursing home at the edge of town if I don't go outside at least once a day. As a boy, I could spit water like an archer fish. One time in grade school, I bet my friends a full carton of cigarettes that I could spit twelve feet, six inches. Or was it seven? No, it was six. Regardless, now I can barely work up enough saliva to lick the roof of my mouth. Age really does make you dry.

My professor said her father worshipped you is what I think I hear her say when I spot my wallet cowering beneath the table, gutted and stretched out like taffy. I worry for the person who could commit such a cruel, surreptitious act. I outta care more about cash. But I'm no good at differential equations.

She wrote your name on the white board and then underlined the title of your book twice is what I think I hear her say when the room becomes dizzy, forcing me to set the cellular telephone on the table and turn on speaker mode. I stick my head between my legs and knock over the black tray table holding the phone book: Joann's phone number circled like a windstorm in red pen. I'm glad she remembers my forgetfulness. The crash of the tray makes me smile. At least I can still feel vibration in my one good foot.

It sounds like somebody is slamming doors, gramps. Is mom there? is what I think I hear her say as I bring the cellular telephone up to my big, cold ear. Even as a burgeoning teenager in the winter of 1942, cutting down White Pine trees with my father and his bearded crew of sardine smelling men, my ears were big and cold. I've always been disproportionately generous in all the wrong places. Last January, waiting hatless for the old people's bus to come pick me up and transport me downtown to the aquarium where I get to watch sea creatures watch me watch them swim around in a big blue tank, I heard the red-haired boy across the street tell his mother I look like a prehistoric gargantuan. He's right. Call it like you see it. That's what I do. Or did. When I could.

When I told the class you were my grandpa the teacher just about swallowed her glasses is what I think I hear her say when I stand and limp my way to the front door. A delightful wind nibbles my neck the way Sheila, my wife, used to nibble me during long, quixotic weekends at the lake house—a time when feeling numb was a good thing. God, I yearn for her signature touch, her thick scent of femininity huddled up against my skin, her morning shuffle beside my novel gait walking up and down Sycamore Street on pain-free bare feet we absolutely took for granted. My poor hands—misshapen barnacles of smoking-arthritis. My poor fingers—all ten tips have forgotten their names.

After class, my teacher asked me if you were still writing, but I didn't tell her what happened to you, gramps is what I think I hear her say as I press my Skechers (with memory foam) tennis shoes into the dew-laden grass and stare into the eyes of mistress sun, heavens loveliest paramour, who continues to offer herself up for the carnal pleasure of mankind. Beauty for the taking.

My teacher said she heard something about your stroke but wasn't sure how accurate the information was, given the source is what I think I hear her say when I step indoors, shut the front door, and pull my leg in the direction of the bedroom, leaving the strawberries in the bowl on the kitchen sink for whatever hungry critters might eat here overnight. I nod at the silver-tip knife dripping red juice on the white countertop, neither bloody enough to file fake charges nor thick enough to congeal into anything useful. The clock in the hallway is perpetually stuck on seven-thirty, proving how little I care anymore about revolution. I stumble to the toilet seat and take an emasculating pee, glad that Sheila isn't here to see how shriveled up my bladder, balls, and beard hairs have become. I blow my nose into a t-shirt. As much paper as I've wasted over the years, it's the least I can do.

My teacher wanted me to convey her sympathy and ask if you might sign for the silent auction this fall a few copies of your book Pandemic Seeds of Murmuration, *which she says is her total fa-*

vorite of all time is what I think I hear her say as I lie on the mattress and settle into the thick impressions my body has carved over three decades, ten years now without Sheila who left me alone with the living task of spreading each year a few more of her autumnal ashes amongst the springtime flowerbeds, thriving from her death. God, I long to see her, to leap bombastic bones between the clouds and ascend into heaven.

If you could do that for me, gramps, I'd be uber-appreciative is what I think I hear her say as I close my eyes and mumble goodbye: I have nothing more to say; nothing else to write; nothing left to do. I've signed my moniker to everything Joann and my granddaughter need to prosper. My epilogue, however embellished, is ready for print.

Just sign the books and give them to mom when you see her next Friday and then she can send them to me ASAP. Is that okay, gramps? gramps. Grandpa. Grandpa Joe. Grandpa Joe.

All Thixthy Thix Bookth

My spirituality became a lot more devout on September 5, 1992, the first day of sixth grade confirmation class at Emmanuel ELCA, when the teacher, senior Pastor David VanOrman, who the girls called Pastor VanHormone, announced we had eight months in which to memorize in chronological order all sixty-six books of the Holy Bible. Adding, "If you want to be properly confirmed under the auspices of the church, the Lord Jesus Christ, and the Holy Saints, you will readily stand in front of the congregation and recite them out loud, proving to me and to God above your affinity for godly fortitude demonstrated by biblical dexterity." Then he announced the big clincher: "The student who can recite all sixty-six books the fastest, and the most coherently—okay—will win four tickets to the Minnesota State Fair and fifty dollars for rides, treats, and souvenirs." Right then I realized two important things about myself. One, life is a price tag, and two, I could be bought.

In less than a month, in eight seconds flat, I nailed like Jesus to the cross the twenty-six books of the New Testament. Names like Matthew, Mark, Jude, and Peter were so easy to pronounce, even a kid could do it. First and Second Thessalonians proved a bit more challenging, but after I changed first and second to one and two, biblical dexterity flew out like an evangelist's spittle. If Pastor VanOrman took issue with the minor changes, I was ready to quote Matthew 18:3: *Unless you change and become like little children, you will never enter the Kingdom of God.* If he still wasn't convinced, I'd quote James 3:8: *Let no man tame the tongue.* I was ready to use God's word against him, willing to back him into a corner from which I hoped he'd feel the hot-word squeeze.

The thirty-nine books of the Old Testament, that boring anthology of begets and behooves and bereaves, proved inarticulately tongue twisty, especially to a boy with a first class overbite and interdental lisp. Coherent took on a whole new meaning.

Genesis. Exodus. Leviticus. Numbers. So many of S's to slur through. Almost unbearable.

Thank god for Deuteronomy.

Joshua, or as I called it, Jothua.

Judges sounded a lot like Judgeth.

Good ole Ruth.

First and Second Samuel. First and Second Kings. First and Second Chronicles. One and two. One and two. One and two.

Ezra.

Nehemiah.

Esther.

Job.

Psalms. S at the beginning and at the end. How alpha and omega.

Proverbs.

Ecclesiastes. Seriously?

Song of Solomon. No way in hell.

Isaiah.

Jeremiah.

Lamentations.

Ezekiel.

Daniel.

Hosea.

Joel.

Amos.

Obadiah.

Jonah.

Micah.

Nahum.

Habakkuk. I've always loved Habakkuk. Just listen to it. Habakkuk. So many easy K's to pronounce.

Zephaniah.

Haggai.

Zachariah.

Malachi. Such fluidity. Almost like a song.

I spent a majority of weeknights, and most weekends, in front of the mirror holding my mother's tape recorder to my lips. If practice made perfect, and perfect made loser's winners, I was a shoe-in to not come in last place, my biggest fear. I wore out two blank cassette tapes in the first month, goddamn Ecclesiastes.

Two weeks before confirmation Sunday, Pastor VanOrman announced an impromptu in-class practice session.

"We'll start with the girls," he said. "Let's see what's going on inside those cute little sweaters and pretty little hairdos."

Not one of the girls carried the sixty-six books without a fumble. But some were fast. Jill Ward, the most popular girl at school, and church, finished the list in 25 seconds. Yeah, she mixed up Hosea and Joel and called Zacheriah, Zebania, but she was coherent and formidable and eager to win. I saw those State Fair tickets and that fifty dollar bill slipping out of my hand and diving head first into her glitter-pink *Duran-Duran* purse. She had to be defeated. By me. No more excuses.

"Now for the boys," Pastor VanOrman said, unenthusiastically. He took a seat and crossed his long legs and skinny, hairless arms.

Chris Pendelton made it to Nehemiah.

Andy Bollant called it Third Kings.

Patrick Olsen said, "Memorization, like confirmation, is a huge waste of time."

Lance Kurtz strangled his neck and blamed laryngitis.

Tim Wegshied had a really, super, terrible, unbelievably wicked, maybe-contagious cough.

Alan Schneider, whose father was the single attorney in town, asked for a temporary recess to which Pastor VanOrman responded, "Not in my court, mister. Now get up here and confess." Alan botched the Torah and after the book of Ruth, excused himself to the bathroom.

Then it hit me. I was one of two boys remaining. There was a fifty percent chance that it was either going to be me or my school tormentor, Tommy Pokorney, the mayor's son. Then it hit me even harder. How in God's good graces was I going to do this in front of the congregation? I barely spoke a word to anyone, not even to my parents, who, lucky for me, were field workers and not mealtime talkers. At school, and at church, I pretended to be deaf, walking around with a wool-knit-cap pulled over my eyebrows and ears. I never spoke in class unless I was called upon, which was rare, as I was quite adept at keeping my head down and tucking my hands between my legs. I knew Jill Ward and her shimmer-minions called me Liplock Lonnie. I also knew most of the boys called me it, too. But because I was the only fifth grader who could touch the bottom of the basketball net with very little effort, the boys never said it to my face. Except for Tommy Pokorney, who started the nickname and kept it rolling, ruining my attempt at achieving invisibility. Like most nicknames, it caught on fire and spread like childhood gossip up and down the white-brick walls.

"Lonnie Lancaster." Pastor VanOrman called my name. "Take off that hat and get up here." I made my way to the front. My legs were chains. My cheeks felt hot and wet. A quiet hush took over the crowd. Feverish and dizzy, I turned around and faced six rows of smiling smirks, brooding eyes, and a bunch of oddly-shaped noses sticking up in the air. Not one friend in the bunch.

"Well," Pastor VanOrman said.

Hat in my hands, I shrugged.

"You can't or you won't."

"Uh, i…i…i"

"Liplock Lonnie," Jill said with a cough.

"You've had seven months to prepare," Pastor VanOrman said, waving an index finger. "How many times do I have to tell you that a sluggard is worse than a pig on vacation?" He'd never before said that to me. Not once.

"Thonnie's just-tho th-scared." Tommy mocked. The class erupted in giggles. Right in front of Pastor VanOrman. No shame at all. The audacity. The gall. A mounting pressure to punish them infused my bones and supercharged my tongue. I had no choice but to surrender and proclaim the good news.

"Genethith," I blurted out. A surge of relief swept over my body.

"Exthoduth." I couldn't contain it.

Leviticiuth." My lips were ablaze. Even if I wanted to stop, which I didn't, I couldn't, spitting out the sixty-six books so fast, Pastor VanOrman took to his feet and bumped backward into the chalkboard. Jill wrote 29 seconds on her left palm and circulated the news above her head. Tommy, Alan, Tim, and Lance sat straight up, their stupid mouths hanging wide open. After I finished, I smiled at the ungodly degenerates and crossed my arms, as if to say, top that, mother fuckers, if you dare. Pastor VanOrman pointed me to my seat, and said, "The tongue is a tool often measured by lies, but sometimes it is also an instrument of courage." I wasn't sure if he was paying me a compliment or calling my tongue a tool full of lies. I didn't care. He told us to bow our heads and pray quietly, which is exactly what I did. I prayed to win. I prayed Jill Ward would lose. I prayed Tommy Pokorney would die a painful death of arthritis and gout. Those were the only two diseases I knew back then, so they'd just have to do.

On May 9, at 10:18am, I stood in front of the congregation in my first white collared Oxford shirt, black tie, pleated khaki pants, and black dress shoes and recited the books in eighteen seconds. Flat. None of the girls laughed and none of the boys pointed. Tommy Pokorney clapped along with everyone else, including my parents, who sat in blue jeans and plaid shirts in the back row. After church, Jill Ward's mother unexpectedly invited my parents (and me) to her house for a congratulatory brunch. I almost swallowed my tongue when my parents accepted the invitation to go and sit in Jill Ward's parent's sunflower-wallpaper dining room and eat soggy pot roast and drink warm 2% milk. Jill's mother rambled on about my victory as if she knew all along that I was going to win and that Jill was going to lose. "Who are you planning to take with you to the state fair?" Jill's mother asked me.

I shrugged.

"Well, I know someone who'd really like to go with you." She and my mother giggled. Jill's father shook his head. My father, like usual, said nothing. Jill stared blankly ahead, neither giving a look of disgust, nor one of approval. Just boredom. Until she smiled and said, "Congrats, Liplock."

After brunch, Jill's mother pushed me and Jill out the back door. "Go do whatever it is kids your age are doing these days." I followed Jill to a patch of wet grass behind an old tool shed where we sat Indian-style: face to face, eye to eye, chin to chin. Jill picked a handful of grass and blew from her palm the blades which tickled my face. I closed my eyes and replayed the highlight reel of my eighteen second win: my tickets, my cash, my tongue, my win.

"If you show me your tongue I'll let you touch my boobs for two seconds," Jill said. I stuck out my tongue and waited. Why not? I was the champion. Have at it. She clamped onto my tongue with two cold fingertips and pressed up and down, side to side. "Well, it feels normal." Then she let go and wiped her fingers on my pants. "Tongues are gross anyway so if I were you, I wouldn't worry about it."

We sat quiet for a short time, listening to and waving away the sounds of a fly-zone-choir.

"Well, go ahead," she said, uplifting her chest.

Now that experience was truly a revelation. Revelation. Not on S to slur through. Not one fear to overcome. Just one excellence squeeze for two, maybe three, seconds. Until a light flashed on, and off, in my brain.

As for Jill, she never called me Liplock Lonnie again. Unfortunately, she told everyone I touched her boobs. I wanted to deny it, but I wasn't courageous enough to admit disgust.

As for my overbite and lisp, I learned to accept the benefits of speech therapy. Thanks, Mrs. Weggum.

As for the tickets to the state fair, I sold them to an upper class-man from church who easily convinced me that by going to the state fair, he and his girlfriend would reach their ultimate fantasy. How could I refuse such stupid simplicity? Besides, my parent's didn't go to places like the state fair. Looking back, I'd have liked to see my parents eat corn dogs and ride a rollercoaster, waving their hands like they just don't care.

As for the fifty dollar bill, I still carry it with me in my wallet. Folded and tucked underneath my driver's license and credit cards, it leads me back home, sometimes in tears, to that wildly frightening, madly exhilarating, spiritually innocent, tongue-twisted gloriousness.

The Way We Drive

I sat fully clothed on the edge of Christopher Buckner's bed, longing for nakedness, wanting to reach out and touch his forbidden year-older skin and finger through shiny black hair swept to the right side of a perfect skull. Square teeth. Satisfying lips. A tugging smile that nineteen years later still pulls me sideways. I couldn't speak up, whisper please, shout yes, or swear loyalty and secrecy to whatever secrets he needed me to be loyal.

He played with silk-thin fingers a brand-name red electric guitar. My jealous heart sought ways to steal it and carry it close to my chest, to tighten it when things got loose, to pluck it when other sounds lured me away—such a tempting life. All that mattered was his brand on me.

He invited me to join a summer road trip to Alabama. A visit to an older sister. Two men. Two bucket seats. Side-face to side-face fact. Seven-hundred and twenty miles round trip. Love and lust mingling like erupting repression. Rolling along. Forging ahead. Michael W. Smith blaring through the speakers. Amy Grant concert on September 10. Shit. College starts September 8.

"What are your plans for the fall?" I asked.

He sat quiet for a while. "Not sure." Voice of seventh heaven. "My dad fixes broken watches. Maybe I'll do that."

"Not interested in college?" Come with me. Share a room, stories, classes, and walks. Best friends having and doing it all. I knew exactly what I wanted.

"School isn't me."

A high school senior when we met, I didn't know the thrill of studying with him. I'd have let him cheat if he asked. I hated every son-of-a-bitch who helped him multiply and divide, read O. Henry, sing tenor in the choir, and divvy up art supplies, every asshole who sat on the edge of his bed when I was missing. In person.

His sister in Alabama was plain, unlike his hazel eyes, nothing plain about him. But if he said he loved vanilla most, then so did I.

I'd have changed anything he wanted me to change, apart from the one thing I didn't know how, or want, to change, because I believed he also possessed the change, and shouldn't he, being older, be the first to confess and open the window of hope my truth needed him to open so I could open mine and climb through, to be with him, happy on the other side. Two bona fide men living the art of realization. I can admit it now: there's nothing more damaging to lying than knowing.

I saw us as old men. Years of speaking sweetly, so speak sweetly, say something raw and real to unleash my tortured tongue. Ignite the 18-me and the 19-you to talk outright about the bond growing between us inside a pickup truck sputtering to and from Alabama. Entice my lips with tenderness. Release my fingers with honesty. Impress my disbelief with conviction. Suffuse my heart's pride with sincerity. Smile whenever onlookers glanced over and saw us as a couple. A smartly pair. Youthfulness maturing into soul mates. Destiny. Fate. Textbook partners. Just as we were. Are. Am.

"Let's switch places," he said.

"While we're driving?"

"You ever drive clutch before?"

"Clutch?" I'd never before said the word. Was that a bad thing? Did that make me less in his eyes? Did he use the word on purpose? Had I, sometime in the past, no doubt daydreaming of him, told him about my clutchlessness? "Did I tell you that?"

"No. I just figured."

"Figured how?"

"Figured you hadn't. Your cars an automatic, right?"

"Totally automatic." God, I loved driving a Ford Escort with him in the passenger seat. Going slower than necessary. Sponging up his time. Listening to Russ Taff's *Silent Love*. A song for all categories of sexual expression, goddamn it.

"You ready?" he asked. "Think you can keep it in fifth gear while I take a snooze?"

"You want to go to sleep?"

"Is that a problem?"

"No." Fuck yeah, it's a problem, stay awake man, pay attention to what's happening right in front of your eyes. "Do whatever."

Our bodies intertwined. His hand pressed against my chest. His toes rubbed against my calves. His breath immersed into my neck. His masculinity seduced my greediness. Then it was over. Finished. I pumped the gas pedal. He set his forehead on the passenger side window and fell asleep. Shutting me out. Yet again. Jesus, dude, I'm right here. I'm driving us in the right direction. Can't you see how far I'm willing to go for you, for me, for us? Don't you understand how much I could matter to your future capabilities? This is just the beginning. We're nowhere close to the end. Tell me you feel the same. Pick me and save me from a life without you.

Four years at college flew by in fast semesters, me coming and going on holiday breaks, him switching bookstores and heart-wrenching girlfriends. We talked a few times briefly at church, the place we met, in the very sanctuary that said my feelings for him were banned from the Kingdom of God, bullying me to recapitulate the car trip exchange—failing miserably. So many men's hands have been pressed against my chest, but only his left an imprint.

Courtney-Buckner Plith. Instagram Follow. March 2013.

Hi Benji. How's life?

I'm ok. I think of u, ur hubby, and Christopher often. How is Christopher? How r u?

Chris died in 2010 from rectal cancer. He fought hard but God decided it was time to call him home.

Raindrops slide down the windowpane of my street-level apartment, dropping into a shallow pool that flows into the city's sewer system and races out of town.

Sleep well, Christopher Buckner. I will dream of you.

Mini Lift

He asked me to ride along. Rare. He told me where we were going. I wasn't surprised by the destination. Just sad—the one emotion we've so thoroughly expressed during our marriage, it's sure to be the linchpin of our legacy.

In the waiting area, while he filled out contact information, I watched red faces come and go through self-reflecting glass doors. "Gregory," a voice called out. For once, I let him walk ahead.

The hallway was filled with silicone parts sitting atop metal carts with wheels. Perfect. More superficial artificiality staring me in the face.

"Doctor Leigh will be with you shortly."

Gregory sat on the exam table and swung his legs while I sat on a plastic chair and flipped through Time magazine. The room smelled incurably cliché. Like regurgitated sterilization.

Doctor Leigh entered the room fully prepared to touch things, white latex gloves poking and pinching Gregory's face. I wanted to giggle. Might Doctor Leigh's hand job satisfy Gregory's incessant pandering for mine?

"It's easier to see scars on men," Doctor Leigh said, looking at me as if to incite, or read, a reaction. I didn't blink or speak. Like Gregory's toupee, I'm also attached to a head full of secrets.

"Brenda's gonna come in and take some pictures of your face. Just remove your shirt and sit tight."

Shirtless isn't his best look. "Nice boobs."

His eyes grew melancholy, so much so my heart travelled down a road I rarely go anymore: a clear path leading to a furtive pasture where softness begs kindness to be a better person. "I'm sorry."

"Hey guys. I'm Brenda." She pulled from the ceiling a blue screen and grabbed from a top shelf a camera. Without warning, she parted his bangs. I closed my eyes and listened for collateral damage sure to come out of his mouth. He can be quite contemptuous, especially caustic toward black women who wear pink highlights and silver lip rings. "Your hair has a mind of its own, doesn't it?"

He remained quiet, so much so I had time to recall being young and in love, with him, happy even when my parents said, don't you dare go and fall for the first guy with a full, thick head of hair. Which he had. So I fell. Hard. Until I fell again. Out. Of love. Even harder.

"I'm gonna swoop a little hair over your ear, okay."

My eyes popped open. This could get ugly.

He leaned back and looked at me as if to say help, the same look he gave the morning he held in his huge hands our dead son's fetus.

"Could you give us a few minutes?" I asked.

"Sure. Just open the door when you're done."

We stood in silence, so close to touching, so close to giving in to what we once knew.

"Should I take it off?" he asked.

"Is that something you can do?"

"Will you hold it for me?"

"No."

His eyes grew angry, so much so my heart travelled down the road I know best: a secret sidewalk leading up a flight of stairs to a cherry door swinging me into another man's home. I sighed, stood, and left the room. I sat in the car and stared at my face in the pull-down mirror. If age has taught me anything, it's that we don't change, no matter how many makeovers promise a fresh start.

Dates and Times Filled In

My ADHD/OCD friend Mark and I might have walked right past LifePath Christian bookstore if not for the a-shaped sign blocking the front of the store, promising free wassail and yummy Christmas cookies. Hungry since we hit the gym at noon, time edging at 6pm, Target and Best Buy would have to wait. Besides, we have enough karate-dude movies already.

"Dude," Mark said, almost kicking the sign. "They have free shit."

"It's like a zoo in there."

Mark scanned the numerous able-bodies lined up to the back of the store. "Christian places are notorious for food and drink. Trust me, I know."

"Really?"

"I dare you to hold my hand and walk through the store," he said, laughing. "We should totally pretend to make out in front of the Bible section."

"What?" I sneered. "No. I don't think so."

"Chicken shit."

Even if we were gay, which I'm not, Mark's way too beefy and short. More, some best friend boundaries can't be spontaneously tested without suffering serious repercussions, like the two of us not being friends anymore because we pretended to make out in the Bible section in a Christian bookstore. Not even stone cold drunk. Off my ass. In Vegas.

"Come on," he said. "Let's see what happens."

"You know what'll happen."

"No, I don't?"

"Tell me this isn't your coming out day."

"Pucker up and give me a wet one," he said, pinching his nipples with sex face.

The thought of kissing Mark's chapped lips or rubbing my cheeks against his bumpy, red face turned my stomach sour.

"This is weird."

"We do weird stuff all the time."

"I'm not saying gay is weird."

"Couples need to mix it up." He punched my shoulder. "Here's our chance to spar with some of those righty-tighty Baptists and those under-brunched Pentecostals speaking in tongues."

"Someone in there could actually hit us." I pushed him away. "Christians are crazy."

"It's a good thing for both of us that you're a lawyer." He grabbed my hand.

"Stop it. I work in real estate, not personal injury."

"Semantics. Now take my hand and hold me like you love me."

Mark and I never talk about spirituality, nor about anything touchy-feely. Our conversations wrap around busty women, muscle cars, and rich flavors of draft beer. He doesn't know I gave my New International Version Bible to the Goodwill the very same week I graduated from Bible College with a BA in youth and family psychology, or that my brother, Justin, preaches brimstone every Sunday to a wealthy congregation in downtown Chicago. Our relationship, like me and my brother's, is built on the premise of don't ask, don't tell. Mark once said something about practicing agnosticism—or did he call God a she?—but whatever it was, true to our custom, we laughed for a while and then forgot all about it. At least I did.

"Pucker up, love kitten." Mark pulled me into the store. Like Jonah in the Whale, I was swallowed and made to stand in the smell of fishy aromas huddled inside LifePath: rotten old-lady perfume and young-man cologne. I tried to release my hand from Mark's grip, but he had a strong handle on the situation. We walked past a family rife with conservative looking haircuts. The slender father tipped a pair of spectacles and grimaced; the red fingernail mother feigned a smile and pulled her son close to her side; a group of girls, maybe sixteen or seventeen, said, "What the what." People—likely Christians—were making fun of us. For holding hands? I closed my eyes and envisioned busty women, muscle cars, and rich flavors of draft beer. My fingers, however, interlocked with Mark's, felt like soggy talons of chaste humiliation. I followed Mark through the darkness, giggling at the gospel song's irony coming from the speakers: *Just As I Am*.

"Can I help you?" a male employee asked. He didn't make eye contact. His plastic nametag—C.B. Headlish—sat crooked on the right side of a faded dark-blue sweater.

"My sweets and I are here to browse your fine little establishment," Mark said. His voice took on height and, much to my amazement, stayed there rather lithely. "We woke up this morning and I told my snuggly-wuggly bear here that this was a browsing kind of day, didn't I, sweetie?" I stood quiet, unsure what to say. Or do. People were snickering and covering their mouths, ears, and eyes.

"What do you expect to find in here?" C.B. asked.

Mark put his head on my shoulder and stretched an arm around my waist. "Any good books on how to make awesome love even awesomer?"

"We have an extensive self-help section. I could definitely recommend a few titles from there."

"Aren't you a dear." Mark winked at C.B. "Please lead the way."

"You do realize what kind of bookstore this is?" C.B. asked, walking ahead. And fast.

"All I know is you have the cutest little trinkets I've ever seen." Mark's voice couldn't get any higher. "This just might become our favorite new store." He grabbed my cheeks. "You love trinket shopping, don't you my little snuggly-wuggly bear?"

Mark and I hit it off instantly the first day we met at work. Abbott and Costello; Laurel and Hardy; Starskey and Hutch; kindred spirits to those who think, and talk, that way. I haven't met his mother and he hasn't met my wife. I've gathered bits of information about a depressive brother and an alcoholic aunt who lives in Colorado. Or Connecticut. I've never mentioned an abusive father or a meth-head older sister, who I haven't seen in twelve years. As much as we talk, you'd think we'd share stuff like that. But we don't.

"You having a good time, sweets?" Mark was in rare form.

C.B. almost toppled over a kiosk peppered with inspirational bookmarks and bumper stickers, his ample belly fat wobbling like pudding. Mark led me like a submissive bottom and kept whispering, "This will all make sense. I promise," nibbling on my ear in front of a couple who simultaneously leaned backward and grit their teeth. "Shame on you two," the lady said.

"Did you see those friggin' homos?" a teenage boy said to another.

Near the back of the store, C.B. pointed to a row of books on the top shelf: *Reparative Therapy Aids.* "I trust this section will help clarify all your needs."

"Love the wording." Mark pulled off the descriptor tag, stuck it to his shirt, and kissed my hand. "Did you know one of the most arousing sexual positions in the entire free world is called reparative therapy?"

"I hope it's as naughty as it sounds." I have a rare form, too, incited whenever I'm confronted by visible, palpable intolerance.

"Think quasi-missionary position with champagne-scented lube and silk sheets."

"I know what we're doing tonight." I raised an arm and flicked a wrist.

"You're not too sore from last night, I hope."

"Hardly." I licked my lips. "You're such a gentle lover." I chomped the air.

"Will you wear that frilly little eatable outfit I bought you on Valentine's Day?"

"I already have it on."

"Okay, I get it," C.B. said. "We all get it."

"Get what," Mark said, releasing my hand.

"You've proved your point. There's no need to keep throwing

it in my face."

"Relax, C.B.," Mark said, placing the descriptor on his own forehead, his voice returning to medium low. "All you need to do is find a gym with a patient personal trainer."

"What's in that room back there?" I pointed to a small room hiding behind the CD's, DVD's, and communion wafers. Mark and I walked in front of C.B and made our way inside the room, decorated by a long wooden table with twelve chairs on wheels, a white board, and a huge banner hanging on the wall: *Ready To Get Your Bible On?* We made funny faces and posed as rappers snapping selfies with our cell phones. "Hell yeah," I said, spinning an invisible record. "Go Jesus. Go Jesus. Go-Go-Go Jesus."

"This room is off limits unless you're part of a Bible study group." C.B. pointed to the white board, dates and times written on a large calendar. "Unless you two are queer, I mean here, for the prayer without ceasing seminar later tonight you're gonna have to go." His face was flush with sweat.

"Queers like to get their Bible on, too." Mark walked to the whiteboard.

"You can't be in here. It's off limits."

"Hey, wasn't Jesus a fisher of men." Mark gave me the peace sign. "I mean, seems to me he was pretty interested in his own kind."

I took a step backward, as did C.B. Something in Mark's voice necessitated space.

"I gotta get back to the register. Shut the lights off and close the door when you're done."

"Righty-oh, Ceebeepoo." Mark's face took on the elements of anger and mischievousness. Something wasn't right. Something was materializing. Something was about to happen.

C.B., like Moses in the middle of the red sea, walked forward and never looked back. Mark grabbed and uncapped a Sharpie. "Let's do this before he comes back and tries to perform an exorcism."

"Do what?"

DECEMBER

Sunday	Monday	Tuesday	Wednesday	Thursday	Friday	Saturday
				1 The sin of pride 6:15-7:45pm 7:46pm *The sin of dishonesty*	2 *Out & proud porn stars 4-5:30am*	3 Praying Without Ceasing Seminar 6:15-7:45pm
4 **Pray for the wisdom of kindness**	5 Intercessory Prayer Group 6:15-7:45pm	6 *O*	7 *P*	8 The sin of lust 6:15-7:45pm 7:47pm *Butt plug, Inc.*	9 *Give not to receive but to bless the receiver 9am-5pm*	10 Twelve Godly Principles of Tithing 6:15-7:45pm
11 *Seek first to understand*	12 Intercessory Prayer Group 6:15-7:45pm	13 *E*	14 *N*	15 The sin of greed 6:15-7:45pm 7:46pm *The 5 Pillars of Islam*	16 *Pagan dancing at midnight: underwear optional*	17 Cults and Secular-ism: From Mormons to Joel Osteen 6:15-7:45pm
18 *Jesus also wept*	19 Intercessory Prayer Group 6:15-7:45pm	20 *M*	21 *I*	22 The sin of envy 6:15-7:45pm 7:49pm *Hating is sin!*	23 *Family (noun): a group bound by love and affection 6:15-7:15*	24 God's meaning of marriage and family 6:15-7:45pm
25 *Sometimes offering hello is far better than chant-ing ten thousand prayers*	26 Intercessory Prayer Group 6:15-7:45pm	27 *N*	28 *D*	29 The sin of gluttony *6:15-7:45pm All is Suf-fering*	30 *Jesus loves me this I know. For the Bible tells me so.*	31 The truth behind the LGBT agenda *6:15-7:45pm Sad.*

For God so loved the whole world.
Am I not your neighbor?
No more lies.
Mark.

Fist. Pull. Foot. Push.

Lanny tightened his fingers around the bottom rung of the silo's ladder and pulled fifty-four pounds, legs swimming the air for leverage, nose twitching bits of corn dust and hay seed that had escaped through tiny cracks compromising the concrete structure: OFF LIMITS, NO CLIMBING, CAUTION, KEEP AWAY. But he knew the silo so well. He'd been counting the fifteen bars to the tip-top for a year. He'd mapped a diagram. He'd worked the math a hundred times. He'd mastered sit-ups, push-ups, and jumping jacks: ten reps three times a day. A measly one-hundred and twenty feet. Super easy for the world's best climber. No wind. No sweaty palms. Not one drop of rain. It was the right day. The perfect day. To show them all.

Fist. He pressed the soles of his tennis shoes into the first rung.

Pull. He shivered a few goose bumps.

Foot. He kissed both biceps.

Push. He freed both hands from the bar, intentionally losing balance, testing ability, catching weakness, turning fear into fight. His pulse quickened. Senses never more alert. Hot damn.

Fist. Pull. Foot. Push. Every inch a major win.

Fist. Pull. Foot. Push. The Coke bottle sloshed in his front pocket.

Fist. Pull. Foot. Push. He'd take a drink later, though he wanted one now.

Fist. Pull. The engine of his father's Ford pickup truck roared, tempting him to look down or back. He closed his eyelids and counted—not one-one-thousand-one, two-one-thousand two. This was no time to daydream. Just one. Two. Three. Deep. Inhale. Seven. Exhale. Ten.

Foot. Push. The muffler grew louder, angrier, closer.

Fist. Pull. Foot. Push. He climbed faster.

Fist. Pull. Foot. Push. The Ford was underneath him.

Fist. Pull. Foot. Push. Oh, the rush.

The Ford passed like a curse of thunder. Lanny braced a leg around the side of the ladder and threw his hands into waves of fit. "I'm up here." He yelled. "I did it. You were wrong and I was right." But only flecks of dust from the dirt road and a few wayward cottonwood seeds took notice. The mighty muffler, growling down county road 10, slowly dissipated.

Fist. Pull. Foot. Push.

Fist. Pull. Foot. Push.

He set his lips on a square piece of wire mesh at the top, a barrier meant to aerate mold and obstruct hungry crows, squirrels, and mice—everyone wanting a piece of the meal. Drumming the tin roof, his silhouette expanding across the silo, he whispered, "I know you saw me do it."

The sound of his mother's weeping in the vegetable garden twisted his head to the right, turning his stomach three flavors more sour. "Tiny little ant," he said, squishing her head between his fingers. "Tiny little cheating ant." His mother disappeared into the cornfield. He squished the cornstalks, the Guernsey, the Appaloosa, the Great Dane, the Massey Ferguson, and more cottonwood seeds swirling around his achievement. "I'm The Great Crusher," he yelled, squishing a Coopers Hawk flying above his head. "The universe is mine. All mine." He finished the Coke. The bottle slipped from his hand and vanished inside a tall patch of prairie grasses. He flicked the bottle cap and spit at the ground. "You'll never get me."

With a burst of hummy-hums and snappy-snaps his little sister threw open the farmhouse door and skipped toward him, her flowery sundress as bright as her cheeks. Lanny inhaled and pressed his back against the silo. His heartbeat pulsed in his toes. His sister stopped, grabbed the bottle cap, and kissed it as if it were a grand prize. "Tiny little brat," he whispered, squishing her as she spun: limbs a windmill, a jet plane, a rhythmic clap, an elbow-to-hip dance she wiggled so well.

"Achoo."

She looked up, mouth wide open. "You in big twouble, mistah." Pointing the finger of fate. "Up thewe's fow big people, not you."

"I'm nine and a half and you can't even tie your own shoes. I am bigger."

"Daddy says it's dangewous."

"Only for little brats like you."

"You gonna get a spankin' when I tattle."

"Everyone knows you're a big, fat liar."

"Nah-uh, I'm Pwincess of the Wealm."

"Not if you tattle, you're not. Then you're just Freda the Frog with huge, ugly warts and one giant eyeball stuffed with corn-cobs."

She pounded fists against her dress. "I'm not an ugly fwog. Take it back."

"Only if you promise to leave and never tell anyone in the whole world what you saw."

"I pwomise." She repeated the elbow-to-hip dance.

"Hand to heart?" he yelled.

"Cwoss it twice." She made an X across her heart.

"Pinky swear?"

"Ow I'm head lice." She sat and laid on her back.

Lanny squished her head. Toes. Go. Teeth. Get. Away. Silly. Stupid. Girl.

"Is God nice?" she asked, making snow angels in the dirt. "Does he have blue eyes like the sky or gween ones like daddy's and mommy's?"

"How should I know? I've never seen God."

"But you's so close to heaven." She pointed upward. "He's wight up thewe."

"This isn't heaven, dorkus. I'm barely higher than the barn. How stupid are you?"

She sat up and slowly turned her head in the direction of the barn, sun-streaked hair sweeping across her shoulders. Turning back to Lanny, she spread her arms to their limit and smacked her palms together. "You awe too close to heaven. Now ask God to make mommy and daddy bettah or I'm gonna tattle."

"This isn't heaven."

"Ask weal nice."

"It doesn't work."

"Then I'm coming up thewe." She jumped to her feet and grabbed for the bottom rung. "I'm big too ya know." But she couldn't reach it. "Ask God wight now." She sobbed. "Do it." And sobbed. "Now."

"Fine." Lanny screamed. "Cry baby."

"Talk loudew so God can heaw you."

Fist. He faced the sky. "Are you even there?"

Pull. He waited for a response. "I knew you weren't."

Foot. He gave the clouds, the sun, and the dark-blue horizon the middle finger.

Push. He closed his eyes and spread his arms to their limit, too.

Foreign Resources

(oma) = swelling

Ruby Myel-Rasmussen locks her street level apartment door while the three-day-overdue-triplets in her belly kick and fist and twist and jab—talk about womb bombardment. She walks to her car parked underneath the brightest light pole in *The Commons* apartment complex, searching for Soren, her husband, the apartment complex supervisor. The car doesn't start on the first turn of the key. But on the fourth. She reeves the engine, worried that Soren's forgetfulness has forgotten his promise to drive to the Tampa Bay Sheraton Hotel and pick up her brother, Terrell Myel, and his new bride, Pyrrhica, who are flying from Maui into the Tampa Bay International Airport, which sits adjacent to the Tampa Bay Sheraton, returning home from a two-week elopement and wedding in Hawaii. Parking fees are such a wasteful expense. Everyone understands this, except for Terrell and Pyrrhica, selfish, impetuous nitwits.

Ruby can't find Soren—busybody Norwegian—or reach him by phone. He refuses to text, so she's just gonna have to trust in his capacity to stay on course and finish the task. Good thing he's funny. And gorgeous. And BFF.

The October sun warms her face and neck. "If we're blessed with three sons," she rubs her belly, whispering Soren's fondest wish to a roseate sky. "Or three girls. May they each know the warmth of our love." Life, unlike her belly, is finally calming down. Terrell and Pyrrhica are off doing their nuptial thing. Mary Dunkle, Ruby's hospice patient, is more determined than ever to stand and walk and win. And the miracle of motherhood—oh, to hear their newborn babies cry—is reaching its zenith. She and Soren are going to be wonderful parents, determined to redo with future wins past failures of childhood. Triplets. Ready for launch. Definitely this week. Maybe tomorrow. Perhaps even today.

The steering wheel smooches wrinkles across her nursing uniform emblazoned with the Tampa Bay Buccaneers insignia, another one of Soren's fondest wishes. Backing up, she hears the sound of keys rattling inside the glove box. Soren's keys. The apartment complex's master set. His mistake. His forgetfulness. His problem. Not hers. Sunlight spills in through the driver side window and lands directly in the middle of her belly. She closes her eyes and envisions three healthy babies cooing in her arms. Total amazeballs: Abso-fucking-lutely.

Waiting at the apartment complex's only stop sign, she stares at and traces with a finger the word, STUDTRIXX, flashing in large pink letters on the white building across the street. About to turn right, she waves to an old man resting on the stairwell of building number five. Is he going up or coming down? Is it Paul, Patrick, or Philip? She knows it starts with a P, but similar to her due date, she isn't quite sure.

"Hope you reach wherever it is you're going." She hums the tune to itsy-bitsy spider, wondering whether happiness, like the lining of her uterus, increases or decreases once the treasure within it is set free.

$$(gangli) = knot$$

Paddy McBrady stops half-way up the forty-four stairs leading to the fifth floor apartment and waves back to the apartment complex supervisor's wife, some Ruthie or Rose or Ratatouille for all he knows, or cares, lucky bitch gets to drive a car and go wherever the fuck she wants to go. Perhaps he should rent a main-level apartment. Perhaps he should try to renew his driver's license. Perhaps he should walk over to STUDTRIXX and find out exactly what kind of stuff goes on inside the building. But he can't. Similar to his vision impairment and ache-imbued body, his mindset is in no position, mood, or shape to move.

From the metal key ring clipped to his jeans, he sticks the usual silver-colored key into the lock on the front door and turns clockwise. Nothing. "Bloody hell." He tries again, squinting at 5C, definitely his apartment. He brings the key to his eyes. Its jagged edges seem to match what he remembers. He tries again. "God-damn it." He tries every other key. He knows that none of the other keys are going to open the door and let him inside. "Such is my luck," he whispers. "Such is my life."

He shuffles to the wooden-spindle handrail and scans the complex, looking for Soren. Nothing. He tries to lift the window. He pounds on the glass. He kicks the door. He finger shoots his own temple. As ill-tempered as everyone accuses him of being, he ought to be able to turn into The Incredible Hulk, smash through the door, and, if he's lucky, take out along the way the Indian refugees in 5B, the section 8 darkies in 4A, and the ISIS looking headscarf-freaks in 3C. And all of STUDTRIXX, too. "Kooks," he whispers. His wrists, hips, and feet throb. As does his heart. Which he refuses to acknowledge. Or touch. He takes to his knees and, lying face up on cold concrete, stares at a patch of free-range clouds rambling adrift in an unlocked sky. "I know *you* see what I'm being reduced to."

When he was ten years old, his mother took ill, relegating her to a mattress by way of an exponential increase in limb-twitch tremors, skin-rash fevers, and slop-slur speech. For three months, two weeks, and one day, she belabored in the bedroom. His father refused to procure the services of a doctor. Paddy was only allowed to see his mother on Saturday morning, at 10am, for fifteen minutes. His father would open the door, step aside, and point him to his mother who'd pat the left side of the mattress where he'd lie beside her, face up, stare at the ceiling, and inhale the amalgam scents of jasmine tea, black mold, and Vaseline—a poor mask to an unknown disease shrinking his mother to eradication. Every Sunday, she'd release a key from a sleeve. "Being locked out of life is no way to live, son, so be sure to use this key and let yourself in." Paddy never cursed the illness; never asked if she felt locked out of life; never begged to know which key went with which lock; never questioned the gift; never cried when she cried; never wiped away hot tears falling onto his cold arm. Instead, late at night, quiet and tear-free, he'd add the key to a metal key ring which he kept beneath the bed in a plastic bag. After she died and was buried by his father behind the pig shed, Paddy used every key to try and unlock her bedroom door, wanting to take one last inhale before her scent faded away forever. But none of the keys let him in. His father caught him trying to open the bedroom door and banished him from even touching the door, forcing Paddy to lie face up on cold concrete, sometimes for hours, whispering, "Being locked out of life is no way to live, son, so be sure to use this key and let yourself in."

"You okay Mister McBrady?" Soren asks. Paddy sits, befuddled by the bulwark-magnanimity of Soren's cowboy boots, tight jeans, checkered shirt, shag-swag jacket, barbwire neck tattoo, nose ring, and blue Mohawk. A towering wildebeest—and one not to be messed with.

"You don't dress much like a handyman." Paddy offers his hand. "Help me up."

"You need an ambulance?" Soren lifts a cell phone from his back pocket. "It ain't the fanciest or the loudest, but it works the way I need it to when I need it to, so I figure why upgrade."

"I'm fine." Paddy huffs. "Where are all your clanking tools? You off today or something?"

"Nah." Soren pulls Paddy to his feet. "Got some official airport business is all."

"You work at the airport, too?"

"Nah. Gotta go pick up Ruby's brother, Terrell and his new wife, Pyrrhica."

"That's an odd name."

"Ruby says she's an odd gal."

"You haven't met her yet?"

"Ruby says I'm better off." Soren shrugs. "Why were you laying on the ground?"

"My goddamn key doesn't work today is why." Paddy shows Soren the silver-colored key. "Damn thing worked yesterday." *Did he leave the house yesterday?* "No doubt about it. It worked perfect the last time I used it."

"I accidentally forgot the master set in Ruby's car," Soren whispers. "I hope that's something we can keep between ourselves."

"I ain't no snitch."

"You can hang out at my place until Ruby gets home if you like, unless you prefer laying on the ground and talking to the sky."

"Some of the best inventions ever created came from people talking to the sky."

"Like what?"

"Like airplanes. Paintings. Psych wards. Heaven."

"I don't believe in heaven."

"You sound like my gay son, Darren." Paddy didn't mean to say the word gay. Or mention Darren. But now that he had, he couldn't take it back. Better to be out in the open anyway. That's what Darren used to say, when they talked. "Darren used to believe in heaven when he was a little boy but now that he's older and." Paddy pauses. *Who is Darren now?* "Different, all he has time for is that STUDTRIXX place across the street and that alien friend of his, Faheem-Saudi-Arabia-something-or-other."

"You mean that white building across the street?"

"The very one."

"Your son works there?"

"Owner and operator."

"I like how well-groomed they keep the grounds."

"Oh, he's meticulous with outer appearances."

"What kind of business is it?"

"A gay business. Like him. Not that I've seen any of it."

"Work's work." Soren smiled. "Right?"

"If it were only that simple."

"You don't like gay?"

"Do you?"

"My family treats Ruby less on account of her being black, but who are they to judge? Who are any of us to judge other people? I mean, isn't it time to just be yourself and let everyone else do the same?"

"I don't judge him," Paddy lies, descending the stairs with Soren. A bit slower than necessary. But what else does he have to do. He sure can't bring back to life his mother or forgive his father or accept Darren. And Faheem. "I just don't get him." Tears fill his eyes. He doesn't want to cry. But he can't stop the uprising. Nor the outpouring. "This complex is so dirty and dusty. You ought to clean it better."

Soren waits on the last step for Paddy to catch up. "Today can be different than yesterday." Soren puts his arm around Paddy's shoulder. "If Ruby's taught me anything, it's that."

"You ought to believe in heaven." Paddy wiggles out of Soren's arm. "If my mother taught me anything, it's that."

"Ruby gets home about six or six-thirty. I'll try to call her and let her know you're gonna be hanging around the house. I doubt I'll get home before she does."

"I'm a pro at alone time." Paddy sighs. "Super experienced."

"Just promise you won't make any messes." Soren swells his stomach and rubs the exaggerated bulge. "She ain't exactly her jolliest self these days."

"What, she sick or something?"

"Only with our any-day-now-triplets."

"Oh, congratulations." Paddy doesn't mean it, but he figures if Soren's kind enough to let him hang out at his house until his wife, Ruby—or is it Ruthie? *Oh, shit what's her name?*—gets home, the least he can do is say something kind about the upcoming delivery. "Did you say triplets?"

Soren nods. "I gotta get going so here." He places a copper-colored key in the front pocket of Paddy's shirt. "It's 1A. Make yourself at home. If you're into dark beer we got some of that. If not, there's some bottled water around there somewhere. Watch

TV. Listen to the radio. Do whatever. But just be careful and if you use the toilet, be sure to put the seat down. You don't want to piss her off like that." Soren drives off fast, creating a fun, little windstorm that fizzles and dies in the corner of Paddy's eyes. He lifts the copper-colored key in the air, and whispers, "Let's see what this key unlocks, shall we." He shuffles to 1A, curiosity bubbling like anticipation as he opens the front door and steps into the emptiest, whitest, gloomiest apartment he's ever had the misfortune to see firsthand. No couch. No chairs. No pictures. No bed frame. No box spring. One crib in the nursery. Not three. One stroller in the hallway. Not three. One bag of diapers beside a porcelain-chipped bathtub. Not three. No teddy bears or pacifiers or fleece blankets. No lamps or rocking chair or bookcases filled with children's books. "This won't do," he whispers, finding on the kitchen countertop the phone and phone book. He picks up the receiver and dials. Her name has to be Ruby, he supposes. Everyone deserve at least one jewel in life.

(neuro) = nerve

"I'm in," Ruby yells from Mary Dunkle's front door. "You here, too, Marguerite?"

"Present and accounted for. There's lemonade in the fridge if you want some."

"Be there in a few. Pregnant girl here has to pee." She lies. She doesn't have to pee. She's just isn't ready to do for Mary what must be done. How much lotion can skin absorb before pores turn to slush? How many bones have to break before a skeleton slanders its own distortion? How can illness bully some people and snub others? How can a heartbeat losing strength to heart problems pound to any other rhythm beyond that which festers, scabs, and flakes away? If there is a God, he needs a few more lessons in benevolence. Ruby flushes the toilet but stays seated, staring at a picture on the opposite wall of two girls laughing on a two-seater bicycle. A picture of Mary and Marguerite, who has a prominent Adam's apple and a hint of facial hair. Ruby can't be the only one who sees it. Or questions it. Mary's eyesight isn't that far gone. She must know. But it mustn't bother her. Marguerite sounds, acts, and looks like a girl. So she must be a girl. Ruby's not seeing things clearly. Pregnancy's messing with her head. Whatever. She's always believed the secret to perception, like hospice work, is to aim at indifference and hit compartmentalization. Next.

"I wanna change my name to Stormie Soma," Mary Dunkle says to Marguerite LaFlore, who stands tall over Mary's bed fluffing Mary's pillows, trying to make full what is always so flat. "It's time to rid every smidgeon of Mary Grace Dunkle forever."

Marguerite grabs Mary's green pill box and uses it to knight Mary's shoulders. "I officially, declaratively, and most coherently pronounce you Stormie Soma." She nose dives to Stormie's ear. "Does this Stormie chic have a middle name?"

Stormie laughs. "Sunblast."

"Perfect." Marguerite's fists give cheer. "Sunblast and LaFlore amidst transformation."

The yellow-diamonique phone on the nightstand rings. Marguerite picks up the ringer and holds it against Stormie's ear. "Hello," Stormie says. Marguerite leans in.

"I'm trying to reach Mary Grace Dunkle," a woman says, her voice bursting with Spanish flavor. "You wouldn't happen to know her, or be her by chance, would you?"

"Her name's Stormie now but yeah I know her."

"Is she there? I mean, can you put her on the phone?"

"Speaking."

"Oh, well I'm not sure if you're aware of this or not but your father, Bishop Randall Howard Dunkle, passed away three days ago and his funeral is at 6pm tonight."

"Did he suffer a lot?" God, she hopes so, bombast hypocrite.

"Near the end all he kept saying were the words Mary Grace Dunkle and eulogy." The woman pauses. The sound of crinkling paper distorts the silence. "We found a phone number in his wallet which led us to your mother in Ukraine who just this morning gave us your phone number and I know it's last minute and all but you weren't the easiest person to track down."

"I thought your mother didn't have your phone number," Marguerite whispers.

Stormie shrugs. "I didn't give it her."

"So, are you in or not?" the woman asks. "I thinks it's a shame to not honor someone's last dying request."

"I'm not motivated by religious guilt."

"You must be Evangelical Free."

"I'm an atheist if you must know, and if I were you I wouldn't count on me being there." She renders the verdict unfavorable, just like her father. "But I'll let you know what I know when I know if I know."

"I'll be at the church all day, so call if you have any questions."

"How did you know my." Stormie pauses. Can she even call him dad? "Him?"

"Yo soy su esposa. Adios."

Stormie's thoughts overcloud themselves with anger, discontent, and condescension. She was never able to torment her father with the same pervasiveness with which he tormented her and her mother, Aprosinia, from Kiev, with chocolate-raspberry hair and pop-out blue eyes who spoke stopgap English which Mary found amusing and cartoonish as a child but marginalizing and debasing as a teenager. In church, at the pulpit, her father preached name-calling a sin; at home he often yelled *immigrant-slut* and *piece of shit.* Oftentimes Aprosinia taunted back, yelling *baby penis and liar-liar.* Back and forth. Day and night. Scream and point. Cast and engrave. Pushing Mary to take pleasure in earplugs and in reading the all-woman-empowerment essays by Kate Bornstein. Fuck adolescence and marriage and God and men and parents and California. And Ukraine, too.

"What better place than a eulogy to balance the imbalance,"

Stormie says to Marguerite. "Right?"

"As rain." Marguerite whispers, adding, "Isn't it a little odd that Ruby never talks about baby names or car seats or pamper stuff? I mean, aren't women that far along supposed to be gushing incessantly all about booboo-baba-baby-stuff?"

"Maybe she isn't excited."

"The way she rubs her belly makes me think she's excited. I don't know. Maybe it's us."

"How could it be us?" Stormie's never given one thought as to how Ruby feels about her and Marguerite. Come to think of it, she's never asked Ruby anything personal, substantive or otherwise. Maybe Ruby feels like a third wheel. Maybe she's jealous of their friendship. Maybe she dislikes being a PCA. Maybe she hates Stormie. Maybe she disapproves of Marguerite. Maybe she's filled with so much sadness, the only way she can deal with it is to keep the negative feeling to herself, bottled up and masked by a smile. "We should ask her if she's excited."

"Maybe some strange dude knocked her up and now she feels like she has to keep it. I mean, stuff like that happens all the time."

Stormie's thoughts overcloud themselves again, this time taking on the scary elements of a rain-soaked evening fifteen years earlier, when her parent's voices collided like thunder and lightning, her father's veiny hands strangling her mother's veiny neck before tossing her to the floor like a stuffed animal, leaving the front door wide open as he drove off as fast as wild rain, her mother's trembling hands leading Mary into the kitchen to sit on lime-green seat cushions, telling Mary, "Now it's time you hear the sad story of how Aprosinia Plakovich met Randall Dunkle. Are you ready?" Mary wasn't ready, afraid her mother's words might pollute her heart and poison her mind. "So good was he at pretending to be a medical doctor at my orphanage job," Aprosinia said. "Putting a stethoscope to my heart and then to his heart saying that from now on ours beat the same way. But he was no doctor. Just a goody-goody missionary who said in my ear that his manly parts had been snipped so there could be no you to come. But there was you to come and when my real woman doctor told me the news I cried happy tears and then sad tears too because I knew he was a liar-lair and that's when my real woman doctor got her three strong brothers to help your father make up his mind to bring me here to the USA and marry me in a proper church and five months later at the hospital on a stormy night you were born and I was happier than any woman in Ukraine or America could ever be. So now what do you think of your father?" Mary didn't answer. Three days later, she read from a piece of paper taped to her bedroom door: *I have to leave the storm, Mary. Please forgive me. Mama.* Leaving Mary to mature into womanhood with a man who ignored her every step, including the ones she could hardly take at the age of twenty-one, diagnosed with EDMD (Emery-Dreifuss Muscular Dystrophy), one year after she left home and four months after she met Marguerite LeFlore in Nyberg's café, reading at a corner table a book of essays by Kate Bornstein.

"How's my favorite patient doing today?" Ruby says. Another lie. Mary isn't her favorite patient. Why did she say that? "It's windy outside." Another lie. What's wrong with her? Why is she lying so much today? "I say we skip going out there, if that's okay with you."

"Call me Stormie from now on, okay."

"Okay." Ruby smiles. "Stormie."

Stormie looks at Marguerite—nimble, vertical, adaptable Marguerite. "I can't decide which makes me angrier, his death or my mother's life"

"Did someone die?"

"My father."

"I'm sorry. We're you two close?"

"Never." Their lack of closeness emboldens Stormie. "I'll do it," she tells the woman over the phone. "Give me the church's address."

"It's Bayshore Nazarene on 57th Avenue West," she says. "Your name's already in the bulletin so I guess it's meant to be. Please sit in the front row. Gracias."

For the rest of the afternoon, while Ruby rubs lotion on Stormie's body and Marguerite reads Kate Bornstein, Stormie writes a haiku, a tanka, a villanelle, a pantoum, and a sestina with some beautiful inner rhyme, the opposite of her father in every way. Each word is tainted by childish animosity and adolescent rage. She longs for a sprinkle of Marguerite's self-awareness and Ruby's usefulness. Maybe Marguerite and Ruby should write the eulogy. At 4:07pm, Stormie folds a piece of paper and stuffs it into her purse. "I've never before touched or rubbed your belly," she says to Ruby, offering her hands. "Would you mind terribly if I did?"

"Absolutely not." Ruby's and Stormie's hands circle Ruby's belly.

"Are they always this rowdy?"

"Soren, my husband, wants three rough and ready boys but I'd be fine with a gentle girl or two," she says, surprised at the level of disquietude she feels having Stormie's weak, feeble hands atop her own strong, resolute hands. Stormie's life is a lesser life and Ruby certainly doesn't want any lesser life seeping into her baby's subconscious(nesses). Ruby releases her hands, steps back, and groans a fake contraction—another lie, a little white one, nothing to worry about, so easily forgiven.

"Are you and Soren excited about being parents?"

"We are." Ruby exhales. "We really, really are."

"Time I stand up for myself and right that man's wrongs," Stormie says, surrendering her arms to Marguerite and Ruby (this IS the job) who lift and scoot her butt to the edge of the bed so that her feet can dangle just above the tile floor. Right foot. Left foot. Stormie wobbles against the nightstand. So many prescription pills. So much unevenness. So many failures. So many globs of oily lotion. She stands for three minutes and eleven seconds, breaking the three minute and four second mark set in August.

"Want me to get the wheelchair?" Marguerite asks.

Stormie nods. "Today's about staying upright and telling the truth."

"I'm with you all the way," Ruby lies. Another lie. Shit. Stop lying. "I totally believe in ya." Oh my God. Lie after lie.

A warm shower energizes Stormie's skin. As does the soft bath towel Ruby put in the dryer to make warm. Getting dressed is a bone-creaking chore, similar to the car ride to the church in the back seat of Ruby's car. But Stormie doesn't complain—it never helps or changes the outcome. The church stands like nobility in its gray-stucco vestments and six-steeple-ornamentations. Ruby and Marguerite sit in the back row while Stormie waddles the walker with tennis-balls-for-feet the span of thirty-three rows to the front pew where a dozen men dressed in white robes and black shoes slide down in unison for Stormie's sunflower knee-length skirt and yellow blouse which, unlike her father, hug her in all the right places. Each man takes a turn at the podium: three sing hymns about grace; six recite quotes about kindness; two read scripture verses about character; one plays the guitar. Her father was none of those things. Not to her. Not to her mother. Silence fills the sanctuary. Paper tweets rustle the air. Stormie opens the bulletin: Mary Grace Dunkle – Daughter - Eulogy. She stands and makes her way to the podium. The weight of the crowd's eyes upon her disfigurements make her doubt the sonnet. Isn't speaking plainly and quickly always the wisest choice? She irons the piece of paper against the podium. The words reconstruct themselves into her father's bald head and prominent forehead and brown eyes and bent nose and off-kilter jaw and why in the hell was he so unkind to her and to her mother. "A sonnet for my father." A ray of sun from the skylight illuminates the paper, softening it, along with Stormie's heart. A peace offering, she believes, not from Randall's God in heaven but from a galaxy of compassion where honesty through clarity is amassed, recast, and dispersed.

"You lied to mark my mother's womb and swore
with Pilot's lips your head and bed was rift,

no baby's heart could beat within the shore.
So deep my cheeks cried out for Randall's gift
to name me love and show me heaven's lift,
to share with care the air of God's great tongue
you lashed and filled my soul as if I was no one.
I faced your faith, fist-coiled your cruel belief
that tortured me had tortured you, like hell,
my vexing-jointed shell brought you relief;
your seed, my bleed, we bruise in common cells
our skin akin not thin but thick you thieved,
now go and howl your loss in fire's fate
to seer in you the you in your mistakes."

(psych) = mind

Terrell Myel's sister Ruby often tells him, "Not all women are as shallow and appearance-oriented as you make them out to be." On his thirtieth birthday, after thirty years of pining to be herculean, he decides to test out Ruby's opinion at the local gym where he hires Tammy Puchanellee, a ninety-five dollar-an-hour personal trainer who tells him during the first session, "Some dudes aren't meant to have bulging biceps. I mean, then who'd work computer screens or do lawyer stuff or sit around all day at those boring libraries and help people check out books." Not once in eight years has his three coworkers, Busty, Crusty, and Musty— he swears they're women—who sit beside him at The J. R. Ember Library, invited him to lunch.

"Don't all women want a herculean man?" he asks Tammy, during session number two.

"I don't know about all that but what I do know I have this super-talky client coming in later today who says all the time that a real herculean man is one who knows how to lead with both heads and a soft, adaptable heart. You ought to meet her sometime. The way she talks, with those high-bar expectations, I'm pretty sure she's single."

"You say she's coming in later today?"

"She's a little hit or miss but she usually shows."

"She actually used the word herculean?"

"Oh, she's a wordy one. Half the stuff she says I just smile at and hand her a weight."

"What's her name? In case I do come back."

"It's a dozy of a name. I've got it spelled right in her training folder but off hand I think it's Fur-ick-ah. At least that's what I've been calling her."

"Like pyrrhic, as in pyrrhic victory?"

"Now you sound just like her."

"What does she look like? I mean, how will I recognize her?"

"Wait till you see those eyes."

"Why, what's wrong with them?"

"Nothing wrong with 'em. It's just that color green isn't something you see every day."

He decides to not leave the gym but sits instead in the bleach-infused TV lounge for two hours, rehearsing the name, *Pyrrhica,* and, *a real herculean man is one who knows how to lead with both heads and a soft, adaptable heart.* "Alrighty then. Let's go with that."

He first sees Pyrrhica's green eyes, and lush pink lips, sucking to depletion an orange smoothie from the juice bar. Which is better, he wonders, coming up from behind or approaching from the side? "Are the smoothies good here?" he asks from behind.

She turns and faces him. Green eyes, sorceress and thriller, disassemble and reassemble everything he wishes he knew about himself, and her. "Did you say something?" She leans backward. He hopes she isn't frightened. Or sickened. There's no way she could be interested. Intrigued. Infatuated.

"I asked if your smoothie was as tasty as it looks."

"If you don't have a coupon for a free one, I say don't do it."

He extends a shaking hand. "Hi. I'm Terrell."

She extends a steadying hand. "Hi. I'm Pyrrhica."

"Like in pyrrhic victory?"

"You're like maybe the fourth person I've ever met who knows what that is."

He wonders if the first, second, or third person is male. A boyfriend? Lover? Husband? He doesn't see a wedding ring. Or one wrinkle. "I'm a bit of a Western-civilization history nerd," he says. "But Rome is my favorite."

"Here's a question for ya, Mister Rome." She shakes out charcoal hair that sweeps across a delicate neck and slender shoulders. "Let's test that Western civilization nerdiness of yours." She laughs. "You up for it?"

Fuck no. "Hell yeah."

She puts on a serious face. "What significant lesson is to be learned from a pyrrhic victory?"

He knows this one. "That too many casualties sustained by the victor ultimately leads to the victor's defeat."

"That is the lesson." She stares at her hands—a bit red. And callous. And dry. "Okay, here's another question." She crosses her arms. "If I put the A in Pyrrhica, how do you put Terrell into action?"

Action? "You enjoy playing mini-golf?" he asks.

"Not if I don't have to. Why, is that your thing?"

"Not really."

"So what is?"

"I'm a pretty good texter and I have great cell phone reception."

"Smart phone, no doubt."

"Super smart."

"I sense that." She laughs. "And I like that. A lot."

He wants to smile. But he doesn't smile. Such unherculean teeth and gums. But then he does smile. And it feels good. And she smiles back. Which feels better. And they begin to smile. A lot. To each other. Often at the same time. Sometimes lifting free weights on either side of Tammy Puchanelle, who led them to each other, even if she didn't mean to. Or did she?

"Can I get you anything else Mister Myel?" the flight attendant asks, startling him, taking him from the euphoria of Pyrrhica's smile in Maui to the anguish-reality of flying home solo. "We're about to begin our descent into Tampa."

He should have bought some vodka. Real herculean men drink vodka. "No. I'm okay."

"You here on business or pleasure?"

"Neither."

"So what brings you to town?"

He debates whether to tell her anything about Pyrrhica. About the barefoot wedding on white sand. About Pyrrhica's Saffron Crocus bouquet and his matching boutonniere. About the lattice arch and the green ivy poking through its holes. About Fredrick, the crazy-eyebrow justice of the peace. About his regular-fit Ralph Lauren tuxedo. About Pyrrhica's Michael Kors gown with four-thousand sequins. About Alika Kinimaka, from the Outrigger Hotel, with tendon-rich fingers and a virile body who played on a ukulele, *Somewhere over the Rainbow*. About the frequency with which Pyrrhica giggled and winked at Alika before and after the ceremony. About dropping twice Pyrrhica's wedding ring on the ground. About reading handwritten vows. About the waves of joy in his heart when they said I do. About walking hand in hand through the Outrigger Hotel as man and wife. About Pyrrhica's request to keep the elopement a secret from family and friends. About his secret phone call to Ruby to share the news. About Ruby's indifference and subsequent voice message telling him to meet Soren upon the plane's touchdown in the lobby of the Tampa Bay Sheraton, and not in the airport baggage claim area, because parking fees are such a wasteful expense. About searching for Pyrrhica the day after the wedding: circling the hotel, the mall, the hair salon, the coffee shop, the marketplace, the police station. Coming up empty. Heartbroken at 2:43am, reading a text from his new wife: *Alika says aloha and I say manana*. About sitting on the bamboo chair in the honeymoon suite for the rest of the trip. About boarding the plane without any luggage, or purpose, or plan. About closing his eyes for hours, hoping to block with darkness the lightness of Pyrricha's touch.

"I don't need anything, but thank you," he tells the flight attendant, who is gone, out of sight, out of reach.

That evening, after the taxi cab drops him off at home, and after he leaves a voice message on Ruby's cell phone, apologizing for not meeting Soren in the Sheraton lobby, he lays sideways on his side of the bed, a new power bed, and stares at the large oil painting on the wall, a wedding gift from Pyrrhica, of a colossus warrior dressed in Roman heraldry shooting an arrow at the back of a thin man dressed in a toga fading into the chaos of a sandstorm.

(chrom) = color

Soren explores for two hours the Sheraton lobby, waiting for Terrell and Pyrrhica's plane to touchdown from Maui. He uses the men's flower-scented bathroom three times. He steals two apples and four granola bars from the "FOR GUESTS ONLY" snack bar. He singlehandedly empties the water cooler. He sets an ear a half-dozen times against the double doors of The Ballroom and listens to chest-pounding electronic-dance music, his favorite. He phones Ruby a dozen times. She doesn't answer. He doesn't leave a message. Or text. He sets an ear against the double doors a seventh time, opens the doors, and steps into a ballroom sizzling with machismo celebration. Wall-size televisions in the four corners play snippet-scenes of man-on-man pornography. Rainbow-colored banners linked by chains hanging from the ceiling pronounce themes of coalition, endogamy, and pride. The hardwood floor twinkles with spectrum-tint confetti, while a bloated disco ball sprays its hypnotic point of view across homogeneously young men who parade the room, cocktails in hand, in neon-mesh thongs, adding definition to what's already so very well-defined.

"No gentleman and all ladies," the announcer says, gathering everyone's attention. "Squeeze your ass cheeks together and help me welcome to the stage Darren McBrady and Faheem Zubiri, or as I like to call them, sadists with a flair for bareback mavericks."

The men howl, clap, and stomp. Camera's flash and butts shake, reinforcing the atmosphere's thickset energy.

Wait, Soren thinks. *STUDTRIXX*? *Darren*? *Faheem*? Soren knows these names. Because Paddy McBrady told him these names. Is this Paddy's son, Darren? Is this what STUDTRIXX does, and makes? Is this Faheem-Saudi-Arabia-something or other? Soren sits on one of the cowhide stools at the bar. *If they want me to leave, they can ask me to leave.* No one asks him to leave, bombarding him instead with questions about where he bought his outfit. When he says, *custom-made,* he receives as many phone numbers as high fives. Quite easily, he's found acceptance in a group of men who look like him and talk like him and smell like him and smile like him and walk like him and laugh like him. But they aren't like him. And he isn't like them. He can't be. He just can't.

"Hey, hey boys," Darren says, taking the microphone from the announcer. "Ya'll having a good time?"

More howls, claps, and stomps. Soren likes to howl. But he doesn't howl. Not here. He also knows how to clap and stomp. But he doesn't do those things either. Instead, he watches and waits. He's good at doing that. So that's what he does.

Faheem snatches the microphone from Darren's hand. "Go enable your liver at the bar, you cellulite queer bait."

Soren's thoughts drift to Paddy McBrady. Won't Paddy be surprised to learn that Soren met his son, Darren? He has to find a way to meet Darren. To extend a hand. Start a conversation. Develop a network. Build a bridge. Perhaps facilitate the reunification of opposing forces. Wouldn't that be amazing, if he could help Paddy and Darren find reconnection? It's too late for him and his own father. Too late for Ruby and Ruby's father. But maybe it's not too late for Paddy and Darren. This is providential. This is not a mistake. Paddy's not a mistake. Darren's not a mistake. Ruby's not a mistake. Soren's not a mistake. Gay's not a mistake. It isn't. It just isn't. It can't be.

Darren toasts the crowd a martini and walks backward to the bar, laughing as a horde-a-hunk slap his shoulders and ass. At the bar, he sits beside Soren and orders martini after martini, growling whenever Faheem congratulates himself for STUDTRIXX'S fiscally advantageous year. Omitting Darren. Dismissing Darren's input, Darren's accomplishments, Darren's money. Just like Darren's father does. Darren stares at Soren. "Overdressed twiddle bit, stud." He slurs. "Which movie you in? You the big ten incher?"

Soren's never measured his dick. Guess it's big enough. Dick size probably matters here. Ruby's never complained. Or given him a blow job. He'd like one. "My name's Soren."

Darren finishes another martini. "You butcher-an all these fags." Darren grabs Soren's crotch. "Show me so I member."

Soren jumps to his feet. He ought to be infuriated. He ought to punch the mother fucker in the gut. Or at least bitch slap him across the face. But he isn't infuriated. And he doesn't want to bitch slap anyone. Not here. They've been bitch slapped enough. Hurt and ridiculed and scorned for being different. Soren understands being different. Ruby understands being different. That's why Soren hugs her. That's why he extends his arms and hugs Darren, who tightens his arms around Soren's shoulders and rests his head on Soren's shoulder. Like a baby. Sobbing. Why is it taboo for one man to rest his head on another man's shoulder and sob? Soren scans the room. So many bare chests in need of a hug. So many heads in need of a shoulder. So many tears in need of acceptance. Maybe this is the gift he's been waiting to give someone his whole life.

"You ain't one-a my boys. Shhhhh. I won't tell. You sexy fucker. Wanna be my boy?" Darren closes his eyes, lowers his head, and falls asleep in Soren's arms.

"What the fuck are you doing with my husband?" Faheem yells from the stage. "Get the hell outta here. This is a private party."

Darren awakens and grabs a highball glass from the bar. He throws it at the stage. Then another. And another. One finally lands in the middle of Faheem's forehead. A textbook fastball, faggot or not. Faheem collapses, face down on the stage. Darren howls. "Now you in-a right position, you middle-eessshern psy-cho-puh-paf."

No howls or claps or stomps. Just a mass of cash-cow veneers waiting to be told how to feel, where to go, what to say, and who to fuck bareback next. But never why. Fuck why. No one cool and gay asks why. Soren carries Darren through the hotel lobby and through the revolving glass doors. He buckles Darren in the passenger seat and reaches for his own phone. But it isn't in his back pocket. Shit. "I knew you's wazza fag. You be my boy. I be your daddy." Soren starts the car and rolls down the windows. Darren lowers his head and snores. Soren chuckles at Darren's pink tuxedo and purple bowtie. Gay men and color—how cliché. He wants to laugh. But he doesn't laugh. This isn't the right time to laugh. It isn't. It just isn't. It can't be.

(pleg) = paralysis

Ruby enjoys driving during a sunset, a soft reminder of the universe's propensity toward goodwill and unselfishness. She enjoys being at home even more. She unlocks the apartment door but pauses at the sound of unfamiliar coughing coming from the other side. "Soren, is that you?"

"No, I ain't Soren," a man says, coughing. "But I do know him so you don't have to worry."

"How do you know him?"

"I live in building five and my key didn't work today is how. He gave me your apartment key and said I could hang here until you got home. He said the master set's in your car. Well is it?"

She knows the master set of keys is in the glove box. She also knows how much leg energy it takes walking to and from the car. She doesn't want to do that again, especially for some cranky tenant making himself at home inside hers. "I don't know where the keys are," she lies. Deliberate. Flagrant. Premeditative. So many lies today. What's the deal? "Soren must be mistaken."

"Figures."

She squeezes the cell phone in her purse. "Just toss out an ID and that'll be that."

"My ID's in my house."

"Then tell me something only someone who lives here would know."

"Like what."

"If I tell you what to say, it sort of ruins the test."

"I know your husband doesn't dress like a handyman and I know he drives a Fiat 500 and I know he has a blue Mohawk and a nose ring and I know you're pregnant with triplets but you only have one crib and one stroller and one bag of diapers. You want me to keep going?"

"Just one more question."

"I'm seventy-two with a pacemaker. I ain't no threat."

"What kind of tattoo does Soren have around his neck?"

"A barbwire fence kind of thing."

She opens the door, steps inside, and gasps. "What in the world have you done in here?"

"Don't be scared. I can explain."

She squints at a blue couch, two cream-colored chairs, a coffee table, two end tables, two table lamps, and a row of pictures cloistered in the middle of the living room. "Whose stuff is this?"

"Do you like it?"

"Did you bring this in here?"

Paddy nods. "There's some stuff in the nursery, too. And in the bedroom. Wanna see?"

"Did Soren put you up to this?"

Paddy nods. "My mother did."

"Do I know you're mother?" Ruby peeks in the nursery: two more cribs, a dresser with eight drawers, a six-shelved bookcase filled with children's books, and a white rocking chair. The bedroom has a mattress, box spring, and a cherry-stained bedframe with four-posts. The bathroom has a black and white zebra-print shower curtain with matching accessories. "I think I need to sit down."

"You wanna try out the new rocking chair?"

Tears come. Damn it. Now she can't see the old man. "What's your name? I don't know your name."

"I'm Paddy McBrady."

"I'm Ruby." She sits on the rocking chair. "I always wanted one of these." She wipes tears with a uniform sleeve. "I'm sorry if I sounded so gruff earlier. I'm a bit overprotective these days. All bark, though, I promise." She counts a dozen boxes of jasmine tea, Vaseline, and bags of popcorn stacked atop the dresser. "Why would you do this?"

For an hour, while Ruby rocks in the rocking chair, Paddy talks about his mother's life, and death, sparing no detail about the many keys she'd given him during her period of illness. Each memory adds softness to his voice, eyes, and posture, leading him first to take to his knees, then to lying face up on the floor, then to staring at the popcorn ceiling. "My mother used to say that being locked out of life was no way to live, son, so be sure and let yourself in, and after Soren gave me your key and when I let myself in and saw that you guys seemed sorta locked out of life in your own way, I knew what my mother was talking about, and more, I finally knew what she wanted me to do."

"I'm sorry she died when you were so young."

"Me too. I never got to tell her how amazing she was."

For another hour, in satisfying quietness, Ruby rocks and Paddy stares at the ceiling. In different ways, they both believe silence between strangers oftentimes reveals humanity's loudest truths.

Paddy sits and unclips the metal key ring from his jeans. "I don't need these anymore." He shakes out his limbs. "I've been released." He sets the keys on the dresser. "Maybe you could give them to your babies after they're born and tell them how amazing my mother was."

"I can do that." Ruby smiles. "I'll also tell them about a most generous man named Paddy McBrady."

"Soren told me something this morning I couldn't forget. He said that today doesn't have to be like yesterday. He said you taught him that."

"I try to live that way and I do try to help him live that way, too. Not that I always succeed."

"Why do you wear a uniform? You an orderly or something?"

"I was until you got here." She laughs. "I'm a PCA. I work in hospice."

"Do you like it?"

"I like the paycheck and I like that my patient is a fighter."

"Is she really sick?"

"Let's just say I'm happy she has someone in her life who seems to really care about her."

"Is she gonna die soon?"

"I don't know. But it wouldn't surprise me."

"I hate illness." Paddy presses his shoulders and back against the wall. "You ever noticed that white building across the street called STUDTRIXX?"

"I see it every day and trace it every morning on my way to work. Do you know what it means?"

"I do, unfortunately."

"What's unfortunate about it?"

"It's destroyed the relationship between me and my son, Darren."

"How can a building destroy a relationship?"

"He's the owner and operator of what goes on inside."

"What goes on inside?"

"He stopped talking to me years ago."

"You live across the street from your son's company but you don't talk to him. Why don't you just go over there and say hi."

"He doesn't know I live here."

Ruby's cell phone rings. Stuffed deep inside her purse, sitting on the floor, it looks a million miles away. She doesn't budge.

"Want me to get it?" Paddy asks. "As you can see, I'm pretty good at poking around other people's stuff."

"Would you? That'd be so kind."

The phone stops ringing. "Perfect." She inhales and exhales. "If I don't know who it is then I don't have to do anything about it."

"That's exactly how Darren and I feel about each other."

"You hungry? I can make us a little something to eat if you like."

"I hope your babies like you more than Darren likes me."

The cell phone rings. It's has to be Soren. He's so good about calling back. She bends over to grab the phone but half-way down grabs her stomach instead. "No no no no." The babies have shifted. A lot. "For the love of all things offspring."

"You okay?"

"Grab the phone, flip it open, and yell Soren into the speaker."

Paddy grabs the phone. "I don't have a cell phone. What do I do with it?"

"Just flip it open and say Soren." Ruby knows a rupture of membranes can happen spontaneously. She also knows that it only happens to about twelve-percent of pregnant women. The odds are deeply in her favor. Nothing warm is trickling down her legs. There's no green or brownish fluid emerging from any orifice. No chills. No pulsating sensation in her vagina. Plenty of time to get to the hospital. She's fine. They're fine. Everything's gonna be absolutely fine.

"Soren." Paddy brings the phone to his ear. "Went straight to answering machine."

"Okay, say mom."

"Mom." Paddy shakes his head. "Same thing."

"Say Marguerite."

"Marguerite." Paddy swallows. "It's ringing."

"Give it to me." *Pick up. Pick up. Pick up.* Nothing. "Alright, this is what we're gonna do." Ruby closes the phone and stands. "You're gonna grab the car keys from my purse and bring my car up to the front door. It's the red Hyndai parked underneath the light pole."

"What about calling 911?"

"We don't need them." She knows the insurance plan doesn't cover the complete cost of an ambulance ride. Paying thirty-five percent might be considered a nominal fee to some, especially under the circumstances, but she and Soren cannot afford it.

"A red Hyndai, you say?" Paddy grabs the keys.

"Sometimes it doesn't start right away, but it eventually will, if you keep at it."

"Guess I'll see you outside." Paddy shuffles to the car, able-body and able-vision enough to be of service to a pregnant woman who needs his help. He feels awkward sitting in the driver's seat, starting the engine, holding the steering wheel, pushing the gas pedal, taping the brakes, backing up, driving forward. Ruby opens the passenger door and slides into the seat. "Ready. Set. Go."

"I haven't driven in years."

"No one forgets how to drive. Just give it some gas and stay on the road."

Paddy gives it some gas and stays on the road. Sort of. Inches from sideswiping a yellow Ford pickup truck, the same color and model as his son's Darren's pickup truck. "I'm nervous." He taps the brakes at the stop sign and stares at STUDTRIXX sign. Blinking. Gay. Straight. Hate. Father. Decay. Love. Mother. Death. Age. Sit up. Forgive. Swallow. Blink. Don't blink. "Did you know you're almost out of gas?"

"Am I?"

"The needles almost on empty." Brakes. An odd sound comes from the glove box. Like rattling keys. "That sounds like keys. Are they keys? Is the master set in there?"

"Soren," she yells into the phone, motioning for the old man to turn right. ONE MISSED CALL flashes on the screen: TERRELL.

"Why did you lie to me?"

"I didn't know you when I lied so it doesn't count."

"Is a liar the kind of mother you want to be to your babies?"

"Mom," Ruby yells into the phone. Nothing. "Mary. Stormie. Marguerite. Bayshore Nazarene. Terrell. Pyrrhica. Darren. STUDTRIXX." Damn. Damn. Damn. The old man swerves onto the highway and weaves into traffic, earning him as many middle fingers as honks.

"You shouldn't lie to people. Nothing good comes from lying."

"The speed limit's sixty-five," she screams, sounding nothing like her timid brother, Terrell, but a loud, angry pregnant black woman whose water broke a half-mile back. She tries breathing homeopathically, interrupted each time she has to help steer Paddy away from hitting a median, two Sedans, a minivan, a hitch-hiker, and the unraveled remnants of a tire strewn across the road.

"I take the bus everywhere I go."

"Take exit 47. It's the one for the hospital, the airport, and the Sheraton."

"I hope we don't run out of gas."

"We won't." She rubs her belly, taking her eyes off the road. For a second. Maybe ten. "Soren," she yells in to the phone. Nothing. "That man!" Paddy takes exit 47 and brakes hard at the stop light. Ruby looks up and squints at a Fiat 500, Soren's Fiat 500, waiting idle at the stop light across the four-way intersection. "Is that Soren's car?" She honks the horn, trying to get his attention. Unsuccessfully. "It is his car." She honks and honks. "Who's that guy in there with him?"

Paddy shrugs. Leans forward. Squints.

"Okay, when the light turns green, you go slowly and I'm gonna honk really hard," she says.

The light turns green. Paddy goes slowly. Ruby honks and honks (and honks). Soren drives forward, his eyes focused on the road ahead. As they should be. Goddamn it.

"That's my son Darren in his car," Paddy says, making a sharp U-turn.

"You can't do that."

Thump! Crash! Whack! Boom!

Ruby's seatbelt tightens. Her head whips forward and back. Her arms smash against the air bag. The stink of sulfur, hot metal, and broken glass confirm her suspicion of being hit headfirst by a large van. Hot steam rises. She blinks and blinks, trying to make sense of what appears to be a head poking through the windshield. That can't be right. She taps her feet against the floor, trying to find the cell phone. Nothing. A copper-colored key, her apartment key, the very key Soren gave to Paddy sits on the driver's seat. Gleaming. Why did Soren give it to him? None of this would have happened if Soren had remembered to take from the glove box the master set of keys. Stupid man. Vertigo dampens her senses. Add fogginess. Spasms. Pain. Shock. Darkness.

"Ma'am, can you hear me?"

Ruby awakens, taking an ambulance after all.

"Are my babies okay?" She presses both hands against her stomach, praying for one teeny-tiny kick. Nothing. "I shouldn't have lied so many times today. I don't know why I lied so many times. It's not like me to lie."

"We're almost to the hospital, ma'am. You're lucky we were so close by."

"What about the old man I was with?"

"I'm sorry, but he didn't make it. The cops will stay with him until the hearse arrives."

"A hearse. What? That can't be right. Is he dead? He can't be dead."

"We're almost there, ma'am. Try to relax."

Ruby closes her eyes and tries to relax. But she can't relax. Held captive by the earsplitting inactivity of her belly. She and Soren didn't yet know the baby's genders; hadn't yet given them names; hadn't yet had the opportunity to stand over the cribs and smile in admiration; hadn't yet hummed the tune to itsy-bitsy spider; hadn't yet rocked them to sleep in the new rocking chair that a kind stranger named Paddy McBrady, who's dead, bought and had delivered from a store of which she doesn't know the name. Opening her eyes, terrified that the baby's in her belly might be in the same condition as the old man with a gay son named Darren, who sat in the passenger seat of her husband's Fiat 500, she weeps and weeps (and weeps).

Starved

Rule 1: Don't kill yourself with food at home—kill yourself by eating out in public.

I prefer PlayThings Bar & Grille, especially the high-back corner booth beside the single occupancy bathroom. Unfortunately, a cackle—or is it a prattle?—of thinner, younger men beat me to it, forcing me to sit belly up to the glass bar opposite a small stage where revolving drag queens impersonate Lady Gaga, Cher, Madonna, Bette, and Hillary Clinton. I finish a second pint of Crispin Cider—must keep the throat lubricated—doing my best to not digest the double cheeseburger, curly fries, coleslaw, warm bread-pudding, and cold strawberry cheesecake ice cream I inhaled like some fat kid at a county fair. There's bloated and then there's distended exacerbation. Stomach sucking is pointless. The best way—the only way—to bring back the washboard abs I need everyone to see and compliment is to deposit the goods by way of manual-finger-regurgitation.

"Thank ya'll shady bitches for coming," a drag queen impersonating Nikki Minaj says, twirling. "Any of you damn fools have the slightest idea what it takes to look this good?" Everyone laughs. "Fuckers." The drag queen steps off the stage and disappears into the bathroom. Before me. Shit.

Rule 2: Before and after mealtime, especially in public, it's imperative to keep one eye on the bathroom door and the other eye on the clock. Timing is everything.

"Can I buy you a drink?" a strange man standing to my right asks. Yeah, I'm sexy. Boyish face. Firm chest. Hazel eyes people say sparkle whenever I talk. All I see is hunger.

"I just finished eating, but thanks."

"Dessert then?"

My stomach grumbles. "Just the bathroom and then home for me."

"You don't eat dessert?"

"Love it actually." I point to an empty dessert plate, follow the zigzagging chocolate and caramel lines. "As you can see, I'm good."

Rule 3: Top off every meal with warm bread pudding and cold ice cream. PlayThing's offers both. Famous Dave's is good, too. Just remember, whatever goes down must come up.

"You must really have to pee," the strange man says. "You always this fidgety after you eat?"

"The food isn't sitting well with me, mister officer bathroom monitor." I can be frank and candid, especially if my routine gets interrupted.

"Maybe you just need to give it some time. Maybe we could go for a walk."

"Feel free to start. I trust you know where the front door is."

FYI: food begins to digest thirty minutes after consumption. It's been twelve minutes since the drag queen took the bathroom. It's a forty-nine minute drive home. Do the math.

"I've got some Tums in the car," the strange man says. "Want me to go get them?"

"Please go." I stare at the bathroom door with laser precision, a dead giveaway to anyone who suffers with my kind of disease. Lucky for me no one really pays attention to anyone but themselves.

Rule 4: Always pick a bathroom with a dead-bolt lock. I can't stress this enough.

The drag queen, now an ex-drag queen, wearing blue jeans, less makeup, and a wife beater t-shirt emerges from the bathroom in a burst of energy some might mistake for white powder or thin needles. But his/her high isn't the result of a quick snort or a thin stick, but from a more cunning place where malnutrition through obliteration is released and released (and released). We exchange glances. The ex-drag-queen curtsies. I notice his/her bloodshot eyes and the dark, heavy bags sagging underneath, the result of his/her—our—semi-cannibalistic lifestyle.

"You're up," the ex-drag queen says. "Left it nice and clean for ya."

A good bulimic can always spot their counterpart coming out of or going into the bathroom. The best bulimics, like me, push the dead-bolt lock, snatch some toilet paper, wipe the toilet bowl, and stick my fingers so far down my throat, I heave, cough, spit, and choke up everything of substance. There goes my face. My mind. My soul. My world. Everything stops. The voices, too. For a moment. Emptiness. Peace. Daze. Cohesion. My heartbeat slows down as I wash sticky goo from my fingers and rinse the taste of vomit from my mouth (lukewarm water is best). I squirt two drops of Visine in both eyes to erase the red and gather up my torment in the mirror and emerge from the bathroom in a burst of energy, much like the ex-drag-queen, for I too am a very good actor on life's stage. An impersonator. A curator. A caricature. Fourteen years of perfecting the artwork of bulimia, I've become top-notch. Except sometimes (mostly during insomnia) I wonder if there's something out there more fulfilling than bulimia, and if so, what is it, where is it, and how does someone like me find it. Bulimia requires three fingers now. When will it require four? What if the dizziness and blackouts never fade? Can hair and gum lines recede to bone?

Rule 5: Don't ask questions you refuse to answer. The deed is done. That's what matters. Bask in the freedom. Rub over the flat abs.

I flush the toilet with the bottom of my shoe, watching pieces of cider, meat, cheese, coleslaw, bread pudding and strawberry cheesecake ice cream swirl round and around, taking with it thirty-four dollars and eighty-three cents. It's costly. It's dangerous. It's value that never comes back.

Rule 6: Look away from the toilet once the task is completed. If you don't, bad memories will arise and shame your struggle with self-worth.

The first time I binged and purged was on Thanksgiving Day,

after I had my fill on the annual cafeteria buffet. My college friends had travelled home, aggravating my loneliness in the dorm. My parents, like always, were strapped for cash. Sweating in the laundry facility, watching with a bloated belly cheap clothes spin dry, I took a man filled with sexual orientation discovery and childhood disenfranchisement into the bathroom only to come out a full-fledge member of a group I didn't know existed. From that day, meal after meal, I courted the laundry facility bathroom—it had a very solid dead-bolt lock—a favorite dumping ground for every feeling I couldn't share, control, or comprehend. I lost twenty-seven pounds by the end of the semester. Everyone said I looked super-hot. Like the jeans I stole from Macy's, my body was completely ripped. "Diet and exercise," I told anyone who asked about my process for shedding pounds. Few people asked. Most American men are excused from body-shame. And more, people forget male bulimics exist.

Rule 7: Establishing a permanent place to binge and purge engenders ownership to task (FYI: purging at home necessitates superfluous clean-up).

Deep inhale. Longer exhale. Open the bathroom door. Ride the high. Smile. Skip. The strange man waves me over. "What took you so long?"

I don't make eye contact or speak, walking dizzy to the front door.

"I don't know who you think you are," he says, laughing. "But you're not all that."

I know exactly who I am—and I am—the finest jaw-dropping-finger-licking-bulimic in the world.

Rule 8: Always leave them wanting more.

7:37 at I-Hop

Chuck and I haven't spoken for ten days. We've gone without speaking before, but not for this long. Nor with such outward disdain—or is it called inner pleasure? There was the week Chuck decided to stay in Baton Rouge to work the sales convention floor; the rainy week I decided to stay in Colorado to snap a few more photographs of family-summer-fun for the Aspen tourism brochure; the stretch of days after my mother died from a heart attack; the week after my father asked if he could move in with us; and the week after that week, when Chuck said, "We're in no position to take care of your father's special needs," and the week after that week, when I finally had to phone my father to tell him, "It's a nice assisted living complex. You won't be alone. You'll make tons of friends. You'll love it." Big moments filled with big circumstances that neither Chuck nor I could articulate with any number of spoken words.

See, generally, we're idea guys, and respective to our professional fields, we're pretty successful. Some even call us innovators. Chuck can sell webinar kits to the technologically challenged without using the words webinar and challenged, and I can capture through a camera lens images of humanity, wealthy people, often strangers, cry, applaud, and buy. We belong to the culture class beefing up the Upper West Side. Not that either of us care about status or titles. We're not emotional anthropologists who (re)actively dissect human predilections, nor are we the type of men to express our thoughts about weather patterns, political agendas, historical wars, house projects, or who paid what to whom. You know, real life stuff. We just are. Us.

There are some days, though, like the day my mother died from a heart attack, when I think I'd like it if Chuck knew more about blue, my favorite color—white is his favorite color—and I think I'd like it if I knew something more about his mother besides an unexplained nickname, Boots, and the bizarre infatuation she has with a set of leather hardcover books delineating The Rise and Fall of (insert any president here). How unpatriotic. And then there are other days, like the day my father asked if he could move in with us, when I think I'd like it if Chuck could speak from one corner of his heart—I've heard deeply feeling people do this sort of thing—look in my eyes, and ask me to share a sad moment or two over the last year and what I did or didn't do to overcome it. I know I can think of two.

And then there are tragic days, like the day I had to tell my father, "It's a very nice assisted living complex. You won't be alone. You'll make tons of friends. You'll love it," which we all knew was a lie, when I think I'd like it if Chuck could sit beside me, hold my hand, and talk late into the evening about our own aging bodies comprised of seventy percent water, one-hundred and twenty-thousand veins, and two-hundred and six bones. Just once, I'd like to share something fascinating with him—did you know oxygenated blood is bright red?—without hearing, "I already knew that." Maybe we could even get into a little tiff before bedtime, and call each other a few cruel names—I've heard people at the end of frustration do this sort of thing—maybe kiss each other goodnight and wish the other sweet dreams. Is that too much to ask?

Lately, I've been thinking a lot about who I am without Chuck. Ten years cycling through the same routine with the same person feels a lot more like twenty. We've been we for so long, I'm not sure I exist anymore. I figure that's why I've been thinking a lot about asking Chuck, "Have you ever felt old, poor, and sad?" I think I'd like it if he whispered the response in my ear—I've heard people in love do this sort of thing—laying naked beside me on the living room floor, playing footsie, basking in fusion affection. Then I think I'd feel comfortable enough to ask him a follow up question. "Do you believe everyone's veins are patterned to run blood the exact same way, or are veins, like fingerprints, uniquely different?" I think I'd like it if he put his fingertips on mine, and whispered, "Now at least ours are the same." Sometimes I really do want to be close to him.

Ten days ago, eating breakfast at I-HOP, just as I was about to take a sip of coffee, Chuck asked, "If you were a fatal disease, which kind would you be and why?"

I dropped the fork. It clanked against the white plate and bounced against the green carpeting. Which is where I left it.

I checked my wrist watch. As a young boy, a ticking clock during moments of uneasiness comforted me. My parent's relationship, much like the outside clothes line, was pulled taut with tension. They sat at the kitchen table, and staring in opposite directions, crunched toast and swallowed scrambled eggs. No good morning. No how did you sleep. No tell me everything about your wildest dreams.

I stared at Chuck, whose usual calm demeanor seemed agitated, similar to the way hot, black coffee changes color and temperature once creamer is added. For once, he was asking me a substantive question about human predilections. Very much, in fact, like an emotive anthropologist.

"What did you say?"

Shooing me away, he said, "Just so you know, you're not a better of a listener than I am."

The image of my parents seated at the kitchen table crunching toast and swallowing scrambled eggs had grabbed and held my attention. "Please ask me again."

"You're the reason I didn't want your father to move in with us," he said. "No one, not even him, should be subjected to that much alone time."

My stomach turned queasy. My heart felt wounded—I've heard people with wounded hearts often have queasy stomachs. Now, had we been anywhere else, say at a bookstore or a photo gallery, I wouldn't have been offended, I'd have been distracted by everything. And everyone. I'd have kept walking and let it go. But because we were sitting and eating at I-HOP, and people we're staring, I felt the need to defend myself and add critique. "I'm not the problem and you're ridiculous."

"I'm over it." He stood. "And done."

I sat alone for a short time.

Fuming in the back seat during the ride home, I came to the decision that outward disdain and inner pleasure are not mutually exclusive but simultaneously unsatisfying, like trying to guess the end of a movie before it has the chance to start. I wanted Chuck to admit he's an unhappy, desperate man who understands very little about himself, or me, or any human predilection. I wanted to tell him that I felt the exact same way. But he didn't speak. So I didn't speak. And the wheel of silent dysfunction kept on turning.

Then there are days like this morning, both of us dressing in the same mirror, when I think I'd like to stop snickering and start talking openly, as adult men, about the future and our roles in it. Which is why I said, "I guess I'd be localized gangrene in need of an appendectomy. What about you? Which disease would you be?"

"Final stage of cirrhosis of the liver." He opened and closed the door, leaving me unable to weep, pack, or text—I've heard people under extreme duress often sit motionless in the bathroom—and following the example of my parents, I did nothing at all.

Grocery Ballet

The metal cart is stuffed with food she can't afford or pass up: twenty-pound turkey, u-shaped boneless ham, oddly spelled cheeses, round fruits, colorful vegetables, thin crackers from Sweden, and funky shaped cookies from Saint Petersburg, Russia. The deli section smells tantalizingly delicious, each dish similar in texture and color to the grainy pictures in her favorite cookbook, *Going Gourmet on a Budget,* the only gift her mother gave without conditions. She chooses tuna casserole, imitation crab, and Mexican pasta salad. Her toddler-daughter pulls the hem of her oversized sweatshirt. "Hold me, mama, please."

"Stop it. We can't slow down." She readjusts the blonde wig and pulls the cowboy hat to the top of her eyebrows, dragging the girl, who refuses to stand, down the coffee, ice tea, and lemonade aisle. Turning the corner, she and the girl almost smash into a pyramid of pasta sauce waiting like a trap door.

"Please mama."

"I said no."

She and the girl speed through the bakery section, grab a bag of chocolate glazed donuts which she tucks between white wonder bread and overpriced brownstone.

"I'm tired and my tummy hurts."

"You have to be quiet." She sets the girl in the cart and swerves to the back of the store. "If you ruin this today, I'm gonna spank you." She covers the girl's mouth with her own hands. "Please be a good girl."

A few shoppers take notice. Some whisper. Others scowl. Two old men turn and look the other way. She needs to blend in, slowly dropping into the cart diapers, dog food, and a bag of multi-colored suckers. Which she opens. For the girl. Who sucks and hums. "Don't hum." She points to the space underneath the cart. "Will you be quiet if I let you sit down there?"

The girl nods. "Is it time, mama?"

"Not yet. But soon." She lifts the girl from the cart and pushes her underneath. Then she pauses at a crate of oranges, holds a 20-pound bag close to her breasts, smells vitamins and nutrients she and the little girl aren't getting. She throws the bag into the cart only to pull it back out. "I will have you someday," she whispers. "Weight and all."

The girl pops her head out, showing off bright blue lips and a matching tongue. "I'm the sky, mama."

She smiles and whispers, "I hate how important you are to this."

"It's yummy." The girl claps.

"Don't clap." She strolls—mustn't appear flustered—through the fresh flower section, bright pedals poking from steel buckets. Then through an aisle of organic zucchini, toward the fire alarm, located ten feet from the dining area packed with old people talking about vacations, cars, grandkids, trouble with the IRS, and body pains that won't quit. She feels nauseous. Like pregnancy nauseous. She touches her belly. "God no." She stops. Why is she stopping? She must keep moving. Who cares about old people's vacations and cars and ailments? It seems she does. A short break. Then she'll finish the task. She closes her eyes and listens to strange voices talk about Paris, Cadillacs, and two-story homes with nice neighbors who wave and say hi neighbor, how are you, I hope you're well.

"Aren't you a little sweetie." An old lady startles her out of the dream. The girl whimpers. "You must really like suckers." The old lady looks up. "How old is she?"

"Have you really been to Europe?" she asks. Why is she asking a question? Never talk. Never reveal your voice. The biggest no-no, maybe the top no-no in this line of work. What's wrong with her today?

The old lady smiles and steps back. "I go to Spain every year. Have you never been?" Many of the other old people spread out like varicose veins, diverting the staff's attention, exactly what she's been waiting for. It's time. Why is she still standing around talking about places she'll never get to go? Why is she not following the plan?

"Have you been to France?" she asks.

"Twice."

"Have you been up close to the tower?" Her grandest wish.

"Been on all three levels. You should go if you haven't. It's stunning." The old lady nods. "Well goodbye."

"Mama, I need to potty."

"Beep-beep," she whispers. The code word. The girl turns into a ball.

"Hold on tight." She blows her hands for good luck and pulls the fire alarm, races through the electronic doors, pushes hard the cart through the parking lot, luckily without security cameras. The girl screams, "weeeeeeeeeeee." Her husband, reeving the RV's engine, waving with both hands, mouths, hurry up. "Forgive me," she whispers to the sky, wondering if the easiest, or the hardest, part of the day is behind her.

Back Room Far Right

At minimum, I want to smell flesh.

In the rearview mirror, he counts twelve haphazardly parked cars in front of a red, vinyl-sided building that isn't exactly a barn although his experience inside does prove it's filled with pigs, bears, and cocks—ravenous creatures looking to feed, seed, and breed. Cannibals of sorts. Horny. Desperate. Men. Like him.

SHOCKWAVE PLEASURES - FOR ALL YOUR ADULT NEEDS!

A red hot Jaguar pulls up fast and stops even faster. A beef-stud wearing an Atlanta Falcons baseball cap emerges and quickly disappears through the front door.

Why does this place make me so sweaty?

Inside, he's unimpressed with the scent of bleached floors, latex gloves, and spice-apple air fresheners. Sex shouldn't smell clean. The twenty-something girl at the cash register nods.

"Good to see you again, sir."

"Hello." He uses a butch voice, the one solely reserved for this place.

The girl laughs. "Lots of new stuff hanging around. Have fun."

He scans the store like a pretend virgin, inspecting with as much luminosity as amusement the glass butt beads, battery-operated vibrators, sixteen-inch dildos, spearmint-glazed eatable condoms, and a rack of poorly stitched lingerie—MADE IN USA—no doubt sewn by ex-porn stars who've lost everything except bad memories of better times. Beef-stud's browsing a rack of interracial DVD's—how bi-cultural, and sexy, and downright electrifying.

"Sup," Beef-stud says, inciting a rock hard reaction. Not that he needs much help. Beef-stud walks to the back of the store and vanishes through a wooden archway, home to twenty viewing booths he secretly calls, The Petting Zoo. The chase. The pursuit. The rush. The prize. He winks at the hard-body magazine rack and flicks a red-licorice horse whip: $49.99. The air surrounding the Petting Zoo moans a savage, hunger song. The booths sound busy. Each one includes a tube-type-TV, a plastic chair screwed to the floor, an almost always empty roll of toilet paper, an almost always full trashcan, and a black slot blinking a cherry-red enticement for green cash. If you want it mother fucker, then you have to pay for it mother fucker.

He peeks in every booth on the left side, yearning to confront Beef-stud's wears. If privacy matters here, he's never brushed up against it. A consortium of men are pleasing themselves. And each other. "Come on in," they whisper. He always declines, although he does enjoy the foreplay. He thinks about the sun-peeled picnic table in the parking lot. Available for anyone to use. Including his family. Come. Sit. Bring KFC. Laugh at the scenery. Throw a Frisbee. Or an insult. Draw a chalk-heart on the sidewalk. Or write the word pervert. Or queer. Or climb the oak tree at the end of the parking lot and sit and watch the commotion like a bird. A spy. A nymph. A judge. Play ring-around-the rosy or hide and seek. However unlikely, the possibilities do exist.

Beef-stud's thrumming sweat in the last booth on the right. Hat brim turned backward. Belt and pants pushed to the top of snake-skin cowboy boots. Black t-shirt rolled like burnt bread dough above pink, erect nipples. "Sup." Beef-stud's hands move like ointment around his skin. Wounds require treatment. Beef-stud's a great kisser, super talented at unbuttoning, panting, and fondling. Slobbery wildness. Striptease discovery. Unrestricted barbarian. The perfect man.

"Get down and stay down," Beef stud commands.

He drops to his knees. Sunday lips that condemn sodomy tighten and gag, worship and lust, suck and swallow.

"You're really good at that."

He wants to be good. At something. To keep men like Beef-stud satisfied. Which is why he lifts his legs and bends over and shuts the fuck up like the fat old queer that he is. Is there anything more tragic than an aging queen? Or a submissive bottom hard-wired to the auspices of dominance and humiliation. No emergency room. Yet. Maybe someday. Hopefully not. In this world, lying is hiding's strongest aphrodisiac. Game on.

"You like the way I pound you, don't you, you old cocksucker?"

He closes his eyes and dreams their making love in sunlight, in an open field, on the very planet God created and called good.

Beef Stud lets out a loud groan. "Now get." He tucks, buttons, and buckles.

"You from around here?"

"I'm in and out kinda dude. I don't do personal shit in here."

He laughs. Men don't come here to exchange phone numbers or find a date. Duh.

In the car, he smears hand sanitizer on his lips, hands, and ass. The Ethol Alcohol stings, another reminder of what he's done and what he's likely to do again. Soon. Maybe later today. A small boy bursts from the green rambler across the street, arms splayed like a jet plane, propelling him with lip-sputter speed. A pack of teenage boys in a blue minivan drive by and honk. A dozen times. Two of the boys moon him. What if he's discovered? That'd be bad. But also good. How exhilarating it must be to live one's truth out in the open in any and every situation.

Three texts await his reply.

Two hours for pizza bites and ice cream, hon? Seriously?

Are you hurt, sweetie? I mean seriously...

Daddy, we're pushing play! Seriously!

The billboard sign above Shockwave Pleasures flickers on, casting a neon web to the traffic whizzing by on Highway I-95. A strand of red and green Christmas lights wrapped around the building's framework pops on, giving him the warm, incandescent feeling of being home.

Gigi and LuAnn

Before this round of sobriety, I was seriously contemplating how to snort my mother's cellulite, figuring we'd both benefit from the process. Colors had lost all excitement. Seasons had become a series of black and white John Virtue paintings. Days, months, and years had blended into an amalgam of seismic coddiwomple and race course immovability. Party-fun, my kind of fun, craves continuation even when the brain, suffering from actual starvation, begins to lose its mind, its reality, and its two little girls. I've always been attracted to desperation. And White China cocaine. Black Tar, too. And booze. All trademarks. All heads. All right. Open vein: insert fairytale. My mother gave up on me years ago. My father died of alcohol positioning when I was nine. My attorney moved to Barbados and my parole officer promulgated .;two options: straight-and-narrow-rehabilitation or prison-cell-recidivism. For once, I chose temperance over temperament. For me. For mom. For dad. For my two little girls. For my exhausting ex-wife. Drink coffee. Stay wired on caffeine. Document the journey in a pocket size journal—I'm on the last page—a gift from Eric, my sponsor/accountability buddy, the strongest voice of influence I've ever known. In case I do relapse, at least I can retrace some of the steps I did climb. Step six: We're entirely ready to have God remove all defects of character. Booyah, if that isn't me.

Every morning, I swim a few laps in The Uptown Gym pool—scholarships are offered to the clientele of The Promise Heart Sober House, my and nineteen other slow-track-back-to-civility living situation. Eric says submersion, even with chlorine, helps detoxify maladaptive behavior. After the swim, I walk across the street and order a large caramel latte at the Starbucks inside Target Greatland. Eric says isolation is deterioration's fondest aspiration. Being alone, he says, like Benzodiazepine, masturbation, and video games, can become a replacement addiction, if one isn't careful. I hate, and love, that he's been clean for twelve years. He's forgotten that abstinence to an addict often activates the compulsion to avoid it. Every month I add another shot of espresso. I'm at five. I want to be at six. Eric says seven is God's magic number. So seven it is. I quit cigarettes, too. All or nothing this time. I can be a bit of an asshole sober. I've thanked Eric a billion times for the journal, in which I've written a personal mission statement: *stay clean, be kind, and strike up a meaningful conversation with someone new every day.* Eric believes meaningful conversation advances a mindfulness narrative. Fucking optimist. He's handsome, has bundles of hair, works in marketing, and drives a cappuccino-colored BMW. I'm on government assistance with thinning hair, no job prospects, and three pair of Guinness flip-flops—it's called osmosis. Keep up.

I spot two teen girls sitting at a red table, slurping strawberry Frappuccino's and giggling about whatever teen girls find funny, probably me. I name the chunky girl Gigi, huge boobs like my Aunt Gigi, and not that I know any, the other girl looks exactly like LuAnn. God, I miss my little girls.

"What can get ya?" Bob, my favorite dead-eye barista, asks.

"Large caramel latte with seven shots please."

"Seven?" He sounds impressed, holding up as many fingers. "Feeling dangerous today, are we?"

"You have no idea."

"If you can stand it, you can do it," he says.

"That used to be my life mantra."

"Used to? What is it now?"

"Isn't the weather great today? The birds are singing. The sky's so open and blue. I sure can't get enough of days like today, no siree bob." I talk loud, trying to say normal things normal people say to a barista. I'm about as normal as a goat without legs. Eric calls us moment men, says our troubles begin and end with life's harshest drug—impulsivity. I have a hard time imagining him stealing his grandmother's pearls to buy heroin or breaking a cop's jaw during an arrest for a fourth DUI. He, however, didn't seem a bit surprised when I told him about an attempt to outrun the cops—blood alcohol level at 0.22: fourteen points over the legal limit—driving 105 MPH down Jolsen Road, smashing headfirst into the back of a Sedan, injuring two teen girls who were waiting for a red stoplight to turn green. Eric says an admission of guilt exhumes from rock-bottom collapse first-rate forgiveness. I hope he's right. He also recommended I title the last page of the journal, CLARITY, and then wait, with expectancy, for revelation to reveal itself. He tries so hard to be helpful. What I really need is a mind reader who can rewrite my code and turn me into salient sustainability. Eric says a life devoid of wishes is already dead. Maybe he's right. Maybe he does get it. I add eight Splenda to the latte and take a seat at the red table beside Gigi and LuAnn. Bring on some meaningful conversation, bitches. I dare you.

"This place is super creepy today." LuAnn stands, glaring at me for a second before facing Gigi. "I need to get going anyway. My mom's on her broomstick again about me cleaning my room."

"Be nice." Gigi stands. "For real."

I set the journal on the table and twirl a pen between my fingers, a task designed to prove that I have both the skillfulness and the determination to accomplish the task. Eric calls it control-based fidgeting. So what if it is.

LuAnn walks away, disappearing through the electric doors. Gigi lingers. "Cool trick. You a magician or something?"

I stop twirling the pen and set it atop the journal which I slide *up up up* and away. Go away. She doesn't move, ogling the journal and the pen. Fourteen. Ten. Eight. I also like to count backwards, and never in order, another way of conciliating a severe social anxiety disorder. I quit Effexor, too. Eric doesn't know this. Neither does my doc. Eighty-eight. Three. Four-hundred and six. She steps back. Not nearly far enough. Six-thousand. Eleven. Nine-hundred and fifty-nine. "I've definitely been under a few spells in my life."

"So you believe in the supernatural?"

Nosey little chubster. "Like palm reading and tarot card stuff?"

"Palm reading is for amateurs, and tarot cards, like fortune cookies, offer silly ambiguity."

Articulate little bitch. "Do you believe in the supernatural?"

"I'm a mind reader."

"Really? Are you any good?"

"Did you hear about that school teacher in Lansing who sold research papers to students for profit?"

"No."

"Called it." She snaps. "And that was two months before my paper-trail investigation had even started. I knew that teacher was up to something sinister, I could feel in my senses, keeping after class C and D students who never turned in a research paper a day in their life. And all of sudden they're A students." She laughs an unfunny laugh. "No, I don't think so. Not on my intellect."

"What happened to them?"

"What do you think happened? They were found guilty and punished. Failure gets what failure does."

Damn. She's harsh. "How much do you charge for a reading?"

She sits across and pulls from a yellow purse a thick, pink notebook. "Ten bucks for fifteen minutes and one dollar for every minute after that." She opens the notebook. "You got ten bucks?"

I remove from my wallet the ten dollar bill Eric gave me for an emergency—cash to be spent on something spontaneous and useful; something unexpected, besides narcotics, that generates joy. I wonder if my little girls have their own thick, pink notebooks. And if so, what, if anything, have they written about me. So many months away. So many failures. So much for being a hands-on dad. Or a positive influence. Or their, or anyone's, hero. I slap the ten dollar bill on the table. "I'm in."

"I'm Sarah by the way." She turns a page and writes on the top the date, time, and place. Her handwriting, similar to her voice, is a combination of uphill highs and traceable lows. "I don't do height and weight and age stuff. What I do is observe, ask, process, and offer insight based on germane findings. Are you ready?"

"Insight away."

"What's your name?"

"Greg." I straighten my posture. Eric says good posture conveys the impression of active involvement. He needs to stop reading so many self-help books. And I need to find out what this mind reader chic knows. Or doesn't. Ahem.

She writes, Greg, followed by a question mark. "Mindreader dot come says a name reveals what sort of storm percolates within. Typically, the shorter the name, the bigger the cyclone."

"Actually, my name's Peaches Honey Blossom Trixie Belle Tiger Lilly."

She laughs. "Good one. Greg."

"I have to ask, why mind reading and not cheerleading or lifeguarding?"

She studies my face, similar to the way my little girls stare with fascination at the mop-top mannequins at the mall. "You're skin tone reminds me of the color of beer my dad drinks." She pops her lips. "You ever heard of Duvel?"

"I have." Wonderful. Now I'm being compared to beer.

"You ever drank it?"

"Yup."

"Is it good?"

"It's not my favorite but yeah it's pretty good."

"What happened to you teeth? Why are they all chipped and yellow?"

I cover with a hand my mouth. "My dentist does meth."

"That's not true," she says. "What happened to your eyes?"

Fifteen. Ninety-nine. Four. "What do you mean?"

"You have sad eyes. Why are they so sad?"

"Aren't you supposed to tell me?"

"My dad's eyes are sad, sadder now that his mom, my grandma, died. Did someone close to you recently die?"

"I guess you could say that."

"Might that someone." She pauses, staring at my trembling, dry-from-chlorine hands. "Be a part of you."

OMG. "Mindreader dot com is no joke, is it?"

We sit quiet for a short time. Now that her voice is off, I suddenly want it back on. Perhaps she is a mind reader. Perhaps she is clairvoyant. Perhaps she does know the whereabouts of this clarity I seek.

"You have children, don't you?"

"I do. Two girls named Robin and Roxanne who live with their mother, my ex-wife, in Milwaukee. They're twelve and thirteen."

"I have a sister, too. Her name's Melia. She just turned ten."

"Is she a mind reader?"

"She's a cheerleader and a lifeguard."

"Really?"

"No." She smiles. "But she is an all-time brat."

"That's too bad."

"What's wrong with your hands? Why are they so dry and shaky?"

I set my hands on the table. Eric says transparency, even shaky transparency, is healthier than opacity. "I swim in the morning and the chlorine hates my skin."

"My dad's hands shake a lot, too. I think it's partly because my mom calls him a huge disappointment. But I also think it's because he drinks too much Duvel." She scribbles Duvel in the notebook. "My hunch is that you also drink Duvel. Maybe not exactly Duvel, but something within its family." She stares at my coffee cup. "I also sense that you're not drinking Duvel these days, drinking instead a substitute liquid to help meet your need for oral, mental, and physical satisfaction."

I can't speak. Or move. Crippled by insight. From a pubescent. I finish the coffee and hand-smash the cup as if it were a can of Duvel. "You're good."

"I also sense that someone, probably more than one person, has called you a disappointment."

My stomach turns sour, as do a million neuron synapses exploding like bombs throughout my body, jolting me closer to the many names I've been called over the years: disappointment, drunkard, druggie, cheat, selfish, jerk, tool, liar, lost, weirdo, dry, super creepy. The part of my brain that craves addiction ignites, causing my salivary glands to want to go out and find as much relief as possible. Stay ardent, Greg. Breathe. Eight. Two. Ten-thousand. Eric says it's best to forgive (and try to forget) the name calling. He says name calling, even nice names, is a risky exercise because it denotes branding and branding is a risky exercise because it denotes leaving an everlasting imprint and leaving an everlasting imprint is a risky exercise because it denotes leaving a scar which is as a wound which is a cut which is a trigger which is a symptom which is a genetic factor which is the start, and end, to it all. I understand. Sorta. Not completely. I believe names have their place, even bad names, clear reminders of the proximity between past mistakes, present struggles, and future authenticities. I want authenticity. My mom wants authenticity. My little girls deserve, and need, authenticity. I grab the journal and offer it to Gigi. "You don't have to read my mind anymore, not if you have this." Eric says the most reconciling thing a recovering addict can do to accelerate healing is to give away a most cherished possession, especially one that holds significant meaning. "Everything about me, good and bad, is in it."

"That I didn't see coming," she says, sticking the ten dollar bill, the journal, and the pink notebook into her purse, hiding my saddest hurts, cruelest blunders, and loftiest hopes. "Sure you're ready to give it away?"

"I wasn't sure until right now."

"How long have been sober?"

"Four months, three weeks, and two days."

"Do your little girls know about your problem?"

"They do."

"Did you tell them yourself?"

"I wasn't sober enough to tell them so unfortunately they had to hear it from their mother."

"Do you think they would have liked it if you'd have been the one to tell them?"

"I think regular dads want their girls to see him as the truth and not as a lie."

"My mom says my dad drinks because he hates himself. Do you hate yourself?"

"Sometimes."

"How can you hate yourself when you have two girls who love you?"

"That's a really good question."

"Do you hate yourself today, like right now?"

"Not as much."

She sighs. "I want to ask my dad if he's got a drinking problem, but I'm afraid of what he might say. I mean, what if he is? Then what will I do?"

"Love him and tell him every day."

"How can I tell if he needs to seek treatment?"

"Maybe you should read his mind."

"I can't mind read my parents. Maybe I'm too close or maybe they're too far away, but whatever the reason, I have no idea what's going on with them."

"Then all you can do is your very best. That's all any of us can do."

"It was nice to meet you. Greg." She lifts the ten dollar bill from the purse. "Keep it. Buy something for your girls. And keep swimming. Maybe one of us will become a lifeguard after all."

"I can do that." Can I? "It was nice to meet you too, Gigi. I mean, Sarah."

"Did you say Gigi?"

Damn it. "When I first saw you and your friend, I named you Gigi and her LuAnn."

"Why Gigi?"

"You know, Gigi Lichtenstein, the top model mind reader

from Paris who isn't afraid to stop and talk to strangers."

"You want to know the name we gave to you?"

Not at all. Three. Two. One. "Sure."

"It's not bad, if that's what you're thinking."

"Name away."

She laughs. "Dr. Doofenshmirtz from Phineas and Ferb." Leaving me with a heart that can drop, surge, and skip after all. Please God, whoever he is, just let him be sober.

Or

Worry bombarded me the moment my wife handed me the positive pregnancy test; lucid flashes of his or her future; stadiums chanting his or her name; penthouse or playgirl viewpoints; hobnobbing in the right or left circles; acting on the big or small screen; jet setting to London or Mumbai: please God, anything but me.

Day of delivery, moments before the birth canal opened, I saw my little boy, or girl, standing beside me, holding my hand, looking up at me with big loving eyes as if to say, hi there, daddy, you're my best friend and my most awesomest champion. I almost fainted or vomited.

I held our boy, Joseph Clarke, falling hopelessly in love with all the tiny, smooth parts. Skin against skin never felt so electric or vulnerable. Half-me in every way. Better schools, clothes, shoes, houses, cars, toys, and friends shot through me like bullets, each one drastically altering the way I smiled at my wife, laying in the hospital bed, smiling at me as if to say hi there, daddy, you're my best friend and my most awesomest champion. I almost cried or dropped Joseph from my wishy-washy hands.

Days and nights grew shorter as Joseph tested the limits of parental love. And won. Mundane tasks like diaper duty, baby lotion, powders, sink baths, and rocking chairs made me forget or ignore the visions I envisioned at birth. Cooing or spitting up has a remarkable way of sticking a person to whatever setting they're in. Or out.

First words, or sort of words, flew like spittle from his mouth. Sitting up wasn't merely an option or a choice, but a laborious effort of it's-just-not-happening-the-right-way. Walking crooked came next. Sucking on everything became pleasurable for both of us. The small house was being overtaken by the littlest or biggest person in the world.

We tried catch and throw but neither came natural. I exemplified speed while he enjoyed taking it slow with two plastic dolls. We sang or hummed nursery rhymes but he sounded more off-key than me. I tried to stretch him out but he refused to grow. Stadiums, penthouses, and jet-setting began to fade or die, replaced by doctor visits augmented by big sounding machines that made Joseph and his mother tremble or cry.

But we, or I, couldn't give up, determined to find our place on the planet. Little doesn't mean useless—or does it? No, it doesn't.

So we tried again, this time with modified shoes and the tiniest glove I've ever seen or held. Kids like to point or laugh at things they don't understand, which made Joseph afraid of kids who point or laugh. So I lied to him (I'm not adept at acknowledging weakness or fabricating truth). "You are no different than anyone else."

"Me bees better net time," he said, my little boy or girl standing beside me, holding my hand, looking up at me with big loving eyes as if to say, hi there, daddy, you're my best friend and my most awesomest champion. I almost fainted or vomited. Or fell deeper in love.

Pieces of Moves

Another long pause.

The man—let's call him Theodore Castle—folds the newspaper and throws it in the trashcan. The woman—let's call her Jocelyn Castle—finishes the coffee and lifts the newspaper from the trashcan.

"Leave it," he says, making a fist.

"I will not let him rot among waste," she says, blocking her face with a forearm.

Like two pawns at the end of a long chess match, they stumble around each other in the kitchen. Neither stand victorious, watching from the kitchen window a night wind stab itself with chilling darkness. Walking from the bathroom, Reverend Olinbrow says goodnight and embraces Jocelyn, but not Theodore, a man not known for hugs, nor religiosity, nor compliments. "Thank you, reverend," she whispers, opening the front door. Standing on the porch, they wave goodbye to Reverend Olinbrow, dropping their hands once the lights of the Sedan vanish and the driveway dirt settles into the rust-colored yard. "I don't want him coming out here anymore," Jocelyn says. "Fine with me," Theodore says. "All he does is stink up the bathroom and tell us how much God hates hate."

Another long pause.

They sit at the table and pick at their skin. What a long day. And brittle autumn. Especially cold for Timothy, their son, who was murdered and branded in the barn (less than fifty feet from the house) by school peers, teenagers, twin boys with shaved heads who call themselves The Hades Heisters.

The man—let's call him Theo for short—turns off the hallway lights. The woman—let's call her Josie for short—turns on the living room lights.

"Hades Heisters," he whispers, taking a seat at the kitchen table. "Did no one see that name as a problem?"

"I thought I knew Timothy," she says, sitting across. "But maybe I was blind."

"We weren't blind. We were right here."

She covers her eyes with her hands, trying to block the image of her son's shaved head, *HH* carved by knifepoint into his forehead. "What was he doing with them in the barn?"

Another long pause.

Theo—let's call him a large appliance handyman—rubs his own eyes and yawns. Josie—let's call her a vegetable gardener—smoothens the newspaper and sobs. Tears fall on the table and meander to the middle. The table had always leaned inward. Theo had planned to fix or replace it, but he never got around to doing it. Jocelyn used to hate the table, especially how it leaned inward. But not so much anymore.

"We should eat something." She stands.

"Nothing for me."

"We could take a walk." She leans against the kitchen sink. "Go out and try to see things more clearly."

"Things seem pretty clear to me."

"Maybe we could have somebody else over."

"Nobody but priest-man wants to come out here and watch you cry."

She looks directly into his eyes. "Well one of us has to cry."

"It's because he was soft," he says. "It's because I didn't teach him how to be tough."

Another long pause.

A large appliance handyman—let's call him a high school dropout—pounds both fists against the table. It snaps and collapses, creating a v-shaped implosion. A large sliver of wood knifes itself between his toes while an even larger piece of wood scrapes his knee. "Why does everything we touch fall apart?" he says. "How did we get like this?

Another long pause.

A vegetable gardener—let's call her a high school dropout—

stands and rearranges by color the cans of vegetables in the pantry, red to green, the way Timothy liked it. "Maybe it's time for a new table," she says. Timothy had told her to make his father buy a new one. "You deserve a proper table from a proper store," he had said, when he was eleven. Twelve. Thirteen. Fourteen. Fifteen. Sixteen. She sighs. Seventeen.

"What if I had a secret?" she asks Theo. "Something I bought that you know nothing about?"

"I'd ask where you got the money."

"What if I told you it was a new table?"

"I'd tell you to go get your money back. I can fix this one. Better yet, I can make a sturdier, stronger, nicer one. I promise."

"What if I told you I bought an apartment in town and that I was moving in alone?"

He doesn't respond, staring instead at the palms of his hands, at the many lines leading to tremors he doesn't know how to stop. He never looked at his son's hands. Nor at his wife's. Never held them, kept them warm, allowed flesh to merge with flesh until there was no differentiation. It seemed like a silly notion, and nonsensical duty, something women and weak men do. Touchy-feely stuff. Not his nature. But could it have been, had he chosen it? Maybe if he'd been softer to his son, and wife, his son would have been stronger, so strong that the Hades Heisters would have left him alone. He heard people on television talk about reverse psychology—the opposite of what is suggested. But does it even work for people like him, his wife, and his son. "You don't deserve us," Timothy had yelled at him almost every day. "I'm done with you," he'd yell. "D.O.N.E." Theo looks at his wife. "If you want to be done, I understand."

The high school dropout—let's call her marinating in self-determination—takes to her knees and lifts from beneath the sink a gray shoebox. She fingers a pair of pink latex gloves and removes the lid. "Wanna take a peek?"

"You don't wear tennis shoes."

"It's not that kind of run."

"I'm gonna go start on making a new table." He stands, moving the broken remnants of the table to the corner of the room, peripherally glancing at the contents in the shoebox. "You want a table long enough for four chairs." He pauses. "Or just two?"

She lifts from the shoebox an electric shaver. "How far are you willing to go for our son?"

"I'm not shaving my head. Or yours."

"It's what he'd want, what he'd like."

Theo couldn't remember how Timothy wore his hair, shaved or otherwise. He never thought to look. Or ask. But now, confronted with whether Timothy had shaved his own head—or had the Hades Heisters shaved it?—Theo found himself lost in the feeling of loss. And care. Deeply. Disgusted by his own capacity to overlook his son's head, and hair, the same way his father had overlooked him, offering only cold, and hot, apathy.

"Okay. I'll do it."

Raindrops pound the rooftop shingles and vinyl siding of the little house. Neither knew a downpour was coming, despite hearing on the television and reading (though not really) the local weather report in the newspaper. Neither used an umbrella. Neither wore a wedding band. Neither touched the other's hair. Head. Face. Jawline. Ever.

Ladies first. Odd finger-combing through her hair, long strands tickling the spaces between his fingers, clumps of gray and black falling onto the floor. Her head was a perfect circle, one he'd wanted, more than once, to crush. More than once he'd thumped, pushed, and pulled. All he wanted now, staring at the prickly pate, was to kiss it, round and around, run a hand against the skin on her neck, thumb a line down her spine. Half of Timothy's spine. He held back tears, letting the rain speak what he couldn't say. "Guess it's my turn," he says, handing her the shaver.

"I wish we wouldn't have buried him in all black clothes," she says, setting the shaver in the middle of Theo's forehead, moving quickly up and back, side to side. So much hair. Growing like porcupine quills for twenty-three years. A face bloated with leather bumps she'd never been able to read, or write, or understand. More gray than she realized. His skull was a perfect egg, one she'd wanted, more than once, to hold. More than once she'd begged, curse, and cried. All she wanted now, staring at the prickly pate, was to finish and to be finished. "Looks good on you. You should wear it this way from now on."

"Do you want me to sweep it up?"

"Do you know where the broom is?"

He nods. "Does it feel weird having no hair?"

"No." She holds the shoebox. "It feels like freedom."

"What else is in the shoebox?"

She lifts a rectangular piece of red felt, revealing an Elk Ridge Ultimate Hunter Fixed Blade Knife and a Smith and Wesson matte silver revolver with a pink handle. "Does this surprise you?"

The high school dropout—let's call him flabbergasted beyond verbalization—steps back and looks at his wife in a most unaccustomed manner, as if seeing her for a first time, maybe ever: popcorn textured skin, lazy right eye, Vulcan-pointed ears, and a dozen or so other odd features he'd poked at until they became scars. If only he was the type of man compiled by an apologetic nature. Which he isn't. So he doesn't. Apologize. Ever. "What kind of gun is it?"

"It's a 442 Moon Clip."

"Why do you keep it beneath the sink?"

"Because I knew you'd never look there and find it."

"Why do you have it?"

"For protection?"

"From who?"

"Who do you think?"

Another long pause.

"When did you get it?"

"I chickened out the first time," she says. "I just couldn't make myself hold it."

"Where'd you buy it?"

"In the nastiest pawn shop I've ever been in."

"Who drove you?"

"Timothy."

"Whose car did you use?"

"His friend, Sam's."

"The kid you told Timothy not to like or trust?"

"I don't like him. Or trust him. But he had something I needed so I pretended that I did."

"Did Sam and Timothy know where you were going?"

"They're the ones who convinced me to do it."

"So this Sam kid knows you have a gun?"

Another long pause.

"Was it hard getting the permit?"

"The clerk said it'll leave a golf-ball size wound."

"Did the store ask for ID?"

"I shoot five blanks at a mounted deer head hanging in the back."

"How much did it cost?"

"The cashier called it a sweet piece."

"Where did you get the money?"

"I didn't shake one bit while I was shooting. I just marked the target and pulled the trigger, just like he told me to do. I couldn't believe it was me doing it."

"How long have you had it?"

"One finally has to surrender to what one can't sustain."

"Doesn't your God take issue with killing?"

"He's no longer my God."

Another long pause.

"Did you buy any bullets?"

"I want to do this, but I want to do it my way." She sets the shoebox in the sink. "And I want us to do it together, The Shaved Shysters, The SS, if you will."

"No one in town will feel sorry for you anymore," he says. "Not your church lady friends or Reverend Olinbrow or anyone."

"Everyone has always underestimated my capabilities."

They turn, as if being pulled by invisible stings, and stare at the empty 8x10 photo frame hanging crooked on the wall, still awaiting Timothy's senior picture, already two months late.

Theo and Josie—let's call them united, resolute even—take turns pointing the gun and carving SS into the kitchen countertop.

"Do you really think this is what Timothy would want us to do?"

"I think Timothy was embarrassed by you," she says, flinging the knife at a picture of The Virgin Mary hanging on the opposite wall. Tip in, first throw, dead center in the middle of Mary's forehead. "And broken for me."

Another long pause.

At One Time or Another

A television commercial advertising Justin Bieber's world concert tour turned the girly chatter in the lower lever of the house into synchronized ear-deafening screams, clenching hearts, and oh my god, yes yes yes. As if by rope, the five girls clung to each other, and to every word coming out of Justin Bieber's mouth.

"He's a little overrated," Hasha said, lying face up on a camouflage sleeping bag. "And I do think he's struggling with some shit." The darkest of the five since kindergarten, Hasha has been the darkest ever since her white mother had a one-night stand thirteen years ago with some black man Hasha has never met, who all five girls, at one time or another, have called Spermy McSpermyson. In elementary school, being Mulatto with a single, white mother inured eyebrow-raising whispers, but in junior high boys prefer snow white to milk chocolate which, although Hasha has never admitted it aloud, doesn't bother her one little bit.

"I'm glad he's getting taller," Tree said, bouncing with the other three girls. The tallest of the five since kindergarten, Tree became a Tree and continued to grow through elementary school much the same way, causing all five girls, at one time or another, to call her Tree. In junior high, however, boys prefer to either climb trees, shoot air-guns at trees, or ignore trees altogether. "I'm not sure I'd invite him to a party, though," she said, lying face up on a Denver Nuggets sleeping bag. "He seems a bit ungrounded and unwise."

"Okay, here's the game." Kodi, the host said, turning down the volume on the big screen television before plopping onto an *Inside Out* sleeping bag. "We each get to invite five guys to a party and they have to come." The chubbiest of the five since kindergarten, Kodi has been the chubbiest ever since she started eating the family chef's food served by maids on handcrafted china from Denmark, the birthplace of Kodi's mother, who the girls, at one time or another, have called Horsejaw-Teeth-Face. In elementary school, being the chubby girl raised the lunch lady's spirits, but in junior high boys reject chubby as the quantifiable equivalent to not being hot, but a super-chunk-fat-ass-gross-piggie-face. "None of us can pick Shawn Mendez, One Direction, or Zane," Kodi said. "Because we all know we're in love with them." She opened a *Brave* spiral notebook and uncapped a feather-friendly pen with which she wrote each girl's name at the top, separating each name by a thin, straight line. "Tree, you go first."

"One, I'm not in love with Shawn Mendes," Tree said. "And who says I want only guys at my party?"

"Lesbo," Hasha said.

"My house." Kodi sat Indian-style. "My rules."

"I could totally kiss a girl," Clumzilla said, tripping over Kodi before falling onto a *Hello Kitty* sleeping bag. The clumsiest of the five since first grade, Clumzilla wasn't clumsy at all during kindergarten, but became clumsy in first grade, during the week she moved from Colorado to Kentucky and then back to Colorado, bringing with her a lopsided haircut and a black eye which she told the girls she got from cutting off her own hair and from falling off a dog that belonged to a cute neighbor boy in Kentucky who dared her to ride it, which she did, and subsequently fell off the dog, causing the girls, at one time or another, to call her Clumzilla. In elementary school, moving three times to two states in one week was nobody's business so nobody talked about it, but in junior high boys make it their business to stare in admiration at Clumzilla's 34c boobs and long blonde hair that stretched well below the middle of her back. "I'd have no problem being a lez," Clumzilla said. "Except for those short-dykie haircuts. That I couldn't do."

"I hate the word, dyke." Hasha said. "I'm not a lez either, but if I was, I sure as hell wouldn't want you guys calling me a dyke."

"Weiners actually do look like hot dogs," Dino(trope) said, lying face up on an *Aladdin* sleeping bag she'd borrowed from Kodi. Like always, Dino(trope) had forgotten to bring one. The dumbest of the five since kindergarten, Dino(trope) has been the dumbest ever since she brought to show-and-tell a green, plastic dinosaur, telling the class, "This was my brother's dinosaur, Dinotrope, which I found floating in the bathtub while my brother was laying on the bathroom floor with a belt wrapped around his neck and there was a piece of paper taped to his chest that said I'm sick of feeling extinct, ya know, like the way dinosaurs are extinct and since he won't be able to bring it in here and show it to you, I thought I better do it for him."

All five girls, as if it happened yesterday, remember the green, plastic dinosaur and Dino(trope)'s speech. Kodi remembers hearing Mrs. Crarry, the teacher, gasp. Clumzilla remembers sitting quietly at her desk and finger-twisting her own bangs. Hasha remembers watching Mrs. Crarry take the dinosaur from Dino(trope)'s hand. Tree remembers feeling happy and honored when Mrs. Crarry picked her over every other student to watch the class while she and (Dino)trope went to see Principal Ed, who sent Dino(trope), according to (Dino)trope, to Miss Clara, the school counselor's office, who asked (Dino)trope, according to (Dino)trope, "How do you feel about your brother's passing?" to which (Dino) trope answered, "It happened and it's over. I mean, people's brother's die every day. I can't change it, just like I can't change that my friends call me Dinotrope." During the third and fourth grade, Tree, Hasha, Kodi, and Clumzilla begged Dino(trope) to let them find and give her a new nickname. "Hell no," she said. "I'm me and you're you and that's how it'll always be." So out of considerable empathy and sadness for Dino(trope), and Dino(trope)'s dead brother, Tree, Hasha, Kodi, and Clumzilla continued to call her a name they despised, until an enlightening day in fifth-grade music class taught them that the word 'trope' means *musical reading of the Bible in Jewish liturgy*, and since none of them were Jewish, and none of them were interested in musical readings, Dino(trope) decided it was time to shorten Dino(trope) to Dino. In elementary school, having a brother who killed himself got Dino(trope) oodles of sympathy from students, teachers, and administrators, but in junior high, boys brand a girl whose brother killed himself as a crazy-whack-job with a vast reputation for giving fantastic blowjobs. "But wiener's don't taste like hot dogs," she said, shaking a bottle of green toenail polish. "That I know one-hundred percent."

"Maybe we should call you Slutetia." Hasha covered her mouth. "I hope you gargle with Listerine."

"Chef say hot dogs are for poor people." Kodi shivered. "What's it feel like to have a dick in your mouth anyway?"

"My dad says hot dogs are a mixture of cow hooves and pig intestines," Tree said. "And can we please not talk about Dino having dicks in her mouth."

"I heard this one girl stuck a whole pack of hot dogs up her vag." Hasha opened her legs and pointed to her crotch. "Can you imagine how bad she smelled?"

"That's not even physically possible," Kodi said, looking at Tree. "So which five guys do you want at your party?"

"Damian Lillard," Tree said. "And I guess I should invite my dad because he's so smart and also my mom because she'd probably be hurt if I invited my dad and not her."

"Why would you invite your parents to your party?" Clumzilla asked.

"Guys only," Kodi snapped. "Follow the rules."

"I know what guy I *wouldn't* invite to my party," Hasha said, pressing her bare feet against Tree's boobs. "Spermy McSpermyson."

"Total rudeness." Tree pushed away Hasha's feet, causing them to land on Clumzilla's boobs.

"Not on your best day, sweetie." Clumzilla pushed Hasha's feet to the floor.

"I'd invite Queen Latifah and Rhianna to my party," Hasha said, lying horizontal on the sleeping bag. "But not Beyonce because she seems like a total bitch."

"You do realize those are all chicks," Kodi said, sneering.

"Is Mariah Carey black or white?" Dino asked, blowing on her toenails. "And didn't Tyra Banks get all chunky-butt and shit."

"No, she didn't." Kodi loaded her mouth with gummy worms. "It's just that all those skinny bitches on America's Next Top Model are so fucking anorexic of course she looks bigger next to them. So would you."

"No way. I've been like a size two forever."

"Yeah, because you're anorexic."

"Jealous much?"

"Can I please finish my party list," Tree said. "Why are you guys are always cutting me off?"

"Then finish already." Kodi gave Dino the middle finger.

"I'd also invite Kerri Walsh Jennings and April Ross."

"Those sound like school teacher names."

"Kerri's six-three and she's a three time Olympic gold medalists."

"You do realize you've only invited one guy to your party and the guy you did invite is your dad. At least Hasha's choices are gender consistent." Kodi glanced at Hasha, Clumzilla, and Dino, who were all texting. "Phones off. Now."

"I overheard two senior girls say Coach Fink has a huge wiener," Dino said. "Hey, maybe we should start calling him Coach Kink. Get it. Fink the Kink."

"Coach Fink's a total perv," Clumzilla said. "Like all the male teachers at that gross, icky school."

"Not every guy's a perv, Clumzilla." Tree stood, looming over the group like a tree. "Why does everything lately have to be about wieners and guys? Remember when we used to just go outside and play and swing and talk about regular stuff besides guys. Why don't we do that anymore?"

"Go outside and swing than." Clumzilla said. "Nobody's stopping you."

"I'm glad I'm still a virgin. I don't care if it's not cool."

"Boys make me horny," Dino said, glaring at Hasha. "Even

though I know not everyone here feels the same way."

"Fuck you, Dino."

"When did you become such a prude?" Clumzilla asked Tree.

"Just because I haven't had sex yet doesn't make me a prude."

"Yeah, it kinda does." Dino said.

"Doesn't it bother you that boys at school call you a slut?" Tree asked Dino.

"Not really."

"Well, it should. It's not something to be proud of."

"I liked you a lot better in kindergarten," Clumzilla said to Tree.

"Yeah, well I liked you a lot better when you had short hair and a black eye."

Silence filled the room. Not one gummy worm, wiggle, giggle, or text. No movement at all. Like five dots stranded in the middle of the night.

"Sorry Clumzilla. I shouldn't have said that."

"I don't want you guys calling me Clumzilla anymore."

"But you're Clumzilla," Dino said. "What else are we gonna call you?"

"It makes me sound stupid."

Tree tried to think of a better, different name for Clumzilla, but all she came up with was Clumzilla. Kodi tried too, ending with the same result. Dino popped her lips while Hasha leaned in and kissed Clumzilla's cheek. "I like you just the way you are. Now what five guys, or girls, would you invite to your party?"

"How about we call you Charmzilla instead of Clumzilla because isn't charming the opposite of clumsy?" Dino asked. "Or maybe Charmy, like lose the zilla part, like I lost my trope part."

"I didn't cut off my own hair or fall off a dog, not that any of you believed it. Or did you?"

"So which name do you like better, Charmzilla or Charmy?"

Hasha's phone rang. "Shit." She looked at the screen and pressed the mute button. "Goddamn stalker."

"Phones off for the rest of the night," Kodi said, turning off her phone, and the television, throwing her phone into the center of the circle.

"Fuck that." Dino pressed her phone against her chest. "Some of us have other friends who we need to stay in touch with."

Tree shut off her phone and threw it in the middle of the circle. "I don't have Instagram or Snapchat so it's fine with me."

"You don't have Insta or Snap?" Dino asked. "I thought you were rich like Kodi."

"Having Instagram or Snapchat doesn't make you rich."

"But it makes you cool and I like being cool."

"You're not that cool."

Hasha tossed her phone in the circle. "Take it. Please."

Charmzilla grabbed Dino's phone and tucked it inside her own bra. "Out of sight, out of mind."

"Bitch, give it back. I'm waiting for a real important text." Dino snatched the phone from Charmzilla's bra. "Now my phone's gonna smell like your boobs." Dino glanced at Hasha. "Bet you wanna smell it, don't ya?"

"Fuck you." Hasha walked to the far opposite corner of the room and switched on a floor lamp. Black linear shadows danced across the earth-colored terrazzo floor and up the stucco walls. "I hate being in the dark." She sat on her sleeping bag. "I guess white is better."

The girls sat quiet for a moment, tightening the circle with incremental scooches forward. Not since kindergarten had they been this close.

"What happened to you when you moved?" Tree asked Charmzilla.

"It's so embarrassing." She sighed. "So crazy...and so mean."

"Secrets here stay here," Kodi shut the notebook. "Everyone swear to it."

"I swear," all five said, at one time or another. What they didn't say is what they were all thinking: how easy it is to break a promise, even a promise to a friend.

"I went to Kentucky with my dad to meet my mom for the first time. When we got there, my dad was so happy to see her. I tried to act happy too, even though I wasn't, and when he reached out and touched her hair, she got really mad and said fuck off, and I felt so bad for him. Then my dad got really mad and started opening and closing the cupboards in the kitchen which were pretty much empty and then he asked if I was hungry and I said that I was, so he left to get some food and that's when my mom took off her wig and I'd never seen a bald woman before and I guess I was probably staring which must have made her mad because that's when she grabbed my hands and put them behind my back and sat me on a chair and tied my wrists and legs with dishtowels and I was like what the fuck is this woman doing to me and where is my dad. I yelled for him to come back but he was gone and that's when she grabbed a steak knife from the drawer and sliced off my hair and I was just sitting there thinking who is this crazy bitch and how could my dad be happy to see her. Pieces of my hair were floating in front of my eyes and they were landing on the floor and that's when she opened the window and left me alone for like two hours and it was so cold in there and I started shivering and I wondered if my dad was ever gonna come back and I was so tired but I didn't want to fall asleep because I didn't know what else she might do if I fell asleep, but then I must have fallen asleep because I woke up to the sound of her hand slapping my face and all I could see was blackness for a second and then I heard my dad's car engine shut off and she must have heard it too because she ran upstairs and slammed the door and when my dad came in and saw me, he dropped the Dairy Queen bag on the floor and scooped me up and we drove straight back here overnight. I don't think we stopped once. Not even to go to the bathroom. Maybe we did, but I honestly don't think so."

"Damn." Kodi chomped watermelon-flavored bubble gum. Hasha covered her mouth with her own pajama sleeve. Tree bowed her head as if in prayer. Dino bit her fingernails and sucked the blood.

"I wasn't even seven." Charmzilla gathered her hair into a ponytail. "I mean, I didn't even know her middle name." She sighed. "I still don't know it."

The basement door opened. "Girls, girls," HorseJaw-Teeth-Face yelled.

"What," Kodi yelled back. The other girls jumped a little.

"You go from sounding like a herd of buffalo to not even a peep. What's going on down there?"

"Buffalo?" Kodi shrugged. "Nice touch, mom."

"I better hear some noise soon or I'm coming down there."

Kodi turned on the TV to volume 20. "There. Now go away."

"You want me to bring down some more snacks?"

"Go away, mom. Jesus H. Christ."

Kodi turned the volume to 25, mouthing *teethy be gone, teethy be gone.* The girls smiled, but no one laughed. This was no time to laugh.

"I'm sorry that happened to you," Tree said. Kodi turned the television volume to 15. Hasha and Dino scooted their sleeping bags even closer to Charmzilla.

"My dad still won't talk about it. Whenever I ask him, he says some things are best left to sit in the quietness of their past."

"Where was the house?" Tree asked, patting the space between her legs. Charmzilla crawled over and sat in front of Tree, resting her back against Tree's big trunk, smiling at Tree's ridiculously big feet. Hasha and Dino sat quiet while Kodi opened a box of Goobers.

"Some town in Kentucky, I don't know the name." Charmzilla leaned her head back as Tree finger-brushed her hair. Dino and Hasha hugged themselves while Kodi finished the box of Goobers. "All I remember is that the house was close to a playground and a few miles from the Dairy Queen."

We ought to call Clumzilla, Bonita, Tree thought. *That is her real name.*

"Why did you say you fell off a dog?" Kodi asked.

"What would you say if your mom cut off your hair and slapped you in the face?"

"I'd definitely come up with a better lie than that."

"Someone should go slap your mom," Dino said. "Hurting kids is wrong."

"I wish my dad would talk to me about it, but I know he never will."

"I saw our neighbor guy once beating his wife," Dino said. "But she was crazy tough and fought back and I was happy to see that she wasn't gonna take shit for him."

"No offense you guys, but I'm sick of the name, Clumzilla. I mean, we're not little girls anymore." She turned around and faced Tree. "Do you even like being called a Tree?" She looked at Dino. "You honestly can't like the name Dino." She looked at Kodi. "Lose a few pounds and people will stop calling you those cruel names." She looked at Hasha. "And there's nothing wrong with being mixed race." She laid face up on her own sleeping bag. "I'm Bonita Clum, and even though I hate that it's her name, too, it's who I am and I have to learn to accept it. If you guys want to call me Bonnie or Bon that's fine, but no more Clumzilla. I mean it."

"Bonita sounds like your one-hundred years old," Dino said.

"Better Bonita than Clumzilla."

Tree hadn't given much thought to the notion of liking or disliking the name Tree. Her father, a geologist, said trees were strong, noble tenements grounded to the earth. Tree's mother, an interior designer, said the best furniture came from the trees. "I don't mind if you guys call me Tree in private but maybe at school you could call me by my real name, too."

"What is your real name?" Dino asked. Kodi, Hasha, and Bonita giggled.

"It's Lydia and your names Jessica, remember?"

"Nah-uh, I'm Dino."

"Jessica's a much prettier name than Dino," Tree said.

"But I'm Dino. That's who I am and who I always wanna be."

"Doesn't it remind you of your dead brother, though?" Hasha asked.

"I'm not Jessica. I don't ever want to be Jessica. Not now. Not ever."

"Fine." Kodi turned off the TV. "Dino."

Bonita crawled into her sleeping bag and pulled the zipper up to her neck. "I was really glad to come back to school and see that you guys were still in class. I honestly don't know what I'd have done if I'd have come back and you weren't there."

"I'm glad you came back, too," Tree said, with a wink. "Bonita."

"I think I like Bon better."

"Bon it is."

""Let's watch a movie. Something funny." Dino stood. "Fuck all this serious shit."

"Sit your ass down." Kodi opened a pack of licorice. "We aren't finished playing the party invitation game and it's my turn."

Dino stuck out her tongue. "Fucking boss. Go then."

"Robert Pattinson because he's a hot Vampire and Taylor Lautner because he's a hot werewolf." Kodi talked fast, the words popping like spittle from her tongue. "Robert Downey Jr. because he's super cute even though he's old and James from Big Time Rush because he's way cuter than Justin Bieber and lastly Jonah Hill because even though he's overweight he's still a huge movie star and super comfortable with who he is." Kodi snapped her fingers. "Jessica, you're up."

"That's not my name."

The basement door opened.

"Goddamn it, mom," Kodi yelled. "What?"

"There's some boys at the front door asking for Jessica."

"My name's Dino." She pounded her fists against her legs. "Why is everyone not wanting to call me that anymore?"

"These boys said Jessica texted them to come over."

Dino shook her head and held up her phone. "Na-uh. I only texted Evan Neverson."

"They're in a really big pickup truck. How old are these boys anyway?"

All five girls jumped up and ran upstairs, tripping and climbing over each other on their way to the stained-glass front door. Kodi tumbled out first, running straight into the middle of Evan Neverson's plaid cowboy shirt. Carl Denger, Billy Winthrop, Blake Olsen, and Kyle Hunter, juniors, stood behind Taylor, laughing.

"Sup ladies," Evan said.

Dino moved in front of Kodi and poked a finger into Evan's chest. "You promised it would only be you."

"Chillax, my love. Me and my posse bring no harm."

"I'm sorry boys but you're going to have to leave," HorseJaw-Teeth-Face said.

"They're just guys from school," Kodi said, shooing her mom away. "Go buy something online."

"Do not make me be the bad guy and start calling parents. You've got exactly fifteen minutes to do whatever it is you're doing and then ya'll have to go."

"Fine." Kodi slammed the door and looked at Hasha. "And you think your mom's a stalker."

"It wasn't my mom."

"So which of you lovely ladies wants to take a walk with us this fine evening?" Taylor said.

"Me me me." Dino clapped, jumping into Evan's arms.

"Guess I can go, too," Bon said, taking Blake's hand. "It's not like this overnighter can't stand a break."

Kodi, Tree, and Hasha stood quiet. The other three boys turned and walked to the pickup truck.

"But we haven't finished the game," Kodi yelled. "We're not done playing yet."

"Total rudeness."

"Dino," Hasha yelled. "Clumzilla, I mean, Bon. Come back."

"Go play your silly little game," Dino said. "These *are* the guys we invite to our parties."

"Fine, leave then, but I'm erasing you both from the list," Kodi yelled, stepping into the house. Tree and Hasha followed suit, sitting on the marble bench in the thirty-foot high foyer. Tree stared at the large beech tree blossoming in the middle of the room. "I think my dad's right." She stood and touched the tree trunk and its leaves. "Sometimes maturity requires pruning." She sighed. "Bon's right, too. We aren't little girls anymore."

"We should go out there and bring them back." Hasha stood. "That's what I'm gonna do."

Kodi stepped in front of Hasha, blocking her hand from grabbing the door knob. "They've made their choice and we're not it."

"Get out of my way." Hasha pushed Kodi aside and grabbed the door knob. "You can't stop me."

"I said no." Kodi pushed Hasha, who fell to the floor. "Nobody out there wants you, you fucking dyke." Kodi pressed her back against the door. "Especially not Dino, who I know you're in love with."

"Kodi," Tree yelled. "Don't call her that."

"Stay out of it, Tree." Kodi glared at Hasha. "It's no wonder your dad doesn't want to see you. I mean, what dad wants to see his daughter turning into a man."

"He does too want to see me, you fat bitch. I'm the one who keeps saying no to him. You have no idea what's going on with my life. Or with his."

"I know you went down on Bethanny Clarke in the music room last spring."

"So what the fuck if I did."

"So you're a fucking dyke is why."

"Stop it, you two."

Kodi and Hasha looked at Tree. "And you." Hasha said. "We don't call you a tree because you're tall. We call you a tree because you're so fucking awkward."

"The dyke's right." Kodi opened the basement door. "You're nothing more than an awkward tree who invites her parents to her party. And to top it off, you're the biggest nerd in the entire school."

"At least my mom's name isn't HorseJaw-Teeth-Face."

"Don't you dare call her that."

"You're the one who started it."

"No, I didn't." Kodi pointed to Hasha. "Ethnicity orientation over there did."

"No, I didn't. It was Dino's who started it."

"Yeah, it was Dino." Kodi slammed the basement door and foot-pounded downstairs. Hasha stepped outside and disappeared into the night. Tree stood quiet, unsure what to do, where to go, or whether or not to hold onto or to let go of the childhood friendships grounding her to Kodi, Hasha, Dino, and the newly-minted Bon.

Time with The Thompsons

During a day trip to the North Shore, the mid-thirties newly-weds found and rescued the square baby blanket from the $2.99 bargain bin at Claire's Antiques. The blanket's skin was stamped with clarinets, Arial's favorite, and snare drums, Ronn's favorite. Ronn named the blanket, "Little Jazz," to which Arial applauded. Right then, they created a marriage-motto: "Life's a compromise linked by collaboration." For three years, Little Jazz was the least expensive item in the house and also the couple's most cherished possession. Arial washed and dried him once a month. Ronn ironed him twice a year. Arial danced the Cha Cha with him on the front porch during the summer. Ronn read to him The Count of Monte Cristo on the back porch during the winter. Arial sang him bedtime lullabies. Ronn gave him a morning embrace. Sweetness. Satisfaction. Kindness. Love. Little Jazz wasn't known as one to doubt his existence.

Little Jazz soon became Saint Little Jazz, comforting the couple's sleeplessness, underemployment, and costly root canals. During an infertility phase, he became a wad of cotton shoved into the left corner of the couch, but reappeared good as new once Arial's belly began to protrude, bestowing upon him the name Grand Protector, soothing what Arial (and sometimes Ronn) called the blessed-bulging-beast. Little Jazz enjoyed pulling all-nighters, working double shifts, serving as scabbard, therapist, and nearest/dearest friend. He cherished his roles and accomplished his tasks with unyielding finesse. He wasn't known as one to complain.

Autumn introduced to the house Jacqueline Claire who kept Little Jazz to herself, imprinting him with burps, slobber, hiccups, and snores. On Christmas Eve, Arial laid him like a ball beneath Jacqueline's crib. He needed some respite, which turned into a long stretch of loneliness: four months to be exact. Finally the spring birds returned, sitting and chirping on the ledge outside

Jacqueline's window. Ronn scooped Little Jazz from the floor and whispered into his heart the letters S.I.D.S., before tossing him into the wicker hamper, a gloomy place that smelled a lot more like death than life. S.I.D.S. What does it mean? Something I Don't See? Shoved Inside Dank Smelliness? Surely I Deserve Salutation? Silently I Digress Slowly? He wasn't known as one to underthink.

Forty-one days passed before Ronn came upstairs and snatched him from the hamper. Ronn washed and dried him, ironed him, and laid him beside Arial's face on Ronn and Arial's mattress. Arial's cold hands pushed Little Jazz off the bed and onto the cold hardwood floor. "I don't want to see that thing ever again." Her words and tone, similar to the way he tumbled in a clothes dryer, lifted from his body some of his youth. But he didn't hate or judge her, happy to perch like a toddler in the passenger seat of Ronn's Nissan 350Z. "I'm sorry she rejected you," Ronn said. "But she'll come around. You'll see. We just have to give her some time." Every night, Ronn set Little Jazz beside Arial's face. Every night, she pushed him away. "I think you're really hurting his feelings," Ronn told her. "Probably," she said. "But it's time we both grow up and stop pretending some blanket is gonna make everything okay." Ronn carefully folded Little Jazz in half and tucked him in the bottom drawer of the nightstand. Which was fine. Little Jazz wasn't known as one to question his position.

One summer afternoon, after Arial left for the grocery store, Ronn fell asleep in the hammock in the backyard and accidentally dropped Little Jazz from his hand. The neighbor's Maltese, Nebuchadnezzar, gnawed, shook, and salivated all over Little Jazz's body. Ronn awakened and ran Nebuchadnezzar away with a soft slap to the butt, but not before Little Jazz had been ripped and bruised. Later that night, Ronn took Little Jazz into the garage and patched him with superglue and duct tape. Then he folded Little Jazz in half and stuffed him inside a translucent, plastic bag where he remained for six weather cycles. Then, on one particularly cold evening, Ronn's warm fingers pulled Little Jazz from the confines of the bag and shock him out, took him inside the house, and handed him to Arial whose fingers and face felt like sateen sheets. Her belly was protruding. Again. Her laughter had returned, too. And her lullabies—*where troubles melt like lemon drops, high above the chimney tops, is where you'll find me*—brought light to the clarinets and strength to the snare drums. For five months, Ronn and Arial called everything heaven, the place Jacqueline Clair was said to have gone. But where was heaven? Was heaven the reason Ronn had said S.I.D.S? Why was her pink room now blue? Little Jazz wanted answers, but Ronn and Arial never mentioned S.I.D.S. again, at least not in front of him. So he continued to hypothesize. He wasn't known as one to quit.

March brought Primrose colors and Peony pedals to the flower beds outside the house. April rains thumped the roof and siding. May provoked a twister that cracked the windows, rattled the floors, and unearthed part of the house from the foundation. Little Jazz, tucked between the couple's heat, flew around the room before getting wrapped up like a cocoon with the ceiling fan. Arial and Ronn twisted and thrashed around the room like puppets. A hole in the middle of Arial's body rid itself of a bloody human boy who bounced like a ball against the walls. After the storm had subsided, while Arial laid quietly beside the mattress, Ronn unwrapped Little Jazz from the ceiling fan and placed the bloody human boy atop his clarinets and snare drums. Ronn tied together Little Jazz's four corners and carried the soggy bundle downstairs, to the car, to the hospital, to the morgue, to the church, and to a wooden coffin buried in a country cemetery beside Jaqueline Claire's headstone. Ah. This must be heaven. At first, Little Jazz heard faint traces of Arial's lullabies and Ronn's reading from The Count of Monte Christo. But soon he heard nothing at all. He did his best to remember in darkness all he had heard, seen, and known in the light. Someday I'll Definitely See-Them-Again. He waited and waited. He wasn't known as one to forget.

Bryan with a Y

Riding high on cardio endorphins, I spot Bryan with a Y standing tall at the top of the stairs, sporting the crimson-colored basketball shorts and the gray *All For One* t-shirt I bought for him during a boys-only weekend trip to Boston five months ago tomorrow. When we make eye contact, he turns around and takes the stairs while I lunge forward, mister quads and delts leaping over YMCA-stickered stationary bikes, treadmills, and free weights. People, both acquaintances and friends, ask, "Dude, what's the hurry?" Similar to Lycra in Zumba class, I can't ignore the noise. At the bottom of the stairs, I yell his name, trying to box him into a fluorescent corner with nowhere to turn but straight into me.

"Bryan." I reach for him, grabbing air. "Bryan."

He stops and turns around. "Cheating on Gold's Gym now, too, I see." His tone bites. Like venom. And fury. I can't blame him. *When did he color his hair? When did he pierce both ears? When did he stop wanting me and my heart?*

"I guess Gold's gym understands me." I touch his shoulder, wishing to touch everything else. Now. Here. Out in the open. Who the fuck cares.

"Someone should tell him what a futile effort that is."

"I think he already knows." I smile. He used to say my smile soothed his unhappiness.

"I see you're still running." His tone bites again. Less venom. Same fury. Beautiful, beautiful man.

"Not as much as I used to. Trying out a few new things. You know, mix it up a little."

"I have no doubt. I gotta go. But take care of yourself, okay."

"Wait." Months of unanswered questions grab his wrist. "Give me a minute." I release the grip. "Please."

He leans against the wall, lips as kissable as they are full. "You have one minute. Go."

I wonder if he still thinks about me. I wonder if he knows how much I still think about him. "Why did you give up on us? I thought we were figuring things out."

"Not here, Tommi."

I widen my stance. "Nobody here cares what we're talking about."

"So you're out now." He crosses his arms. "Free from all the ladies and the lies."

I offer a hand. A peace offering. "I'm sorry if I hurt you."

"Don't touch me." He taps the back of his head against the wall, the same action he made in Boston, in the hotel room, after I said I wasn't in love with him, that I couldn't pick him, that I didn't want birthday's and holidays and Gold's gym and vows and fidelity and reliability, that I'm not the man he needs. Or deserves.

"I do miss you."

His eyes and shoulders soften, luring me back to steamy showers, matching Red Sox baseball hats, Drag Race, sex—so much sex—and Maxi, a three hundred dollar poodle he bought for me on our three month anniversary. "How's little Maxi doing?"

"He ran away after you moved your stuff from the house. I made a few signs but nobody called, so like I had to do with you, I let him go."

"You should have called me. I could have helped look."

"It's kind of hard to call a blocked number."

"You have my work number."

"I'm not calling you at work." He scoffs. "You and all your goddamn secrets. Don't call me until nine-thirty. Don't stand so close. Don't sit beside me. Don't touch me in public. Don't play with my hair." His eyes turn glossy. "Don't say you care. Don't say you love."

"It was all so new to me. I didn't know how to do it. But as you can see, I am changing."

"Never fall in love with the darkest part of the closet." His voice cracks. "How many times have I heard that? How many times have I told others that very same thing?"

"I just couldn't figure a way in. Or a way out."

"In," he whispers. "That's all you care about." His magic fingers slide down a vein-stemmed neck and magnanimous chest. "I should hate you," he says. "But I don't. Because there's nothing I could do to you that's worse than what you do to yourself."

"I am sorry."

"I see you're wearing your wedding ring again." He wipes his eyes, bedroom blues that haunt my wildest and wettest dreams. "Always pretending to be something you're not."

"I am this, though."

A tear falls from his chin. "If you say so."

"I'm just trying to be honest."

"Honesty isn't lying. Not to yourself. Not to me. Not to her. Not to anyone. You don't have to stay married if you don't want to. That you can change. That you can do. Now leave me the fuck alone." He takes the stairwell one and one, leaving me to marinate in my own secrets and lies, along with a question I ask myself innumerable times a day: how many steps does it take to live an honest life?

At the top of the stairs, I hear my other name, the one I first heard three years ago at the breakfast table: Pupa with a U. I turn around and see my green eyes and pointy nose and my wife Susan's curly red hair on a precious little boy, Tommi Hunter Jr., dripping wet and waving a flimsy piece of paper in the air. "I did it, Pupa." He jumps up and down. "I swam the pool back and forth twice. They gave me two gold stars. See?"

I wiggle my tongue, because he loves me silly, and award a hearty two thumbs up before waving him back to his mother who's no doubt beaming with pride and ticked off with me for missing another family milestone, which I have, she's right, I'm always one or two steps behind. He bounces away, unaware of the power he holds over me. I turn and nod at Bryan, running fast into a glistening sweat. One final acknowledgement of what was and what will never be. He doesn't respond. Nothing. Kaput.

Zilch. And I know how we met is why we must end.

I spot a mat in the stretch and bend area where a large black woman is sprawled flat on her back, as if posing for some crime scene investigator to white-tape her outline. "It doesn't get a whole lot easier," I say. "But we can't give up, now, can we?" She stands, shakes her head, and limps to the water cooler.

"No pain, no gain," I say. She laughs out loud. As do I.

Catching me off guard, my everyday life walks toward me, confining me to the straight and narrow facade they expect and need me to be. Susan waddles like a duck, resting her hands on a distended belly that'll soon produce Ashleigh Rae, another reason why I had to walk out and close the door on Bryan. And the many men before, and after, him. Hunter bounces around the walking track, ignoring Susan's pleas to come back, to get over here, to obey and stand still. She's right, he and I are very much alike.

Suddenly, I'm struck with a moment of clarity. Which rarely happens. Perhaps I fell for the wrong man. Perhaps Jason, the human resources hottie at work who's always asking me to lunch, is better equipped to accept the limitations of my situation. Perhaps he can treat with casual contact my terminal ailments. Perhaps he can adapt to my responsibilities and not beg to become the highest priority. Perhaps he hates Boston and little dogs. Perhaps he's also married to a woman. Perhaps he can save me and I can save him. Perhaps, if I'm lucky, he can help erase the uselessness of still being in love with, and without, Bryan with a Y.

Parade Drain Paranoia

"Hello Mister King. I'm detective Marianne Halvero. May I sit with you?"

"It's your room."

"Would you like some water?"

"They gave me a sandwich and an apple earlier. Call me Barney."

"Who's they?"

"Where are you all coming in from anyway?"

"All who?"

"Forget it. Ask me whatever. I have nothing to hide."

"Just a few questions. In and out, I promise."

"Have they found Abby yet?"

"We have many skilled people looking."

"I offered to help look for her, but they told me I couldn't leave this room. If she's still able to hear voices, I know she'd respond to mine the fastest."

"Tell me about this morning, Mister King, before the parade."

"Why can't I see my other girls, Carlie and Kaitlyn? Who are they with?"

"They're with Marianne Pribanue, a social worker. Very professional. Very caring."

"I don't want them going to my mother or my mother-in-law. They're both crazy. They'll say things about me that aren't true. Have you gotten in touch with my sister?'"

"So far she's been unreachable by phone."

"Did you try her cell phone? I think she got a new cell phone."

"We've been trying for hours but still nothing."

"She and my wife used to call each other kindred spirits."

"Did you notice the sewer drain when you sat down?"

"I know that the second button on my shirt popped off. Doctor Vindigo says I'm using food to stuff my emotions, but in all honesty I'm just stuffing my face. I really don't care how I look anymore."

"So you planned to attend the parade beforehand."

"I thought we could all use some time out of the house. I even pre-packed the diaper bag and sun block. The forecaster on TV said there was a chance of thunderstorms but I was so glad when I woke up and knew he was gonna be wrong. Fucking experts think they know everything. But they don't."

"I hear your wife recently passed away. I'm sorry for your loss."

"Yeah, me too."

"You must have a lot on your mind?"

"Well, I know the name Susan G. Komen if that means anything and I know that a casket costs as much as a grave stone and I know I'm supposed to smile real big for the girls and just go on living life even though I wish it would stop and rewind."

"Sounds frustrating and confusing."

"You think?"

"Did the girls seem excited about the parade?"

"Abby kept sticking out her tongue going, 'Pllllllllllllllllll, which made all of us smile and that's when we saw the tall, blonde woman walk by and Abby said, Mama, and I saw the same pain in Carlie and Kaitlyn's faces like the day of their mother's funeral and I thought they were gonna cry but they didn't and I knew right then that life really does move on."

"Did you walk or drive?"

"We live right off Radcliff. It's like six blocks away. I wanted to make sure the girls didn't have to sit behind anyone this year."

"Do you remember what the girls were wearing?"

"I sure do. We wore the same red, white, and blue outfits my wife picked out last year. They're a little matchy-matchy but I figured that was the point and besides I didn't have time to go out and buy anything new. Carlie hardly fit into her shirt, she's growing so fast, and I distinctly remember bending down to kiss Kaitlyn's sparkly pink headband because she really likes my kisses even though I don't wear chap-stick which she thinks I should because boys need soft lips, too. She's very thoughtful like that. And I remember sitting up real straight and thinking if my wife were alive how proud she'd be of the example I'm setting for our girls. She was very proper, my wife. All her ducks were in her row. Every T was crossed and every I was dotted. She was very orderly, and very fashionable, too."

"The older girls said Abby was only wearing a diaper. They said you refused to put clothes on her."

"That's not true. I remember putting her arms through the shirt holes. Why on earth would they say that?"

"They did. Two different times."

"My wife wouldn't want me to take her outside in just a diaper."

"The Superintendent at your school said you've taken a leave of absence."

"What? Oh, yeah. They've been very understanding."

"How long have you been off work?"

"I don't know. Three, maybe four months."

"An officer reported finding eighteen prescription bottles in your nightstand."

"So what? They're all prescribed by a doctor."

"Almost every bottle had a different doctor's name on it."

"That's not a crime."

"It's called doctor-for-pill-shopping and it doesn't paint a very good portrait of you being a dutiful father in total control of your surroundings."

"Fine, I went to see a few doctors. My regular doc wouldn't give me anymore pills and then after a while he refused to see me at all. I mean, I lost my wife. I needed some assistance. I was in pain. Call him. Ask him. Ask any of them. They all know what happened."

"So much pain that you might have forgotten to put clothes on Abby?"

"I told you, I put her arms through the shirt holes."

"Fifteen of the seventeen prescription bottles were empty, Mister King."

"I'm not talking to you anymore. You're accusing me of doing drugs and being a bad father. I held Carlie and Kaitlyn in my arms the first three nights they came home from the hospital. Ask anyone who knows me and they'll tell you I was a wonderful father and devoted husband whose girls wear shirts all the time."

"I'm simply trying to map out a timeline."

"Ask Carlie and Kaitlyn who I am. They'll tell you."

"They said you sleep a lot during the day."

"I make them breakfast every morning."

"They said they're afraid of you a lot of the time."

"Afraid of me. Yeah right."

"Kaitlin said sometimes when you're lying on the couch she thinks you're dead."

"You talked to her? Did she ask about me? How did she look? Is her knee still bleeding?"

"She's safe, Mister King. I promise."

"They're not telling you the whole story. I mean, they're little girls. They don't see things the way you and I do. They're not with my mother or mother-in-law, are they?"

"No. They're with Marianne Pribanue, a social worker."

"Oh yeah, you told me that. I forgot for a second, but now I remember."

"It's okay."

"My wife's name was Marianne. Did you know that?"

"Tell me what happened when you arrived at the parade."

"A few people were sitting in plastic chairs and there were lots of people speaking Spanish which didn't surprise me as much as it angered me because it's like America's birthday and shouldn't we all be speaking English on that day, and then some African American family plopped down beside us but they didn't stay very long, because the mother said something about being smelly or stinky or something strange like that."

"You thought she said smelly or stinky?"

"We were sitting there awaiting the first float and the older girls were knocking their knees together and Abby was fussing between my legs. Then Carlie mentioned wanting a lollipop and Kaitlyn said she loved marching bands which made me happy since that's what I do for a living and I knew she really meant it."

"Did she say stinky or smelly?"

"I don't know. Floats and streamers started passing by and all the kids were screaming and grabbing candy from the ground. Usual parade stuff. I was just thrilled to see the older girls doing something besides sitting in their rooms or asking me questions about cancer that I don't know any of the answers. I'm no doctor. I teach spoiled rich kids without rhythm to play the drums."

"Then what happened?"

"The girls said they were hungry so I went for food."

"Did you leave the girls by themselves?"

"They weren't alone. Those Spanish speaking people were still there and I distinctly remember asking the lady in a blue bonnet to keep an eye on them."

"So you do remember leaving?"

"Kaitlin said she was sick of candy and Carlie kept begging for a corn dog with lots of ketchup. She loves ketchup. Kaitlyn prefers mustard like her mother and I'm not sure what Abby likes yet, but yeah, they said they were hungry and a good father doesn't let his girls go hungry."

"Do you remember how long you were gone?"

"I told you, a couple of minutes, maybe two. Five minutes tops. No more than a blink. And the whole time the tall vendor guy was breading the corn dogs I was looking at them over my shoulder."

"The girls said you were gone for more than an hour."

"They're mistaken."

"Tons of eyewitnesses said the same thing."

"They're lying. I distinctly remember the short vendor lady in the red hat was deep frying cheese curds which is why I blew on them so hard when I walked back and that's when I heard everyone screaming that a little girl had fallen into the drain."

"So which is it? Vendor guy or vendor lady?"

"What?"

"You first said it was a tall vendor guy and then you changed it to short vendor lady."

"Vendor person. I don't know. They all look the same."

"Eyewitnesses said you weren't holding any food in your hands when you returned."

"I knew they couldn't be screaming about Abby. I knew it had to be somebody else's baby. I knew my wife was watching down on us from heaven and that she wouldn't let anything else bad happen to us."

"Eyewitnesses said you were shirtless when you did return."

"We all wear shirts all the goddamn time. Why does no one believe me?"

"They said you were panting really hard and super sweaty, Mister King. Mister King. Mister King!"

"What?"

"You were snoring."

"Marianne said I didn't snore."

"Are you okay to continue?"

"Like you care."

"We're almost finished. Stay with me, okay."

"I wish you'd stop accusing me of doing something wrong. You know what? I'm done with you. I mean, you won't even let see my other girls so why in the hell should I help you, when you won't help me."

"I can leave if that's what you want."

"Where are you going? Come back. Okay, fine, I'll tell you more. Just please don't leave me alone."

"Hello Mister King, I'm detective Marianne West. May I sit with you?"

"It's your room."

"Would you like some water?"

"They gave me a sandwich and an apple earlier. Call me Barney."

"They who?"

"Where are you all coming in from anyway?"

"All who?"

"You didn't see the lady who just left?"

"I'm the first person to come in here."

"She was just here. Blonde hair, green eyes, fashionable and orderly, just like my wife, Marianne."

"Excuse me, Mister King."

"Where are you going? Come back. Okay, fine, I'll tell you more. Just please don't leave me alone."

"Hello Mister King. I'm detective Marianne Atridge. May I sit with you?"

"Stop tormenting me. All of you. I know who you are and I know what you're doing."

"Hello Mister King. I'm detective Marianne Whitmore. May I sit with you?"

"What do you want? You want me to admit that I pushed her in the drain and ran away. You want me to say I'm sorry, well I'm not sorry. You want me to say I failed them, fine, I failed them, but I don't see it that way. I see it like I saved them, like I saved all of us from living life without you, which I can't do, if you really want to know the truth. Well, do you? Do you?"

She Only Wishes For, and Only Gets, Five

Twelve days after Christmas, prowling the attic for her mother's prescription pills, Melanie finds beneath the toolbox a prescription bottle filled with finishing nails. Apparently Ativan and carpentry were so last year. She shakes the bottle, creating a manufactured hailstorm. The noise brings clarification to her New Year's resolution to hang clothes on her bedroom walls—except for space above the headboard plastered with a 20x40 poster of Tom Selleck's hairy-chest. She fills the inaugural wall with black pantyhose, a blue bra and lace panties, a gray mini skirt, and a zebra-print blouse and belt. Finding a new way to get high until the old high is reinstated is still a type of high. Ah-ha moment number one.

"Where'd you get the money for the clothes?" her mother asks.

"You have your secrets and I have mine."

"On that, we're in agreement."

On Valentine's Day, after vomiting sixteen boxes of candy hearts in the backyard, Melanie uncovers from beneath an arborvitae a sandwich baggie laced with Percocet, Cyclobenzaprine, Codeine, and Vicodin. She binges for a week. She blacks out on the mattress on Saturday morning and has her stomach pumped at Regions Hospital on Saturday afternoon. On Sunday morning she's admitted to rehab where she convinces herself that life, like twenty-eight days of sobriety, sucks. During rehab, her parent's find Jesus at Lakewood Baptist Church and begin hosting a potluck brunch for an after-church crowd. After rehab, Melanie stays in her bedroom and dreams of getting high. On something. Or someone. Soon.

On Memorial Day, a new couple, Doctor and Mrs. Jacobsen, show up at church and brunch, carrying a fruit tray and a bottle of Merlot, wearing cream-colored linen and leather sandals. Karen

Jacobsen works as a cartoonist. Tom Jacobsen works as a neurologist. Similar to Melanie's new perm and Tom's poolside physique, the summer of 1985 is shaping up quite nicely. Lots of bounce and swagger. Lots of hometown appeal. Lots of rod and reel potentiality. Yummers McNummers.

Two days after the 4th of July, Karen and Tom purchase the rambler to the right of Melanie's parents two-story home, relegating Sunday brunch from all-are-welcome to five, then six, once Betsy, Karen and Tom's first child is born. Melanie's bedroom wall, thanks to the many inattentive employees at JCPenney, is an homage to America's love affair with red, white, and blue. Spandex never looked so cheap and easy.

September arrives and Karen and Melanie's mother hang around town like mosaic drapes while Tom and Melanie's father smoke cigars and drink Merlot in the basement. Melanie babysits Betsy, a stinky, slobbery ten dollar an hour job that Karen and Tom could easily afford to pay fifteen. For twenty bucks an hour she might even clean up after Betsy. Okay, make it twenty-five. Even then: no.

For Halloween, Melanie hangs on the wall a blood red tweed jacket, a black and white checkered shirt, two lime green socks, and a Ronald Reagan mask from Spencer's. Which isn't the easiest place to shoplift. Thank God she's Caucasian with straight teeth. White people really do get all the breaks. Ah-ha moment number two. Karen and Melanie's mother practice in the den their Twiddle Dee and Twiddle Dumb marching song while in the guest bathroom, adjacent to Melanie's bedroom, Melanie's father perfects a bad impersonation of Captain Morgan while Tom rocks in the full-length mirror a Tarzan loincloth and sexy, hairy chest. Ah-ha moment number three.

"Jane likey," she says as Tom passes the bedroom.

He stops and backtracks. "You okay doing candy patrol all by yourself?"

"Sugar's a girl's best friend." She lifts from the dresser an orange bowl filled with candy bars and lollipops. "Comfort food for at least a month if nobody shows."

He scans the bedroom. "So you do this on purpose?"

"Do what?" She undresses a lollipop and sucks.

"Dress the walls."

"Tom, we're leaving," Karen yells from the kitchen. "Come on already."

"I'll join ya on Blackberry Street." He winks at Melanie. "Melanie and I here are discussing appropriate candy to kid ratios."

"Don't bore her with all your stupid mathematics stuff," Karen says, disappearing down the street, alongside Betsy and Melanie's parents.

"Why on the walls and not on your body?"

"I can't wear them until their ready." She sets the bowl between her legs. "They need time to familiarize themselves with the new environment."

"How considerate. How long does it usually take to break them in?"

"It depends on their virginity."

He laughs. "You're funny."

"You find my clothes virginity funny?"

"I've never heard you talk before."

"I can stop."

"No. I'm definitely interested in what's going on here." He widens his stance. "Please continue, candy girl."

"Once the fabric bonds with my skin." She looks directly in his eyes. "I know things will never be the same."

"How perceptive. And analytical. You should be a doctor."

"It only works when the time is right." She closes the window blinds, eviscerating the yellow light streaking in from the street lamp. "Like right now." She drops to her knees and rips off the loincloth. Ah-ha moment number four.

"Here it comes."

She swallows and pushes him away. "I need Percocet."

"I can't do that."

"Not even for a fifteen year old girl?"

"I thought you were seventeen."

"I need Vicodin and Ativan, too."

"Tom, where are you?" Karen yells from the front door.

Tom cowers behind the mattress while Melanie sticks her head out the bedroom door. "I'm afraid he's already come and gone."

"Did he say where he was doing?"

"Something about going downtown."

"Did he change clothes?"

"Oh, he changed alright. That I can tell you for sure."

"Well, if he comes back, tell him Betsy was crying for him."

"You can count on me to tell him exactly what he needs to do. And know."

Twenty-seven days later, during Melanie's father's funeral, while her mother and Karen sob, and while Tom reads scripture verses about friendship, faith, and finding eternal peace through rest, Melanie, riding the high on Percocet, Vicodin, and Ativan, sits quietly between her mother and Karen, cradling Betsy as if she were her own. Ah-ha moment number five.

What I Learned about Love and Hate from Socrates Tremapolos and His Wacko, Sicko Parents

The man I still love, and hate, who lied to me for eleven months about his age, along with a few other things, still wants to take me on a first-class tour of Greece, the birthplace of him and his parents. Or so he says. I adore Greece, what I've read online and seen in picture books. Santorini Island sits on an active volcano. How dangerous. And picturesque. I've never travelled outside Green Bay, Wisconsin, my birthplace, which is pretty cool if the Packers football team matters most.

The Packers are responsible for bringing to me the man I still love, and hate, which is why I still love, and hate, the Packers. Every Sunday, during regular season home games, I sell fried corndogs and eight-dollar Corona on the main level of Lambeau Field, the Packers birthplace. The man I still love, and hate, attends like clockwork every home game, by himself: section 133, row 47, seat 8. A season ticket holder. Grandfathered in, thanks to some deceased Uncle Nikolas he never met. Fans tell me the strangest things. The flirtier ones, like Socrates, stand around in bedazzled paraphernalia until my shift is over and then, once we're alone, ask, in a whisper, for a date. Yeah, I'm a looker, if pretty-boy-androgyny fields your dreams. I usually decline the invitation, citing a jealous boyfriend or some newfound sexual continuum that includes girls. But I said yes to Socrates, mostly because of his huge hands and rolls of cash, but also because I love, and hate, the way his accent takes charm to the summit of the most mesmerizing eyes and bubble-butt I've ever seen. Still. From the very beginning, he was a temptation I couldn't refuse, a game I wanted to play, a devil disguised in the physique of a god, a man's manly man, a bona fide charmer, a real mother fucker.

On our first date, we walked the perimeter of Lambeau Field. I said very little while he replayed with his lips and hands the game highlights, as if I hadn't just worked a shift and clocked out. He isn't the first guy to confuse my working at Lambeau for wanting to be at Lambeau. But it's a bi-monthly paycheck for five, often six, months of the year. Its food in the fridge, electric bills, black toenail polish, and Indie flicks on weekends. It's learning through experience to be okay with whatever team I'm playing for at the moment. My deceased parents, who never saw the inside of Lambeau, called Lambeau incredible. I never asked if by incredible they meant absurd or awesome or noisy or what. I should have asked. But I didn't. The man I still love, and hate, will never get to meet my parents. Which is fine. I haven't met his parents either. At least not in person.

The man I still love, and hate, has given me some great sex in my apartment. He's a passionate lover, eager to teach me lots of things about my body, mostly to appreciate the youthfulness within it. "I'm not doing too bad for forty-eight," he likes to say, flexing and kissing his biceps. His driver's license, which I peeked at while he was going to the bathroom, says fifty-eight. I don't think fifty-eight is old. He still has broad football shoulders, a rigid tummy, a cellulite-free ass, and a cantaloupe-shaped head marked by hectic black and gray hair. I enjoy looking at his red face, no doubt the result of too much outdoor-stadium sun, a lack of fruits and vegetables, and oodles of eight-dollar Corona. He'd benefit from a good clay mask and some anti-bronzing concealer, although I'd never tell him as much. He may talk and act tough, pounding his chest and growling like a Packer, but I can see within the shallow spaces of his mannerisms a vibration of softness, especially malleable whenever we hug and he calls me his sweetest one, his Packerette, his pro-everything, his real-life dolly-doll. It's hard to not fall in love with that kind of presentation. It's harder still to fall out of love once the presentation, with all its sideshows, begins to crumble. And it always crumbles. For me. It's too bad my sexual continuum doesn't include girls.

242

The first time I invited the man I still love, and hate, to my apartment, I worried his flashiness might pock fun at its starkness. Except for the mattress and box spring, it's all previously used, and in uniformity to the cabinets, closet doors, and countertops, the rent's pretty cheap. He didn't say a word, big brown eyes skimming the space. I should have asked if he liked it, or if he didn't like it, and if so, why. But I didn't. Instead, I became distracted unzipping his pants and tearing off his shirt and rolling down his socks which I like to throw on the carpet and use after sex as stepping stones going to and coming from the bathroom. He prefers the apartment dark, which means we spend a lot of time tip-toeing around and bumping into each other. After a while, I figured he never said anything about my apartment because he couldn't see anything inside my apartment. That's fair. I get it. It's okay.

Three months after we started dating, I asked the man I still love, and hate, about siblings, cousins, parents, friends. It seemed odd that he'd never mentioned anyone except for Uncle Nikolas. He snickered and said he wasn't ready to talk about stuff like that, not yet, but soon, someday dolly-doll, I promise. The dismissiveness hurt my feelings. But I let it go. For two months. Then one day, after sex, while he was in the bathroom, I turned on a reading light, scrolled through his cell phone contacts, and wrote down three phone numbers attached to three names—Mom and Dad, Packers Pro Shop, & VIAGRA69.

A week later, I phoned his Mom & Dad. More out of curiosity than investigation, I wondered if their names actually matched the numbers. And if so, did their accents mirror his? Did they know about me, because he'd told them about me, and if so, what had he said? A simple call. Nothing heavy. I was willing to hang up after they answered, depending on the tone of their voice. Or maybe I'd chat a little bit, depending on the mood of my reaction. Easy breezy. Like Socrates. And me.

His mother answered. "This is Katerina." Sweet voice. Then

Babis, his father, introduced himself on a second phone line in the second bathroom. Pleasant sounding folk, until I mentioned dating their son, the sweetest man and biggest Packers fan I've ever met. They were quiet for a short time. "Are you still there?" I finally had to ask. His mother sighed, and said, "Are you a boy or a girl?"

"A boy."

"You don't sound like a boy."

"I don't. How do I sound?"

She stayed quiet. Babis did, too. "Are you still there?"

"So, how much do you want?" she asked, lingering on the word, you.

"Want what?"

"Hmm," she and Babis murmured at the same time.

"I just called to introduce myself and say hi."

"How nice of you." Her voice turned gruff, infused with grit and cynicism. "You're not the first gender to call, sweetie, and I can assure you, you won't be the last."

Babis laughed an unfunny laugh. "Our son's a packer alright. Like pack-her-him-in."

I remained quiet for a minute, maybe two, wondering about the other boys, girls, genders, who had phoned his parents. How many had there been? The words, "pack-her-him-in" split my heart into fractions, keeping me from deciphering exactly what Katerina had meant by, how much do you want? Was she offering a bribe? Hinting at hush money? Attempting to silence the truth by way of compensation? I should have asked for clarification. But I didn't. Instead, I thought about the word, team. The man I still love, and hate, and his parents are part of a team. The Packers are part of a team. Goddamn strippers are part of a team. But I'm not part of a team. Anger, the kind that lines a body's cell count with goosebumps and vengeance, caused me to say, "A $3,500 cashier's check ought to do it, as that's the exact amount I gave him last month from my savings account for a fourteen-day tour of Greece he said just yesterday he still wants to take me on." The amount was a lie. I'd only given him $500. But I felt betrayed. And greedy.

"He hates Greece," Katerina blurted out, and Babis grunted. "We've asked him to go a hundred times and he always gives us the same answer. No."

I remained quiet, flipping through a picture book of Santorini Island.

"But I suppose," Katerina finally said. "As long as you promise to never tell him we talked and if you promise to cut off all contact with him asap, we can come up with a mutually beneficial arrangement." She paused. "Think you can manage that, deary?"

"You know what, make it an even five-thousand. Call it reparation funds for the emotionally abused." If they can afford $3,500, they can afford an additional $1,500.

"How do we know you'll keep your word?"

"I guess unlike your son, you'll just have to trust I am who I say I am."

"Hmm," they said again is unison. Then I heard a click. "You still there," I asked.

"What's the address," Katerina said, hanging up the moment I finished the zip code. Later that night, lying in bed, with every light in the house on, I spent in my head the extra $1,500 on Chicago Bears gear. That'd show him.

The man I still love, and hate, continued to come over. And we continued having sex in the dark. He didn't mention anything about his parents, so neither did I. Like usual, after sex, he dressed and pushed his feet into Packer-colored tennis shoes. Looking at me from outside the screen door, he whispered, "See you soon, my sweetest one, my Packerette, my pro-everything, my real life dolly-doll. Can't wait to take you to Greece." And so it remained for five months. Coming fast. Leaving faster. Allowing me little time to whisper goodbye or tell him about the $5,000 cashier's check sitting atop the fridge, *charity donation* written in the memo line. I began to wonder where the man I still love, and hate, lives and works. Probably part of some team in some well-lit office in some top floor building with floor-to-ceiling windows. My father said a man's job is a private affair. So I didn't prod. But I refused to give up.

Last month, on the twenty-first, on my birthday, right after we had sex and fed each other Packer-themed cupcakes, and just as I was about to tell him about the $5,000 check and beg for forgiveness, the man I still love, and hate, asked if I wanted to come over and see his home—like soon. His face was redder than usual. I couldn't decide if he was nervous or happy. I picked happy. Why not. I never am.

"Sure, I'll come over."

"I've got a king-size bed and a few other amenities I think you'll really enjoy," he said. "I'll shoot you a few dates and times later this week." Two days later, at 6:16pm, he texted, *I've got off tomorrow from noon to three, to show you more about you and me.* The rhyme scheme made me giggle. And soften. And forgive. And hope.

R u picking me up or do I need to find my own way?

I'll pick you up at noon, dolly-doll. Don't keep me waiting.

"Should I be dressed or what?"

Me thinks wearing a Packer thong beneath a Packer robe is super sex.

Go Pack Go.

My Packerette.

The man I still love, and hate, was prompt. Right at noon. I jumped into the passenger seat of a green and gold Ford F-350 super-duty truck and set my head on his shoulder while he rubbed his hand up and down my back. I wanted to say I love you. But I didn't. How could I? Knowing what I know. Knowing what he didn't know I knew. Besides, it's pointless to rush a man's tongue to the words, I love you. Men are like babies, capable of expressing love only after their hunger for something visceral and reassuring is routinely satisfied. That's what my mother said. And she was never wrong. Not about men.

The man I still love, and hate, tapped the brakes in front of a large estate with a four-car garage before slowly turning into a wide, slick-polish concrete driveway. Manicured front yard. Six rock beds. Elm trees. Shapely shrubs. Blooming flowers. Light-brown stucco Tudor. Dark-brown trim. Hilltop viewpoint. A bit ornate, but also calming. A place where one-hundred dollar bills could easily grow, hang, and fall from the vines. I held out my hands. Just in case.

"Is this where you live?"

"Come on in and I'll tour ya."

We slipped through a cherry side-entrance door. Once inside, the smell of lemon and lime made me sneeze. The sprawling kitchen had a built-in espresso maker and a two stoves. Seven bedrooms. Seven bedroom sets. Art-deco watercolor paintings. Custom-made tapestries. Eight toilets. Seven marble showers. I'd never before heard the term Jack-and-Jill bathroom. To my surprise, and delight, there were no visible photos of his parents, nor of any other boys, girls, or genders on any of the walls or inside any of the many bookshelves. The in-ground swimming pool had a curlicue slide. The outdoor kitchen glimmered against the sun. Lattice gazebo. Sand-pit volleyball court. Movie theatre. Pool table. Cosmopolitan bar with ten leather bar stools. An entire room was decorated and stocked with expensive Packer memorabilia: signed footballs, posters, jerseys, and hats. The Packer-themed home gym was bigger than my apartment. The sauna was hot and the steam room was sticky. "Made sure it was all on for you, babe," he said, unknotting the belt on my robe. His eyes landed on my chest while his hands worked down my torso to the top of the thong—a gift he'd given with pleasure, no doubt in the hope of one day taking it back by taking it off. That day had arrived. "Me likey you more, and less, in Packer lingerie." He grabbed my ass and pulled my erect cock into his erect cock. All I could do was stand there and wonder: Can life be a fairytale? Do some dreams come true? Is it possible for two people who've connected to stay connected? Especially for people. Like us.

"Do you live here all by yourself?" I stepped back, after we both reached ejaculation, which he wiped up with his socks.

"I take it you approve of my digs?"

"Why does one man need so much space?"

"Because more is more, and even more is better. Haven't you heard?" A pea-green framed cell phone popped out of his front shirt pocket and toppled against the hardwood floor.

"Whose phone is that?"

"Who else's would it be but mine?" He stepped backwards, leaving the phone on the floor.

"Is it new?" I bent over to pick it up.

"Leave it alone." He kicked it across the room. It slammed against the terracotta-colored wall and spun like a top. "There. Happy now?"

"That's not the phone you usually use when we're together."

"So I have a couple of phones. What's the big deal?"

"Why do you need more than one phone?"

"Why the interrogation?"

"Why do you always want my apartment dark?" I couldn't believe I was asking him about apartment lighting, or the lack thereof. I should have been telling him about my conversation with his parents, confessing all that I'd learned, all that I'd said, all that I knew. But I didn't.

He frowned. "What's going on?"

"What color's my couch?" I sat on the edge of a brown, L-shaped Packer-insignia sectional. The cold leather made me shiver. I saw through the sliding glass door a golf course and the back decks of other, even larger estates. The man I still love, and hate, came at me holding two Corona. I hadn't realized he'd walked away. "Here." I didn't take it. "You're really killing the buzz, hon."

"What color's my couch?"

"Really." His shoulders slumped. "You want me to tell you the color of your couch?"

"Yeah. What color is it?"

"I don't know. I mean, have we even sat on it together?"

"How could we. You're always in such a rush to get the hell outta there."

He stood quiet, staring at the Coronas. He finally shrugged and whispered, "I don't know. Black?"

"Wrong." I tied the robe's belt and took two and two the plush-carpet steps leading to the main level.

"Do not go up there." He followed me up the steps. "You can't go up there."

In the foyer, half-way to the stained-glass front door, I stopped at a towering bookcase packed with books about Spain, Packers, marriage and family, horror and mystery, Oceanic Mammals, Qurans. Not one book about Greece. The man I still love, and hate, put his arms around my neck and squeezed, whispering words my dizziness couldn't transform into rationality. I became weak. I couldn't speak. Or yell. Or swallow. I kicked his shin and rammed an elbow into his stomach. Twice. He released his grip and fell to his knees. "Fucking cunt." Then, empowered by a sense of retribution, I pushed the bookcase atop his body, rendering his limbs motionless and askew. Had it been a movie: *Deception at the Not-So-Hot Acropolis.* Liar. User. Thug. I turned on every light. I marred with a cheese grater the Packer couch. I shattered with two bottles of Corona the cell phone. I wiped with a towel every place I had walked, stood, and jizzed. Looking down on him, still immobile, I confessed to talking to his parents, to accepting (and cashing) the $5,000 check, to keeping from him what he kept from me, the truth. We we're never going to be a team. Never going to be a couple. Never going to stand hand-and-hand in the immutable light. The man I still love, and hate, twitched, and I knew what I had to do, which I did—some men need to be tied down; some men need to be set free—after I stared for a while at the life-size oil painting hanging above the transom: a twenty-something dressed in a green and gold sequin vest, bow tie, and cap. The pretty-boy-androgyny made me laugh. And cry. It could have been me, we looked that much alike.

The Other Side of Living

No hope remains behind the bedroom door. A wooden shell. A tomb. Daily, the man works around the door: straightens the bathroom, the office, the hallway linen closet. He takes down towels, puts away paper goods, and cleans the tub every Saturday afternoon at 2pm—the best time to clean a tub, really.

The bedroom door begins to fade, crack, and bend. It's as if the door is calling out for medical attention. I'm famished: that's what he thinks the door is saying. He doesn't answer, worried the door will get worse if he tries to make it better.

The door creaks, pops, and shifts. Like a spirited child restless in bed. He steps forward and touches it, not to leave fingerprints, but to hear with his bones and see through his veins and swear by the lines weaved across the palms of his hands life's incompleteness dying within.

The door opens, on its own, crying all the way to the wall. Light from the window magnifies the silk flowers and craft pebbles scattered across the carpet, illuminating the body-size piece of carpet removed from the far left corner still bleeding red; still jaggedly wounded; still trying to connect the dots.

Of Course

You're standing in front of a bathroom sink in a public restroom rinsing soap from your hands when a blast of hot water splashes your pants and burns the tip of your dick, which happens to every man at some point, especially to slutty, unsafe, pathetic men like you, who seem built to absorb splashes. At the hand dryer, you glance at your Betty Crocker wristwatch, a gift from Pierre Roustening, your French roommate (and first kiss) in 1990—the summer of enlightenment—who you met because of your keen ability to successfully beg your parents to exchange one icky-brown Boy Scout uniform for one week of cake baking/decorating camp, singing playfully, "Baker's man can bake you a cake as fast as you can." But you still remember the tenderfoot motto: *Be Prepared.* Which you're not. Nowhere close. Panic and unrest wallops you upside the head like a rolling pin, causing you to empty the weight of your stomach in the toilet bowl and cry big tears, the kind of big tears you didn't cry at your chronic mother's and vacuous father's funerals who both died as poorly as they lived—drunk, ignorant fools. You rinse your mouth with cold water and spit in the sink, refusing to look in the oval mirror, scared you might see the beginning traces of the HIV test you took last week, the one that may or may not be positive. Who will want to look at you then? You tidy up the bathroom, of course, take three deep breaths, of course, and suck it all in and up, of course.

You resume a hunchback position over on a laptop at a wobbly wooden table two-feet from the restroom and surf the web, nothing in particular, finding on Youtube a same-sex marriage proposal at Home Depot with fourteen million views. You smell a woodsy-scented cologne approach from behind. You spin around and fall fast for a set of sea-blue eyes affixed to lean masculinity wearing model-black hair, a white Ralph Lauren polo shirt, dark-blue Lucky brand jeans, and a satisfying pair of brown curl-at-the-tip dress shoes. Athletic. Tweezed. Six-two. Gay, of course.

You name him Woodsy Wayne and call him a great big dick tease. You like him so much, you lean in and listen for the soft-click-lock of the bathroom door. You can't call the clinic for two more hours anyway so why wait around like absolute despair when you can plan your and Woodsy Wayne's wedding.

Woodsy Wayne from Augusta Maine drinks champagne in a private plane. You suddenly realize you were not some prolific poet in some past life. No matter, you and Woodsy Wayne are busy picking tapestries, bedspreads, and stainless steel dessert spoons on Rodeo Drive. Then come the vows, the rings, and all-the-I-do's. There stands your newly constructed four-story house with a sprawling yard in a gated community. No more trailer houses with mullet-gut neighbors sitting in plaid pajamas on plastic chairs inside a dank garage drinking Boone's Farm from a red solo cup. You deserve a well-made deck, triple insulation, and double-pane windows. You warrant being kissed in public, and often. You love Woodsy Wayne so much for designing t-shirts and running marathons to raise money and awareness for causes like yours. Of course he chose you to be his happy-ever-after. I mean, look at yourself. And him. Together. You're total amazeballs. Everyone believes it and says so. Everyone wants what you have. Everyone.

You're startled when Woodsy Wayne kicks open the bathroom door and leaves a black scuff mark on the bottom of the door, annoyed by the way he scurries off like some bratty teenager and sits across a Hollister-twink with gel-height-hair and V-neck-chest-tightness. Whatever. You detest scurrying; you've had enough scurrying for eight lifetimes. Fuck Woodsy Wayne. And his gay-baiting twinkazoid, too.

You Google WEB-MD: *Six Critical Steps after Initial Diagnosis* when you smell Curry Spice approach from behind. You spin around and recoil in displeasure at a set of mud-brown eyes affixed to fat masculinity wearing scraggly hair, a two-decade-ago-porn-esque moustache, a black sweater, and denim shorts with an unsatisfying pair of penny loafers and black ankle socks. *Please don't be gay. We don't want you.* You try not to lean in and listen to the soft-click-lock of the bathroom door, but bad habits are so hard to break.

You dive headfirst into the informational pool of WEB-MD: *Finding a support group in your area is an essential step to staying physically, emotionally, and spiritually well. For support groups in your area, please enter your zip code.* You type 05602, recounting the seven, one-hundred-and-two-degree fevers over the last month flaming like a blowtorch across your skin. The nausea. Vomiting. Unexplained weight loss. Diarrhea. Dry mouth. Headaches. Dizziness. Isolation. Fear. Every common symptom. All the red flags. Tons of cold showers. Bowlfuls of Chicken Noodle Soup. You're the idiot to blame. You're the slutty, unsafe, pathetic man who did it. You. Yourself. I.

You're surprised by the calm manner with which Curry Spice steps from the bathroom and gingerly closes the door. When he blows dry his fingers, as if playing a flute, you laugh. Which grabs his attention. Of course. He extends a hand and smiles, but you don't respond. You're so not into two-decade-ago-porn-esque moustaches and penny loafers with black ankle socks. Buh-bye.

"Have a good day," he says, taking surprisingly big steps toward a small table in the opposite corner of the café.

Chin in your hands, you think about the words, good day and buh-bye. And judgment. And lack of self-respect. And physical appearance. And aging. And the stigma of HIV and AIDS. Twenty-five million men and women in the world have died from the disease. Tears come. What a pussy. Something you've never tried. Of course. At least there's that.

Curry Spice is behind you. Again. You don't turn around or look up, perplexed and impressed when he lifts your chin with large, warm fingers, and says, "Hey. You okay?"

"Why can't their kind just blend in," a male customer says to another.

"I know, right," a female customer answers. "First marriage

and now this."

"I'm Talan." He sits across the table. "What's your name?"

His foreign accent sounds sexy. Mysterious. Enticing. Upon closer reconnaissance, he smells more like coconut with a hint of lemongrass. And his brown eyes, light-brown eyes, are a few shades lighter than mud. "I'm Ethan."

"Bad day, Ethan?"

"Sadly, it could get worse."

"Perhaps it'll help if you get it off your chest."

So many chests. So many sex parties. So many shots of tequila. So many chances to say no. So many times screaming yes. "I wouldn't even know where to start."

"The beginning's always a good place."

As if unpacking from a long trip, you bring out the tight jeans, the muscle shirts, the multi-colored thongs, and the latest pair of navy-blue eyes that a few months ago left you at midnight in a hotel room sore, sober, and ashamed.

"That many, wow."

You laugh. "I know it's not funny. I know I shouldn't laugh." Your heart ticks clockwise. It's been awhile. Afraid it might stop, or rewind, you keep talking, revealing the upcoming phone call to the clinic and the HIV test result you cannot barter, fathom, or control. "It's just me." You set your forehead on the keyboard, wishing it was Woodsy Wayne who was sitting across.

"Why do you do that to yourself?" Talan asks.

"At first I did it to feel numb but then numb wasn't enough. Now it's about numbing the numb because there's just so much of it."

"I definitely understand feeling numb."

The pre-set alarm on your wristwatch beeps. "Guess it's time." You stand. "Thanks for the talk, though. It was really nice of you."

"I can stay if you want."

"It's up to you."

"I'll be right here if you need me."

256

You step in the bathroom, lock the door, sit on the toilet seat, and pray to a God you don't believe in, unable to recall or recite one encouraging Bible verse from ten years of Sunday School and Vacation Bible School. You dial the clinic's phone number and press send, wondering if life from this day forward holds nothing but a death sentence. You hang up before anyone answers. "Our Father Which Art in Heaven," you whisper. The room spins. The walls shrink. You dial again. Not knowing is the hardest step of all. Ring one: inhale. Ring two: exhale. Ring three: regardless the outcome, you need a pedicure. Ring four: "Hallowed be Thy Name."

"Public Health Center, how may I direct your call?"

Recklessness haunts you. The poppers. The blackouts. The blood on the sheets. The cherry-flavored condom, still wrapped, sitting on the hotel nightstand. Why didn't you ask for his name? Why don't you ever ask for a name?

"Hello? Is anyone there? Hello?"

"Sorry. Doctor Richardson's office please."

"Please hold while I transfer the call."

You bite your fingernails through a series of classical ballads, wishing for a touch of soft, pop rock.

"This is Nurse Fronita. How may I help you?"

"Hi Fronita. It's Ethan Grover. I'm calling about my test results."

"Oh, yeah," she says and pauses. "Hold on a sec." Does the pause mean something bad or something good? When did life become hinged to one specific word? "Cashmere. Cashmere. Cashmere," you whisper, a favorite splurge, a demi-god, a comfort through this whole ordeal. Then Nurse Fronita whispers the one word you've been dying to hear for two weeks, causing you to grow faint and collapse to the floor, inadvertently smacking your head against the toilet bowl. In the darkness, an image surfaces of you and your mother at the beach: building sandcastles, laughing, splashing, dog-paddling. You begin drifting alone into deeper waters. Your mother is calling for you to come back. She uses your full name, waves her arms, jumps, flails, swims out to rescue you, brings you to the shoreline where she kisses, holds, and loves you. She definitely doesn't slap your cheek, push your face in the sand, and call you a cock-sucking faggot. You open your eyes. Your head is resting on Talan's leg. A greasy man wearing a black uniform with a large set of metal keys is standing over you. "What are you two doing in here?"

"How many fingers am I holding up?" Talan asks.

"Two," you say.

"Can you stand?" Talan helps you to your knees.

"You guys gotta get out of here. This isn't one of those kinds of bathrooms."

You bury your face in the center of Talan's black sweater—cashmere, of course—and cry the biggest tears of your life. You wrap your arms around his shoulders and whisper into his left ear, "Sometimes being negative is a good thing. I've been given another chance."

"I'm so glad," he whispers in your right ear. "I wish I'd have been so lucky."

Of course. Of course. Of course.

ACKNOWLEDGEMENTS:

The following stories were previously published
in slightly different forms in the following publications:

"What I Learned About Love and Hate From Socrates Tremapolos
and his Wacko, Sicko Parents," *Pomona Valley Review*
"It's Worth Exploring," & "Preacher Victoria," *Apocrypha
& Abstractions*
"The Cognomen Affair," *Literary Orphans*
"Great Lengths," & "Mini Lift," *Foliate Oak*
"Which Face Today?" & "Starved," *Pure Slush*
"The Weebie's," *Empty Sink Publishing*
"Syntax," *Breathe Free Press*
"Re-Release," *Fix It Broken*
"The Good Life," *A Few Lines*
"Potion Number Us," *Second Hand Stories*
"State Lines," *Dryland Lit*
"Fifteen," *Blackheart Magazine*
"Do You Know What I Mean," *Ascent Aspirations*
"The Way We Drive," *RFD Magazine*
"Dates and Times Filled In," *Flywheel*
"Fist. Pull. Foot. Push," *Dual Coast*
"Grocery Ballet," & "The Other Side of Living," *Full of Crow*
"Or," *Diddledog*
"Elder Mistrust," *Rathalla Review*
"7:37 at I-Hop," *Capra Review*
"All Thixthy Thix Bookth," *Edify Publications*
"Time with The Thompsons" *Linden Avenue Literary Journal*
"The Governor's Table," *Subtle Fiction*
"By Robert McClintock 2017," *The Hungry Chimera*
"Back Room Far Right," *Queen Mob's Teahouse*
"Of Course," *Identity Theory*
"Bryan with a Y," *Literary Yard*
"She Only Wishes For, and Only Gets, Five," *The Bookends Review*
"Parade Drain Paranoia," *Nixes Mate Review*

NOTES:

I wish to express my thanks to the following friends, writers, mentors, and teachers for their advice and encouragement: John-Ivan Palmer, Paul Pederson, Matthew Olson, J. P. Johnson, Lee Henschel, Jr., Bernice Johnson, Eowyn Gatlin, Daniel Rosen, Ted King, Ruben Gonzalez, Yvonne Moore, Kevin Stebner, Kim Macinnes, Steven Palm, Mary Boyd, David Fingerman, LuAnn Rockman, Roger Morris, Dan Budke, Steve Schultz, Cynthia Long, Brent Holt, Tim Jozwowski, Christy Moulton Perry, Frederick Blanch, Kevin O'Rourke, Janet Preus, Jeffrey Whitney, The JOY Project, Sandra Joyce, Chris Palumbo, Nicole and Brett Bundy, Michael Peal, Mark Renner, Marge Barrett, Jacquie Trudeau, Lee Orcutt, Laurel Ostrow, Lisa Wurtinger, Al Reiper, Kurt Duex, Mary Weggum Snorek, Joy Bryant, David Santiago, Hutch Matteson, Wendy Louise Nog, Jorie Miller, Mark Turbak, Tara Lynn Price, and The Loft Literary Center.

Very special thanks to Marc and Ashley Pietrzykowski (and crew) for the great care they put into the editing, inputting, and publishing process.

ABOUT THE AUTHOR:

It began in the countryside where fourth generation farmers tilled the hardy soil exposed in large rectangles, outlined by poplars and jack pine. The old Swedish and Norwegian accents could still be heard in the tinkling voices of the elder women who gathered to weave rugs by hand. The sometimes terrifying solitude of the countryside and the beauty of a nature that would somehow spring up through a deeply frozen land profoundly formed Samuel's perspective.

Samuel E. Cole is a writer of prose and poetry, living in Woodbury, Minnesota. His stories and poems have appeared in numerous literary magazines, including *Rathalla Review, Capra Review, Literary Orphans, Winamop, Empty Sink Publishing, Pure Slush, RFD Magazine, Full of Crow, Jazz Cigarette,* and *Foliate Oak.* His first poetry collection, *Bereft & the Same-Sex Heart,* was published in 2016 by Pski's Porch Publishing. He has won literary awards from The Loft Literary Center and from Minnpost.com. He finds work in event management and is a key player in adding to the paper trail chronicles of The Minneapolis Writers Workshop.

www.facebook.com/coleport

www.samuel-cole.com

FONTS:

Bloodwork is typeset in Adobe Devanagari, a font designed to be highly readable in a range of situations, where the full character of the typeface reveals itself, and Myanmar Text, a business-casual font developed by Microsoft Corp. in 2012.

COVER DESIGN:

Bloodwork cover, spine, and back was designed by Nicole Bundy, a graphic designer living in Coon Rapids, Minnesota, currently employed at Medtronic via Creatis, Inc.

nicole@nicbdesign.com

Pski's Porch Publishing was formed July 2012, to make books for people who like people who like books. We hope we have some small successes.

www.pskisporch.com.

Pski's Porch

323 East Avenue
Lockport, NY 14094
www.pskisporch.com

Made in the USA
Lexington, KY
17 July 2017